U2

D1564902

N095

# THE NEIGHBORHOOD

# THE NEIGHBORHOOD

A NOVEL BY

## S.K. EPPERSON

DONALD I. FINE, INC.

*New York*

*Dedicated to all my friends and family,*
*with special thanks to*
*Michelle Louis, Martha Hodges, Sally Brown*
*and all the neighbors who've made me wonder.*

# PROLOGUE

THE BOARD ROOM IN the hospital was silent. Two nervous, perspiring doctors watched in dread as the chief of staff picked up the chart before him and tore it in half.

"I'm taking him home," he said. "He's my brother."

"It won't work," said one of the doctors. "We'll have to report this at once. We can't keep quiet about something like this."

The chief of staff went stiff with anger. "You haven't considered the consequences. News of what we have here could close the doors of this hospital."

"Temporarily, perhaps. This isn't a Hollywood movie, one patient does not an epidemic make."

"In this case, our government may disagree."

"Has the World Health Organization destroyed the last vials of the virus?"

"It was slated to happen this year, but who knows?"

The other doctor lifted his head. "I thought they destroyed it in 1993."

"No. Scientists hadn't cloned it yet. They think they have it now, the harmless version, anyway."

"A full genetic blueprint?"

"As close as they can get. That's why they want the real virus destroyed now, so no accidents happen."

"Or biological warfare."

"Exactly."

1

"And we're just going to sit here and keep quiet. How are you going to keep your brother isolated?"

"I've told him he has AIDS."

"I repeat: how are you going to keep him isolated?"

"He believes a virus he contracted has weakened his immune system and hastened him into the last stages."

"Is he dying?"

"Almost certainly."

"Does he have the blisters?"

"Yes."

"Has he exposed anyone here, do you think?"

"I admitted him myself, and he's seen only one nurse. I'm going to take her home with me to look after him."

"You're relieving her of duty? Who might she have exposed?"

"No one. She lives alone. No boyfriends, no women friends, not even a pet. Lee Ahrens is her mother."

The three men looked at each other.

"I knew her father," said one of the doctors.

"So did I," said the chief of staff.

"Was she ever inoculated?"

"Yes. But so was my brother."

"Are you certain? Both of them?"

"Yes."

"How do you know she didn't go to the grocery store or the dry cleaners on her way home?"

"I asked her."

"Is she with him now?"

"Yes, she's preparing to take him home. I've asked her to handle the matter without the assistance of any orderly or aide. She has agreed."

"Does she know?"

"She believes the secrecy is due to embarrassment on my part and hasn't questioned any of my orders."

"What happens if she contracts the virus?"

"When my brother dies I plan to send her on an extended cruise. *If* she becomes ill, it won't be here."

"This is insane," said one of the doctors. "We can't go through with this. I can't believe you're even suggesting we hide something of this magnitude."

"And I can't believe you're suggesting we turn this hospital over to the whims of a paranoid government. Do you realize how much we stand to lose? Every bed on every floor would empty out within days."

The three men fell silent once more. The doctor who had made the diagnosis put a hand to his face and rubbed tiredly at his eyes. "I'll be conducting research myself into the nature of the virus, to determine if a mutation of some sort has occurred. I don't have to tell you this is a disease that killed over six hundred thousand people a year for several centuries."

"I still can't believe it," said the other doctor. "The last recorded case was in Somalia in 1977. I thought we had it beat."

"Apparently not," said the chief of staff as he stood and prepared to leave the room.

The two doctors stood as well, and the chief of staff held up the torn chart.

"I'm putting this through the shredder. I don't have to remind you how important it is for your future and mine to keep your silence. The last known case of smallpox in the world will not occur in this hospital, gentlemen."

# CHAPTER

# 1

"A FULL-TIME NURSE just moved into the guy's house," said twelve-year-old Eli.

"Who told you that?" asked Holt, his sixteen-year-old brother.

"Nobody told me. He's sick with that HIV shit and he's gonna die."

"Who says?"

"God, you should have seen her. She was ready to take off her blouse when she saw me."

"She cute?"

"Oh, man. Wish *I* was sick."

Holt snorted. "Listen to you, you little pervert. You've never even kissed a girl."

"I have so."

"Have not. Who was it?"

"Cyndi Melo."

"The girl in your class?"

"Yeah."

Holt eyed his younger brother and took a drink of Diet Pepsi from the can he held. "You only said *her* name because she's missing and I can't ask her."

Eli stopped swinging the porch swing and stared.

"Cyndi's missing?"

"It was on the news all day yesterday. She's been gone since Monday."

"What happened to her?" asked Eli.

"Who knows?" answered Holt. "Her mom said she was riding her bike in the street one minute and the next minute she was gone. They think someone snatched her."

"She lived on Laurel," Eli said slowly. "Just a couple blocks from us."

"Yeah. Her brother's the one with that black-and-gold mountain bike."

Eli nodded. "Yeah. Cyndi was swimming at the Y last Friday. I saw her there."

"You wanna go today?" Holt asked.

"Nah. Don't feel like walkin'." Eli craned his head to see inside the house behind him. "Dad still with his patient?"

Holt shook his head. "He sent her home because of the clouds."

"Did you see the eye patch she had on? It was pink and had a big yellow flower right in the middle of it. Man, I had to hit myself to keep from laughing."

"Dad'd beat the shit out of you if you did."

Eli snorted. "He laughs sometimes. I've seen him."

"He's laughing at *you*."

"Is not. I'm the one who pisses him off, remember?"

Holt smiled. His little brother had that right, but it was only because Eli liked to make fun of the eyeball business. Their dad used to be a policeman, but that career ended when a bullet in the face took him off the force and put him on disability. He used the time and the money to attend the Dean McGee Eye Institute in Oklahoma City. Now he was an artificial eyemaker and medical artist. He liked the job because he didn't have to talk much, and he could work by himself.

The bullet had made him that way. He couldn't talk good anymore, and because he couldn't, he liked to avoid social situations. He was still the kind of person who liked to help others, so he made free eyes for people with no insurance. He once told Holt that his own father had a fake eye, and he hated the thing because it didn't match the other eye and made his dad, the nicest guy in the world, look like a monster. Zane Campbell always thought he could do better.

Holt and Eli's mother was grossed out by her husband's career choice, but her mind had been made up to leave long before the bullet struck him. His behavior after being shot gave her the excuse she needed. She offered to take Eli and Holt, but they elected to stay with their father. They still saw their mother once a week, sometimes more, sometimes less, depending on the real estate market. She was remarried now and had a baby girl by her new husband. Holt and Eli thought the little girl was cute, but they didn't want much to do with her.

The screen door opened and their father stepped onto the porch. "I didn't expect to find you guys here."

Most of Holt's friends thought Zane Campbell sounded drunk when he talked. Holt hated it when they said that.

"Just hangin' out, Dad. Eli says Mr. Conlan has AIDS. They hired a full-time nurse."

"That right?" Zane looked next door to the Conlan place. "Who told you that, Eli?"

Eli's grin was guilty. "Clyde did when he caught me peeking in the window."

Zane's head swiveled. "You were peeking in the window? At what?"

"The nurse. She was moving in. She's got the bedroom right across from yours, Dad."

"What did Clyde say to you?" asked Zane.

"He said his brother was dying and would I please do my best not to disturb him."

"That doesn't mean he has AIDS."

"He's a fag, Dad. What else would he have?"

Zane's brows met and he moved to stand over his younger

son. "The word is homosexual. Don't ever let me hear you call it anything else."

Eli's face turned sullen. "No problem."

Zane shook his head and walked back inside the house. For a moment Holt felt ashamed for Eli. Then he felt hot. He put down his can of Diet Pepsi and peeled off his pullover. Eli watched him and did the same with his own shirt.

"Copycat," said Holt.

Eli gave him the finger.

In the house next door, Abra Ahrens looked out the window and saw the two boys still on the front porch. The younger one had been at her window earlier, peering in as if he expected to catch her either dressing or undressing. Abra was at first irritated, then amused. He couldn't be more than twelve or thirteen.

She left the room and walked into the hall to check on her patient, Thomas Conlan. He was still sleeping, as he had been all morning. He was exhausted after leaving the hospital, where he claimed he couldn't sleep at all.

In the living room she found Clyde Conlan, the man who had employed her. He was hanging up the phone, and when he saw her he smiled. "It's happened. I hate this, since you've just arrived, but I'm going to have to leave. I've got a meeting in Riverside, California, tomorrow."

Clyde Conlan was chief of staff at Riverpark Hospital, and he had told Abra he would be away from home often, but she had no idea he would leave so soon.

"I'm sure we'll be fine, Mr. Conlan. Is there a number where I can reach you in case something comes up?"

"Of course. I always stay in the same hotel. I'll note everything for you after I finish packing." He gestured with his hands. "Go on and familiarize yourself with the house."

Abra looked around herself after he disappeared into the hall. She decided to start in the kitchen. The washer and dryer were in an attached utility room. She opened cabinets and drawers, noting the location of glasses, plates and silverware. The food shelves were fully stocked; groceries were delivered once a week, Clyde had told her.

She would be expected to cook and clean up after herself. Clyde explained that he was in between cleaning services and wanted to disturb Thomas as little as possible. She found a den filled with books and a room with a CD player, turntable and comfortable chairs. In the hall she discovered where the linens were kept. In another closet were bags of disposable plastic gloves, boxes of syringes, alcohol swabs and a number of different preparations and medications. Abra let her breath out in a sigh and closed the door.

"What about the neighbors?" she asked as Clyde entered the living room carrying an enormous suitcase. "Do they know your brother is ill?"

"I think most of them have guessed by now. Thomas was always an outdoor person."

"This morning there was a boy outside my—"

"I caught him. That was Eli, from next door. He lives there with his father and brother. Mr. Campbell is an ex-police detective, so I'm sure you'll feel safe with him nearby. The neighbor to the north is an old woman and her retarded son, and across the street are a young couple with a baby, and in the house next to them a middle-aged couple with a lot of birds. I'm sure you'll see all of them eventually." He paused and felt in his jacket for a pen. "Let me write down those numbers before I forget."

Abra watched him bend his balding head over a pad on the telephone table. When he finished, he handed the pad to her. "If all goes well, I should be back within ten days, maybe less. When I find out, I'll let you know. I will be calling, of course, for periodic updates on his condition. In case of emergency, use the first number on the list and call Dr. Tuckerman at Riverpark.

He's familiar with my brother's case and will advise you in my absence.''

He picked up the large suitcase and walked toward the door. ''I can't thank you enough for agreeing to come, Miss Ahrens.''

His departure was so rushed Abra was left standing in the middle of the room with her mouth hanging open. She walked onto the porch and saw him backing hurriedly down the drive in his dark gray Mercedes. Abra looked toward the garage, where the midnight blue Subaru wagon was parked. The Subaru was hers to drive for the duration of her stay.

She glanced at the neighbor's porch and saw that the two boys had gone. In their place was a man who wore a white lab coat. He was looking at Abra, but when she met his stare with a polite smile he turned his head in the other direction without acknowledging her. He opened the door to his house and walked inside. Abra blinked in surprise at his rudeness. Was he one of those people who believed everyone with AIDS deserved to have it? Abra hoped not. She was about to reenter the house when she spotted a car driving slowly down the street and attaching something to each mailbox. Abra walked out to retrieve the circular. As she turned around she saw him again, the white lab coat in the window beyond the porch. She looked away pointedly and hastened away from the mailbox. She was in the middle of the street when she heard a chilling scream that made her whirl in her tracks and drop the circular she was holding.

In the house across the way stood a man with a large white bird on his shoulder. He made no move to come out, he only stood and watched her as she stared at his bird. The thing shrieked again and Abra's innards tensed at the eerie sound it made. It was like a human scream.

She picked up the dropped circular and turned to see yet another neighbor at his door, watching her from the house to the north. His dark brown face was deeply suspicious as he watched Abra cross the lawn and enter the Conlan house. Once inside, she closed the door firmly behind her and put on the deadbolt. She didn't think she was going to like this neighborhood.

# CHAPTER

## 2

ZANE STRIPPED DOWN TO his T-shirt and went out to the garden to pick tomatoes. He felt like an idiot for turning away from the nurse like that. He didn't know what was wrong with him. She probably thought he was a real jerk for running into the house the way he had. He had no excuse, other than fear of using his mouth to talk to an attractive woman. When he was tense he sounded even worse than usual. He paused to look across the hedge at the Conlan house. Maybe he would drink a beer and take some tomatoes over and apologize.

No. If she smelled alcohol on him and then heard him say something, she might think he was inebriated.

"Forget it," he muttered to himself. He picked half a bucketful of tomatoes and took them in the house. He filled up a shelf in the refrigerator and, after looking around for the boys, decided to take some tomatoes over to old Mrs. Morley and her son. He walked down the drive and out into the street, still carrying the bucket. Out of the corner of his eye he glanced at the Conlan house as he passed, but he saw nothing.

Chance Morley opened the door and stood looking at Zane as if he had never seen him before.

"Hello, Chance," said Zane. "Is your mom home?"

"My mom's home, yeah. You want her?"

"I have some tomatoes from the garden."

11

Chance watched Zane's mouth as he spoke.

"Tomatoes?"

"Like the ones Holt and Eli brought over last week."

"Where is Eli?" Chance asked.

"I'm not sure. He's around somewhere. You want some tomatoes, Chance?"

"I'll get my mom. I can't understand what you're sayin'."

Zane exhaled through his nose. At least Chance, if slow, was honest.

The white-haired Mrs. Morley appeared at the door and opened it wide. "Come in, Zane, come in. Forgive my son for leaving you standing out on the porch." Her wrinkled face was caught between a frown and a smile.

Zane followed her inside to the kitchen and began to take tomatoes out of the bucket and put them in the sink.

"Oh, my, just look at those fat, juicy-looking things. Even bigger than last year, aren't they?"

Zane smiled. She said that every year.

"Yes, ma'am, I believe so."

He said that every year.

Her expression grew serious. "Zane, is it true about Mr. Conlan? Does he have the AIDS thing?"

"According to Eli, but we don't know for certain. They hired a nurse. She came on today."

"Oh. Uh-huh. I guess that would be the young lady Chance was telling me about. He saw her in the street and started hollering at me that she was picking up someone else's mail. I knew that couldn't be right, but then I wasn't sure. She's a young one, then?"

Zane nodded. "Younger than you and me."

Mrs. Morley clicked her dentures. "Have you spoken to her?"

"No, I haven't. I saw her on the street, same as Chance."

The old woman chuckled. "Pretty young girls get him excited. Starts acting crazy. He likes to play with that boy of yours, Eli. I sure do appreciate it when Eli comes around to talk to him. Most people are afraid of Chance, feeling the way they do about different folk. But that Eli, my goodness, he's fearless, isn't he? A real pistol, that boy."

"A mooch is more like it," said Zane. "He doesn't get cooking like yours at my house."

Mrs. Morley frowned. "Moose? No, no, mooch. Okay. You send those boys over anytime, Zane. You've done plenty for me, the least I can do is feed your kids a good meal."

Zane smiled. "They eat just fine at home."

"If they eat what you grow, they do. You ought to think about truck farming, Zane. A man who enjoys working outdoors the way you do ought to be making money at it."

"I'm happy making artificial eyes, Mrs. Morley."

"Making eyes, uh-huh. But only four or five a month, isn't that right? I'm sure you could use extra cash."

Zane shook his head. "If I made any extra, Holt would ask me to buy him a car and Eli would want a four-wheeler. Enjoy the tomatoes, Mrs. Morley."

"I will," she promised. "You see Chance out there, tell him to come on in. I'll fix him a nice tomato sandwich."

Zane waved and kept walking. Outside he saw Chance riding a child's bicycle up and down the driveway. Chance looked up and laughed when he saw Zane. "This my new bike. It works real good."

"That's nice, Chance. Where did you get it?"

Chance's face twisted. "Huh? I don't remember."

Zane switched the bucket to his other hand. "Your mom wants you to go in the house now. She wants to fix you a tomato sandwich."

"Go in? Okay," said Chance, but still he rode up and down the drive, his big knees sticking out as he pumped the pedals.

Zane wondered who had taught him to ride a bike. As far as he knew, Chance's father left when Chance was just a baby. Mrs. Morley had probably taught her son to ride. She was a woman of endless patience.

"Go on in now," Zane said as he turned to walk up the street.

Chance nodded and kept on riding. By the time Zane reached his house, he looked to see Mrs. Morley outside and scolding her son. He thought he heard her ask him where he got the bike, but he wasn't sure. Zane carried the bucket inside the house and took it to the pantry just off the kitchen. He found Holt at the table, finishing a peanut butter and jelly sandwich. He walked behind him to open up the refrigerator and take out a bottle of fruit juice.

"Where's your brother?"

"Dunno."

"Where did you last see him?"

"On the porch."

"Did you see which direction he went?"

"Nope."

Zane removed the sandwich from his son's hand. "It's your job to watch him this summer. We agreed on that."

Holt reached for the sandwich. "I *do* watch him. I watch him all the time. Just not in the last twenty minutes."

"Did he go to Bryan's house to play video games?"

"I doubt it. Bryan's pis—he's mad at him for winning all the time."

Zane gave Holt's sandwich back to him and walked to the back door to yell for Eli.

Holt got embarrassed listening to him, so he left his sandwich and went out the front door to look. He found Eli on the ground under the hedge by the Conlan house. He had his binoculars with him.

"Didn't you hear Dad calling you?" Holt said in irritation.

"I thought he was yelling for his Levi's."

Holt smacked his brother in the head. "That's not funny, you snot-nosed little jerk. Get in the house. You know how he worries. What if someone snatches you like they did Cyndi Melo?"

"I'll kick 'em in the balls," said Eli.

"Oh yeah, you're a real tough guy."

"Tougher than you, numb nuts."

"Where'd you learn to talk like that, you little shithead?"

Eli smiled at him. "Hey, Holt, listen. This nurse isn't much on top, but she's got a great—"

"Eli," said Zane. He walked up and yanked the binoculars out of his son's hand. "Get in the house now."

"Dad—" Eli began.

"*Go.*"

Impairment or not, Zane still knew how to convey the seriousness of a situation.

Eli lowered his head and trudged into the house, his brother right behind him. As they neared the porch, Eli said, "I bet he looks through the binoculars."

"Bet he won't," said Holt.

Zane was tempted—Eli was his son, after all—but he managed to restrain the impulse. He wound the strap around the binoculars and carried them into the house. Once inside, he ordered Eli into his room and went in after him. After lecturing him on respecting the privacy of individuals, he asked him to go around to Chance's house later and take a look at his new bike.

"Chance has a bike?" asked Eli.

"It's a kid's bike. Tell me if you recognize it. Chance said he didn't remember where he got it."

Eli eyed his father. "You think it's Cyndi Melo's bike, don't you?"

"I didn't say that."

"But you're wondering. I can always tell when you get that cop look on your face."

"Just do it, Eli."

Across the street, Craig Peterwell and his wife Louise moved away from the window and their observation of the Campbells.

"That Eli is a felony waiting to happen," said Louise, lifting her voice to make herself heard above the din of the birds caged throughout the living room.

Craig's nod was short. "He's what my grandfather would have called a 'scamp,' only he's almost a teenager now, and what happens to scamps when they grow up to be teenagers? They become punks. Gangbangers. The young girls who were once 'cute' and 'adorable' become sluts. Teenage whores with makeup. It's disgusting."

Louise glanced at her husband. The acid tone was a little too acid. He really had lost all patience with the children in the neighborhood this summer. He cursed their walking down the street and laughing, cursed their riding their bikes at breakneck speed and cursed them for laughing when he rolled down his window and yelled at them. She picked up the hem of her lime green housedress and flicked at what looked like a piece of bird doo. Some days it was more than she could keep up with. She didn't know why Craig couldn't take some of the birds into the basement where he had his workshop. It was cooler and more damp. The birds might appreciate it more and doo-doo less. Louise wasn't the bird person in the house. That was Craig.

She picked up the *TV Guide* and looked to see if her stories were going to be on at their usual times tomorrow. They were. Then she looked at the movies scheduled to be on her favorite movie channel this evening. She just loved all those wonderful old movies. When Craig was home he wasn't much of a TV person. He was too impatient to sit and watch television. He always had to be up and doing something, either taking care of his birds or building things in the basement. Only occasionally did Louise wander downstairs to see what he was doing. Most of the time he yelled at her to get out and leave him alone.

Craig was younger than Louise by eleven years. Louise was almost sixty, and Craig was forty-nine. They had met at the pet shop Louise owned on the south side of town. Craig was always coming in to buy birds from her. Back then it had been parakeets and myna birds. Now it was parrots and cockatoos. When the cockatoos began to scream, it was bad, but when the parrots opened up wide and began to shriek, it was even worse. On the days when Craig was home it was constant cacophony. He worked in maintenance at Riverpark Hospital and carried a beeper with him, and each time the beeper went off, so did the birds.

He had a special permit to keep the birds, given to him by some high-up federal official who was also his mother's brother. Each time one of the neighbors complained, Craig would take out his permit and wave it in their face. He was allowed to keep the birds, the paper said so. They could try to take him to court but he had the paper. None of the neighbors wanted to spend the money to take him to court.

The ones who really grew irate were the young couple next door with the baby. They claimed every time the baby got to sleep, the birds would start screaming and wake her up. Craig and the young husband had exchanged words several times, but nothing ever came of it. The ex-cop across the street came out last time and told them both to back off. Louise had been secretly thrilled. She thought Zane Campbell was so attractive. If she were thirty years younger, she would give him a run for his money. She liked him even better than she liked the men on her soaps. Zane Campbell wasn't necessarily as handsome, but he had such distinctive features and carried himself so well. And he had the strangest multi-colored eyes, with swirling shades of gray, deep green and brown. He was the nicest man to talk to, even with his speech impairment, which only endeared him to Louise even more. She wanted to take him and just hug him to death.

She looked up and caught Craig staring at her. Louise blinked. "What?"

He blew out through his nose in agitation. His color didn't look good. He was much too pink today.

"I asked you what we're having for dinner, dammit. Don't you ever listen to me?"

"I'm sorry, I was thinking of something else. I'll go right this minute and look in the freezer." Louise went to the kitchen to open the freezer. Since selling her exotic pet store last spring, it seemed Craig had no use for her anymore. He was rude, demanding and seemed depressed much of the time. Louise didn't know what to do about it. She had given up her two dogs and two cats for him when they married four years ago, but she missed her own pets. She missed them more than she would miss Craig if he were gone, she thought. She had believed she was lonely, ready to take another stab at love—too bad she had forgotten what living with a man was really like.

"Pork chops," she said a moment later.

"No," said Craig. "It's too hot for pork chops. Make something else, for God's sake."

Louise went back to the kitchen and opened the freezer door again. Chicken and turkey were out—Craig refused to eat anything that had feathers. There was a pound of hamburger with half an inch of ice frosted on top. She could thaw that in the microwave and make some Italian meatballs and spaghetti.

"Doesn't sound good to me," said Craig when she walked once more to the living room and told him.

"Well, what does sound good to you?" Louise asked.

Craig mumbled something under his breath and got up to go downstairs to his workshop. Louise followed him.

"You asked me what we'd have for dinner, and I gave you two choices. Now you tell me what you want."

He turned on the stairs. His face was pinker yet. "Don't come down here. Make whatever the hell you want."

He went down the steps and disappeared behind a door. Annoyed, Louise went after him. "All I asked is what you want. Can't you tell me that much? If we don't have what you want, I'll go to the store. There's no need to be such a baby about it."

She reached for the knob on the door and gave it a twist. As she pushed open the door she said, "If you don't want pork chops or meatballs, then I can—" Her next utterance was a shriek of pain every bit as loud as that of the birds upstairs as

Craig hit her on the arm with a two-by-four. Louise heard a *crack* and thought it was the board, but the board was still intact in Craig's hands. Her arm. He had broken her arm! Louise stared in pain-filled horror at her husband. "Craig—"

He opened his mouth and unleashed a terrible noise. The veins in his head and neck stood out. His face went scarlet.

Louise held her uninjured hand in front of her to ward him off as he advanced. Craig lunged and swung the two-by-four like a baseball bat. The bones in Louise's hand and wrist, all the way up to her elbow, were shattered as the wood connected. "I told you not to come in here!" he screamed at her. "Why don't you listen to me? Why doesn't anyone ever listen to me!"

Louise's mouth worked soundlessly as the pain brought unconsciousness near. She backed unsteadily away from the red-eyed, frothy-mouthed monster who was her husband.

Foam flew from his lips as Craig swung the board once more. He missed Louise and the board crashed into the doorframe beside her. Splinters flew and Louise fell back onto the stairs. She tried to use her arms and legs to scrabble up the stairs behind her, but the pain in her broken arms brought her even closer to blacking out. She gave up finally and began to sob as he lifted the board again.

"Don't kill me," she whimpered. "Please don't kill me."

Craig made a screaming noise through his nose and brought the two-by-four down like a sledgehammer across her legs.

# CHAPTER

# 3

ABRA CLOSED THE FRONT door and rubbed at the raised flesh on her arms. The noise of the birds across the street was positively ghastly. She hoped they didn't carry on like that all night; though with the door closed as it was now she could no longer hear their screams. She slid the deadbolt home once more and walked back to Thomas Conlan's bedroom. He smiled at her with cracked lips and she moved to sit in the chair beside the bed. Thomas was balding, like Clyde, and he looked like his brother, but Thomas's face was more relaxed, his manner less tense and anxious and his smile more sincere.

"Hello, Miss Ahrens. Or should I call you nurse?"

"No," she said. "I don't like to be called anything but Abra."

"As in abracadabra? How do you like our home?"

"I like it very much. You and your brother seem to have an enormous amount of space."

"It's usually filled with furniture, but Clyde has been selling many of our older pieces to buy more stock in the hospital."

"They were that old?"

"Oh, yes. One Queen Anne chest of drawers was worth almost two thousand dollars."

"I see." Abra would definitely have to study up on antiques while she was here.

"I picked it up in Cuba, of all places, but that was the first time I was there. There are mansions full of the most glorious pieces practically ripe for the picking. I'm telling you, it's a virtual gold mine untapped.''

"In Cuba?'' Abra was unconvinced.

"God, yes. You should see some of the antiques picked up from Panama and Haiti. No one ever thinks of those places when they think of antiques, but some of the most incredible pieces in the world come from the houses of former dictators and drug lords. They may be criminals, but they usually have excellent taste when it comes to furnishings. I'm going to miss it all so much. The thrill of the deal and the victory of each new acquisition. In my mind I've already died and gone to heaven a dozen times.''

"Thank goodness the rest of you hasn't given up the fight," said Abra with a smile.

"Not yet anyway,'' said Thomas. "I almost wish I'd had one of those near-death experiences people have written so much about. They say you're much more calm and relaxed about dying after you have an NDE. People who have experienced it feel that after a brush with death one comes back with renewed zest and appreciation for life and even more of the brain is used than before, perhaps even endowing some with psychic ability.''

"That's very interesting,'' said Abra. "But there's no solid scientific evidence to—''

"To hell with solid scientific evidence. Is that going to comfort you when *you* die? It sure as hell won't comfort me. I want the light and the tunnel and all those happy, glowing faces and open arms to welcome me. Who cares if it's just a random firing of neurons in the brain that makes it all happen? I want to feel the perfect love all these people talk about.''

"It's a wonderful idea,'' Abra agreed. "It would be nice if the last thing all of us felt was perfect love.''

"I think I've become a bit psychic even without an NDE,'' Thomas confessed. "Like a blind person's ears become sharper, I think my brain has become sharper. Like when you came in here just a minute ago, rubbing your arms and looking slightly queasy, I knew you'd just been listening to Peterwell's parrots. Were you?''

Abra nodded. "You're used to it?"

"Never. Damned things sound like a human in agony."

"Why do they keep the birds?"

"Because he can. Peterwell looks like a cockatoo himself. His eyes are always red-rimmed, like he hasn't slept in God knows how long, and his hair sticks straight up on his head, almost as if he combs it that way. It's not as white as his cockatoos, but it's close. His wife Louise is a nice lady. One of those gentle pet people who get along better with animals than they do with humans. Clyde said she sold her pet shop this spring and planned to retire, but the sale was probably made to finance another dozen exotic birds for her husband."

"Isn't there some ordinance against it?" Abra asked.

"Of course. But Peterwell has circumvented it. More than once he's dared us to sue him."

"Does he breed them for money?"

"No, he works in maintenance at Riverpark. You've probably seen him."

"What about the man next door?" Abra asked. "The one with the two boys."

Thomas smiled. "What about him?"

"What does he do? Your brother told me he's an ex-police detective, but I saw him wearing a white coat earlier. It looked like a lab coat."

"Mr. Campbell crafts artificial eyes and scleral shells. On occasion he'll make someone a new nose or a new ear. Nice looking, isn't he?"

"Is he? He ducked into his house the moment he saw me."

"Zane's gotten a bit bashful in the last four years. His speech was impaired by the bullet that ruined his police career. He works out of his home and hardly goes anywhere."

"His name is Zane?"

"That's right. What time is it, Abra? My stomach is beginning to rumble."

"Then it's time to eat. I baked some mackerel while you were sleeping. And a potato. Your brother was kind enough to provide me with a list of your favorite foods."

"My brother, the prince. He's incredibly good to me, you know. Works like a dog."

"Yes, I'm sure he does." Abra left her chair and went to the kitchen to prepare a tray. When she brought it to him, Thomas smiled sadly.

"You never saw yourself as a private nurse, did you? A cook, sheet changer and mother confessor. You look like you'd rather be back on the ward, wearing those clunky white shoes and checking your pockets for fresh thermometer covers."

Abra looked directly at him. "I'm a nurse, Mr. Conlan, whether it's here or at Riverpark. To tell you the truth, I feel as if I've been given a working vacation of sorts."

"Not quite," said Thomas with a smile. "I still have my buzzer, and I'll make good use of it."

"Please do so. I'm here to give you all the attention you need."

"Because my brother is chief of staff?"

"Exactly."

"I thought so. Hand me that fork, please."

Abra handed the fork to him and then turned on his television when he requested she punch the button on the remote. She put the remote on his tray and left him to eat while she returned to the kitchen.

From the window she saw the boy who had been spying on her earlier walk across the lawn to a shed in the backyard and take out a bike. He rode across the grass to the front, and it was obvious there was little or no air in his tires. Abra walked to the living room to watch him and saw him ride past the Conlan drive to the house next door to the north, where the retarded man lived with his mother. The retarded man bounded onto the porch, his face alight with joy. He disappeared around the side of the house and soon emerged with a bike of his own. Abra saw the boy say something, to which the man answered and shook his head.

The boy's face reddened and he began to shout at the retarded man and point his finger. The man began to cry and shake his head again. The boy, Eli, got off his own bike and tried to wrest the smaller bike from the retarded man. The retarded man responded by shoving Eli away. Eli fell back onto his own bike and let out a howl of pain that sent Abra rushing for the front door. She ran across the lawn and reached Eli just as he was struggling to rise. A wrinkled older woman came outside and began to admonish the retarded man, who was standing with his head down and his long arms at his sides.

Abra helped Eli up and turned him so she could look for damage. There was a severe laceration on the underside of his left arm, one that would require stitches. The skin was purpling and the gash was welling up with dark red blood. She asked the distraught woman for a clean, dry cloth and gave the jabbering Eli a firm squeeze.

"Calm down now. We'll apply pressure and stop the bleeding. Then we'll get your father so he can take you for some stitches."

"I want my dad now," Eli told her, tears streaming down his white, frantic face. "That's Cyndi Melo's bike."

"Who is Cyndi Melo?"

"The girl who's missing. Chance said he found the bike in the ditch by the bridge. He says it was laying in the water under some weeds and he took it out. He's lying."

"Eli," Abra said firmly. "Take some deep breaths and let them out slowly. We'll go and see your father in a minute. I'm sure he'll know what to do about the bike."

"My arm's hurting where you're holding it."

"I know it is. Here's Chance's mother now." Abra thanked the woman and firmly applied the clean cloth to the wound.

"What happened, Eli?" asked Chance's mother.

"Chance took a girl," said Eli. "He's got her bike. Ask him what he did with her."

"What girl?"

"Cyndi Melo. You ask *him*. Ask him what he did to her."

"Eli, you know Chance would never hurt a soul. It's not in him to hurt anyone."

"He hurt *me*," cried Eli.

"You frightened him, child. Look at him over there shaking like a leaf. He doesn't understand what's going on. All he knows is that you tried to take his bike."

Eli looked at Abra. "Let's go get my dad. He told me to come over and look at the bike to see if I recognized it."

Abra nodded and advised the old woman to leave the bike exactly where it was. The police would probably come for it, and if there was any evidence to support what Chance had said, it was best not to risk destroying it.

Chance's mother agreed, and hurried her still weeping son into the house.

"Goddamn retard," muttered Eli as they walked away from the drive. "Big, stupid, damn dummy."

"Watch your mouth," said Abra.

Holt came to the door at the ring of the doorbell.

"Holy shit," he breathed when he saw the blood on Eli. Then he opened his mouth and began to yell for his father.

Zane emerged with a frowning expression that changed to surprise when he saw Abra and then worry when he spotted Eli.

"What happened?" he asked his son.

"It's Cyndi's bike," answered Eli. "It is. He said he found it in a ditch. When I tried to take it away from him, he pushed me and I fell down on my bike."

"He needs stitches," said Abra. "You should take him to the nearest emergency room."

Zane didn't look at her. He reached in his pocket for his car keys and turned to Holt. "You stay here until we get back."

Holt nodded and Abra stared as Zane pushed open the door

and led his son outside without another word. She went out after them and stood on the porch as they slid into the white Buick in the driveway.

She watched as the car backed down the long drive, and behind her she heard Holt say something. Abra turned.

"Excuse me?"

"I said thanks for helping my brother."

"You're welcome," said Abra. She opened her mouth to say something else, then she changed her mind and walked away.

In the Peterwell house, Craig had just finished dragging Louise into the laundry room beside his workshop in the basement. Sweat poured down his face and he used a handkerchief from his back pocket to mop his neck and forehead. Louise was unconscious. From the pain, he guessed. He had broken both her arms and both her legs. She was already puffy. She'd probably swell up like a poisoned pup. He walked over to a basket of dirty towels and sheets and dumped it out on the floor. Then he dragged Louise on top of the pile. The smell was bad, but she would be more comfortable than if she were on the cold, damp basement floor.

Craig was in a state of shock over what he had done. He didn't know what had come over him. For months now he had dreamed of taking a two-by-four and whacking her with it, but to actually let himself go and do it, well, all he could do was stare blankly at his hands and ask what they had done to him. He was going to be in big trouble if anyone found out. He would be in the worst trouble of his life if anyone knew what he had just done. He would have to keep Louise hidden until he could think straight and figure out what to do.

He thought briefly of going ahead and killing her, getting her out of his guilty sight altogether, but then he would have her corpse to deal with, and Craig wasn't sure he could handle anything like that. He could just see himself struggling with a body and trying to explain it to his neighbors. And he wasn't certain if he actually *could* kill her. Beating her up and breaking her bones was one thing, but to kill her would be quite another. Craig didn't think he had it in him.

He was certainly calmer now that he had worked off some of his tension.

Calm, but exhausted. He trudged back up the stairs and sat down on the couch to think while he rested his aching arms. He would have to feed and water her, certainly. He wondered if he should gag her.

No, he decided. Louise would be indistinguishable from the birds.

What if she peed on herself? he thought suddenly. What if she messed all over that lime green housedress he hated so much?

His lips twisted in disgust. Maybe killing her wasn't such a bad idea after all. Less mess.

He put a hand to his forehead. What in hell was he thinking of? What had he done? He couldn't believe she wasn't sitting there in that chair getting ready to watch one of her stupid soap operas. Craig was convinced even the birds watched her "stories," as she called them. She should have been there. Or in the kitchen. Anywhere but where she was right now.

God, what was wrong with him? He hadn't been right lately. Craig knew that. No one could say anything to him without making him angry. It was just the fact that no one ever seemed to *listen* to him that upset him so. He could talk and talk and people would nod their heads, but he knew they weren't listening to him. Not just the little things, like asking Louise what they were having for dinner, but big things too, things that were really important to Craig, where he thought his opinion should matter, that someone shouldn't interrupt him before he was finished to tell him their opinion, because they hadn't even heard *his* yet.

People didn't listen anymore. They listened to the frigging television more than they listened to the person sitting right beside them. That wasn't right. There was no way that could be right.

Craig considered himself a smart man, an intelligent man, and if no one listened to him, then what was the world coming to?

Sometimes he wondered if he were shrinking and no one could hear him. Or if he was the only one who could hear himself. Sometimes he wondered if he only *thought* he was talking.

But he knew. He was talking and no one was listening.

Except Louise. Craig had guaranteed she would listen to him now. She would hang on every word.

He left the couch and went to the kitchen for a glass of water. He carried the glass downstairs with him, slopping water as he went. When he reached the basement he went to the laundry room and moved to kneel beside his wife.

"Louise?" he said softly. "Are you awake yet?"

A moan came from deep within her. It seemed to take hours, but when she finally opened her lids, fear immediately entered her eyes. Craig saw it and felt bad. It also irritated him.

"I'm sorry," he said. "I didn't mean to do what I did, Louise. You have to believe that. I didn't know what I was doing. It just happened. I wish I could take it back now, but I can't. Here's some water. Are you thirsty?"

"Aaaambulance," Louise managed.

Craig smoothed her hair from her forehead. "I know that's what I should do, but if I call an ambulance for you, I'll wind up in jail, and who would take care of the birds?"

"Won't . . . tell," she whispered.

"You say that now, but who knows how you'll feel once you're pumped full of painkillers and feeling a little better. I can't take the risk, Louise, you understand that. I'll do the best I can for you, but I still have some things to figure out."

Fear brightened her eyes again. "What?"

"How to keep you from pooping all over yourself, for one thing."

"You're keeping me . . . here?"

"I'm afraid to take you to the hospital, Louise."

"I could die. Infection will—"

"I said, I'm sorry. You just should have listened to me. You sold your pet shop when I asked you not to. You put all the money in an account with just your name and I asked you not to do that. It made me sick to my stomach to know how you actually think of me. I know it was your pet shop and this is your house, but I contribute income of my own, Louise."

"You buy birds."

Craig's nostrils flared. "They are an investment. How many times do I have to tell you that?" He put the glass of water down beside her and got to his feet. "See? See what I mean about no one ever listening to me? Those birds are worth *thousands* of dollars. Any child on the street knows that. Do you ever wonder why the neighborhood kids are always coming over here? Because they like to look in the windows at the pretty birds. People like pretty birds, Louise. People buy pretty birds, and they spend good money for them. Those birds will pay for my retirement some day. They will."

Before Craig could go on, the doorbell rang. Without actually thinking about what he was doing, he stepped on his wife's broken leg until she blacked out again. Then he hurried upstairs to look out the window.

A police officer stood on his porch.

Craig's vision darkened in alarm and he felt his sphincter loosen slightly as he opened the door.

"Yes?" he said in a tight, tiny voice.

The officer looked Craig over and then checked something on the pad in his hand.

"Are you Mr. Morley?" he asked.

Craig smiled hugely at him and pointed. "No, the Morley woman and her boy live right over there."

"The white house?"

"That's right."

"Okay. Must've copied down the wrong address. Sorry to have bothered you."

"It's no trouble," Craig assured him, and as the officer stepped off the porch, he closed the door.

The man had said nothing about the birds. But then the birds had been strangely silent while the policeman was at the door. Craig crept to the window and watched the policeman back his car out of the drive and move it across the street.

He wondered what was going on over at the neighbor's house.

# CHAPTER

## 4

MARK VAUGHN HELD HIS four-month-old daughter and stared through the smudged glass of the picture window at the police car across the street. He watched the cop get out and approach the door, and he saw Mrs. Morley emerge and start talking with her hands. She was pointing to a bike in her driveway. The cop walked over to look at the bike.

"Valerie," Mark called. "Come and look at this."

"What?" Her voice was muffled. She was still folding laundry downstairs.

"Come up here and look at this. There's a cop at the Morley house."

His wife puffed up the stairs. She was still heavy with the weight gained during pregnancy, and she tired easily.

"What are they doing?"

"It's just one cop. He's looking at a bike in her driveway. Did they ever find that kid who was missing?"

"What kid?" asked Valerie.

"The little girl who was riding her bike when she disappeared on Monday."

"Oh. No, I haven't heard anything." Valerie stood at the window beside him and looked through the glass. She frowned. "Is Mrs. Morley crying?"

Mark squinted to see, and as he opened his mouth to answer,

31

another patrol car arrived. The second police officer got out to look at the bike and the two talked for several moments before turning to Mrs. Morley. Her hands flew to her mouth and she began to shake her head. Both policemen advanced on her, hands out as if in supplication.

"I can't believe this," said Valerie.

"What?"

"They think Chance did something."

"Naw, they probably just wanna talk to him."

"Just watch, Mark. It happens every time. Chance is a retarded adult and in this society it's enough to make him a suspect."

"Val—" Mark closed his mouth as he saw Chance come out on the porch. Chance was obviously crying. His shoulders shook with his sobs.

The policemen talked with Chance, and he pointed several times to the east while he answered their questions. Mark frowned as he tried to think what was east. Laurel Street was east, where the girl had lived.

One cop walked over to the bike again and began a closer inspection. After a moment he began to nod and point with his fingers to several areas on the bike.

Soon he straightened and carefully picked up the bike by the underside of the seat. He placed the bike in his trunk and talked with the other officer before getting in his car again. He started the engine and drove off east.

"He's going to check with the girl's parents, to see if it's her bike," Mark speculated.

"Why is the other cop staying?" asked Valerie.

"I don't know."

They stood at the window, attention across the street, and the baby gurgled, trying to recapture their interest.

Valerie looked at her daughter and poked her gently in the tummy. "Hi, squirt. How's my little 'Lissa?"

The baby grinned wetly.

"He's leaving now," said Mark.

"They'll be back," Valerie said, and she turned once more to the window. Mrs. Morley was patting her son in the middle of his broad back and attempting to lead him inside the house. Chance craned his head to see the policeman's departure.

"Should've gone over and complained about those fucking birds," Mark grumbled.

"Mark, watch the language."

"She doesn't understand us yet."

"She can still hear us, and she hears the emphasis we put on certain words."

"That's why we say fuck. Because it emphasizes where we need it to."

Valerie rolled her eyes. "The police wouldn't do anything about the birds anyway."

"I know. But *I* might."

Valerie had started back downstairs, but she stopped and looked at her husband. "What?"

"You heard me."

"What are you going to do?"

"You'll see."

"Mark, don't you think they'll know who did it?"

"Not if I do it right."

"Wonderful." Valerie threw up her hands. "You're never going to change, are you? You still operate like a goddamned criminal."

He laughed and bounced his daughter until she smiled at him. "Watch your language, Mom."

"I'm serious, Mark. What was your plan? To poison their birdseed? Throw salt on their wings?"

He turned to look at her. "Salt?"

"Come on," said Valerie. "Didn't you ever have a parakeet? Any kid with a parakeet had to check and see if salting its wings kept it from flying."

"Did you do it?"

"We were kids. We also tied our dog's front legs together to see what it would do. Kids do mean things sometimes. Responsible adults don't, if you get my drift.''

"Okay, but don't come crying to me next time the birds wake up you or Melissa.''

"I won't. Don't you do anything stupid. You're still on parole.''
Mark smiled at her. "I won't.''

"Swear to me, Mark.''

"I swear. Okay, okay, I *swear.*''

When Zane and Eli reached home it was dark. Holt had the porch light on for them. Zane opened the door and told Eli to go to bed. He walked into the living room and found Holt engrossed in a television program. Zane plopped down on the couch beside him, and when a commercial came on, Holt turned to look at his father. "How many?''

"What, stitches?''

"Yeah.''

"Twelve.''

"Did he cry?''

"Is that a big deal, whether he cried or not?''

"No.''

"You're just looking for something to tease him about.''

"Yep.''

"Don't. He's pretty upset about Chance having that bike. He thinks Chance did something to Cyndi Melo.''

"Do you?''

Zane put up a hand to rub at his eyes. "Not really. Chance probably found the bike right where he told Eli he did. I think he told me he didn't remember where he got it because he knows I'm an ex-cop and he wasn't sure if taking the bike was right.''

"I saw the cops over there a little while ago.''

Zane sat up. "At the Morley house?''

"Yeah. They took the bike.''

"Mrs. Morley must have called them as soon as we left. They didn't take Chance, did they?"

"Take him? No."

"Good." Zane had been worried about that. They must have found something on the bike to corroborate what Chance told them.

"Dad?"

"Yeah?"

"It was nice of Mr. Conlan's nurse to help Eli the way she did. It looked pretty rude when you just got in the car and didn't say anything. Why didn't you thank her?"

Zane left the couch and stood. "I was worried about Eli. Did you thank her?"

Holt nodded. "She's nice looking. Did you get a look at her?"

"Yeah."

"She doesn't look like any nurse I ever saw."

Zane looked at his son and cocked an eyebrow. "You're beginning to sound like Eli."

Holt snorted.

"I'm going to bed," said Zane. "Turn off the lights when you're finished watching TV."

"I will. Goodnight, Dad."

"Goodnight."

As Zane walked down the hall he felt his face burn at the idea that he had embarrassed his son by his behavior. He had wanted to say something to the nurse. God knows he had tried, but nothing would come out. She was better than nice looking, and Zane didn't know if he could bear to see the pity or the derision that was sure to fill those large blue eyes once he started talking. It was more than a matter of pride with him; it was self-esteem, confidence and everything else that made a human being happy to be in his own skin. He was tortured with the idea that she would feel sorry for him. Worse than being taken for a drunk was being pitied and treated the way Chance Morley was treated, as if he couldn't think for himself and needed help finishing sentences. Zane would rather avoid her for the rest of the summer than spend one minute with her looking at him with a gentle frown of sympathy on her face.

Just being close to her and smelling her skin had reminded him that he hadn't slept with a woman since before his divorce, over two years ago.

He went into his bedroom and closed the door behind him. He stripped down to his briefs and sat on the edge of his bed to look out the window. Across the lawn he could see what Eli had said was her window. The light was on, but the shades were drawn. He could see nothing.

Zane sat in the dark and looked at the starless night. If Holt only knew how he loathed the sound of his own voice. How he would rather say nothing at all than listen to the damaged words that came from his struggling lips and tongue. He knew the agony his son suffered when Zane spoke in front of his friends. He knew the guilt Holt tortured himself with, for being ashamed of his father.

Eli didn't care. Eli was a merciless mimic when he thought Zane couldn't hear him. Zane heard him, but he was amused by his carefree younger son. Zane tried to make fun of himself just as often, to lighten the sometimes oppressive atmosphere of the house.

Things had been different when their mother was here. There was more laughter. More arguing. More everything. Now there was a strange sense of being caught up in time and waiting for something to happen, good or bad.

Zane thought about Cyndi Melo and the bike Chance had found. This was definitely something bad. Someone had snatched a little girl in the middle of the day and no one saw a thing. Snatched her and dumped her bike under the walking bridge in some weeds. Zane considered going over there tomorrow and having a look around, but the police would have been there already to do the same thing. If there was anything to be found, they would have found it.

And if the sun was out, his patient would be coming back. Zane didn't like to make eyes on days that were cloudy. He couldn't see the true color of the good eye and couldn't duplicate it. It was better to wait until he had a bright, sunny day to work with.

He also had to go over and make an apology and say a thank you to a certain nurse, or he would lose what little respect his sixteen-year-old son still had for him. It wasn't going to be easy, but he would do it. He would steel himself against whatever expression entered her eyes and force himself to say the words. Then he would take Eli to Mrs. Morley's house and force him to apologize to Chance. That wasn't going to be easy either, considering that Eli now regarded Chance as a danger to the community. Zane would have to convince him somehow that just because Chance had found the bike didn't mean he had taken his classmate.

Anyone could have taken the girl, anyone at all. It was one of those crimes that would either be solved in the next few days or in the next few years, when someone stumbled across a pile of small bones and recognized them as human.

Zane settled himself down on his bed and closed his lids tight. He was glad to be out of the police business. He was a nicer person now that he no longer dealt with such occurrences on a daily basis. Cops usually saw people at their worst, and after a while it produced a shift in attitude. Zane hadn't recognized this until after he wasn't a cop anymore. In many ways he was grateful for the bullet that changed his life.

Until it came to talking to pretty women.

# CHAPTER

# 5

ABRA LIFTED THOMAS FORWARD on the bed so she could wash his back with the soapy washcloth she held. His skin was covered with red blisters that reminded her of childhood chicken pox; a reaction to the medicine he was forced to take, Clyde had told her. Thomas's hair stood out in spiky tufts above the back of his neck. Blood ran to his face as he leaned over, giving him a strained expression.

"As I was saying, Abra, my brother and I come from a strict Catholic background, so you might guess my father's reaction when we balked at being altar boys. Clyde didn't want to do it because of his allergies. I didn't want to do it because I hated the parish priest. He was a horrible old thing, with yellow fingers and breath that stank of stale, sour wine. Later, when my father discovered I was homosexual, I blamed it on the priest."

"Did he molest you?" asked Abra.

"No, he never touched me. But I had to blame it on someone, you understand. That was what we did in those days. And my Aunt Iris told me to do it."

"Your aunt? Why?"

"Because she hated the priest as well and wanted an excuse to leave the parish, Thomas said with a laugh. "I dearly loved my Aunt Iris. So did Clyde."

"Is Clyde heterosexual?" Abra asked.

"Yes."

"Has he ever married?"

"Twice. Both lasted less than a year. My brother is a very exacting person, Abra. Most people don't live up to his standards. People eventually wind up disappointing him with their humanness. He's happy in his devotion to his work."

"Have you both abandoned the church?"

"Abandoned the church," Thomas echoed. "That's an interesting phrase, isn't it? Our father wanted nothing more to do with the church after I told my little lie. And, naturally, he wanted nothing more to do with me, whom he considered to be sick. He later called Clyde evil and perverted for taking my side and for believing homosexuality to be as natural as heterosexuality."

"Is your father gone now?"

"In mind, but not in body. He's in a nursing home, where people in wheelchairs are parked in hallways and left to rot, and everybody has a rosary around their crooked, gnarled little fist."

Abra finished his arms and pushed him back to bathe his chest and groin. Thomas began to chuckle.

"What?" she said.

"I never get over how impersonal you people are. You're soaping away at a person's privates and you might as well be washing a dog in a tub in the front yard."

She grinned. "To me you *are* a dog in a tub in the front yard, at least while I'm washing your privates."

Thomas started to laugh and ended up in a coughing fit. When he finished he told her to hurry up, he was getting cold.

Abra finished bathing him as quickly as she could and helped him into fresh pajamas. She gave him his medication and then carried the pan of water and wet towels into the bathroom. When she came out, Thomas was asleep.

The bath had worn him out, she guessed. Or the coughing. She was on her way to the hall cabinet to prepare the next round of medications when the doorbell rang. She walked to the door and peered through the tiny window in the top. It was him—the neighbor.

She opened the door and looked at him without saying a word.

"Hi," he said.

"Hello."

She waited, and he opened his mouth and said something she didn't come close to understanding.

Abra said, "I'm sorry, I didn't get that."

He slowed down and tried again. "I wanted to apologize for yesterday. And to thank you for helping my son. I appreciate it. I would have thanked you last night, but sometimes my speech is hard to understand."

"You're speech-impaired."

"Yes."

"Did you manage to communicate with the doctor at the emergency room?"

"Yes."

"Good. How is Eli?"

"He's fine."

"Was anything resolved yesterday concerning the bike?"

He looked at her in surprise and she noticed for the first time the odd color of his eyes. He nodded and said, "I spoke with Mrs. Morley this morning on the phone. It belonged to Cyndi, the missing girl. The police believe Chance found it under the walking bridge, but they're coming back to ask him more questions."

"I'm sorry?"

"I said they're coming to ask more questions today."

"Oh. I hope they don't upset him too much. He was scared to death yesterday."

"So was his mother," said Zane.

Abra nodded and they stood looking at each other a silent moment. Finally she stuck out her hand.

"I'm Abra Ahrens, Mr. Conlan's nurse."

He shook her hand. "Zane Campbell."

"Mr. Conlan tells me you make artifical eyes."

He nodded.

"Sounds very rewarding."

"It is." He backed away from her. "Thank you again for helping Eli. I'm sorry if I seemed rude."

"I understand," said Abra. She cleared her throat and said, "Mr. Campbell, we'd love some of those tomatoes you had yesterday. Would you happen to have any left? I enjoy cooking with fresh tomatoes."

He stopped and stared at her.

"Tomatoes," Abra repeated.

He nodded. "I'll bring some to you."

"No, I can come and get them. Mr. Conlan just went to sleep. Do you mind?"

"No."

She stepped out onto the porch and pulled the door closed behind her. Thomas hadn't slept well last night, so he was sure to sleep for several hours today, and she had her beeper in her pocket if he needed her. She fell into step beside Zane as he walked across the lawn to the front porch of his house.

"Mr. Conlan said you're an ex-detective. How long were you on the force?"

"Fourteen years."

Abra's brows lifted. "Do you miss it?" she asked.

"No."

Abra opened her mouth to make another query, but a yelp from Eli prevented it. The startled boy was in the living room in his underwear when Zane opened the door. Eli made an immediate, diving exit when he saw Abra. She smiled and turned to Zane. "The modesty of a pre-pubescent male is matched only by that of a pre-pubescent female."

The corner of Zane's mouth curved as he led the way to the kitchen. Abra looked around herself in surprise. No bowls half full of milk and floating cereal in the sink. No crumbs on the counters or on the floor. The kitchen was spotless. She followed him to the pantry, where he opened a paper sack and began filling it with tomatoes from the bucket by the back door.

"I love tomatoes," Abra said as she watched. "I saw you taking the bucket to the Morley house yesterday. Is that when you saw the bike for the first time?"

Zane glanced at her. "Yeah."

"I saw the Cyndi Melo segment on the news the other day but thought nothing of it until I came here."

She waited for him to make a comment, but it never came. After two minutes of dead silence, Abra gave up. She thanked him for the tomatoes when he handed the sack to her and turned to find her own way out. He followed her into the living room, and she thought he might stop her, but he didn't. He let her open the door and step outside before saying something she couldn't understand. She thought it sounded like "goodbye." Abra didn't respond and she didn't look back. She carried the tomatoes to the Conlan house and took them inside and dumped them in the kitchen sink.

So much for Zane Campbell.

She walked into the hall to check on Thomas and found him still sleeping. She went to her room to find a book and saw Zane out in the backyard in his garden. She moved to the window to watch him. He was picking green beans.

As if sensing her gaze, he looked up at her window. Abra's impulse was to move away, but she forced herself to remain still. When he looked down again she turned from the window. She went into the hall and paused outside Clyde Conlan's closed bedroom door.

Abra wasn't a snoop, but a closed door was a temptation impossible to resist. She opened the door and looked inside. The room was obviously the master bedroom of the house, with its own bathroom and walk-in closet. Abra slipped inside and looked at the furnishings. The antiques were breathtakingly beautiful, but the room itself lacked warmth. There were no personal items

in view to give the space identity. No loose change on the ma-
hogany nightstand, no paperbacks lying open, no slippers under
the bed. The room was as neat and impersonal as the chief of
staff himself.

Guilt niggled at her and she moved toward the door. On the
wall beside the exit was a framed photograph of Thomas and
Clyde as boys and two stern-looking people who must have been
their parents. Abra made a face and left the room. She intended
to check on Thomas again, but she found herself heading for
the kitchen and the window there. Zane was still in the garden,
shirtless now, with his back to her.

Abra looked at his brown skin and felt her breathing shift. She
knew herself well enough to recognize what she was experiencing
and the knowledge annoyed her. She had better things to do
with her time.

She always did.


Craig hurried home on his lunch break to check on Louise in
the basement. She was just as he had left her—a little worse,
actually, having turned purple and green and yellow and red in
color. She had swelled, as he guessed she would. Only her face
was normal in size. Her eyes opened when he came down the
stairs and he saw pure agony in the glazed, feverish orbs. Craig
felt terrible.

Her lips moved, but nothing came forth except a low, sonorous
moan.

Craig approached and knelt down beside her. "I got some pills
for you from the head nurse whose central air unit I fixed last
month. I told her my back has been killing me at night and I
can't sleep, so she gave me some really good pain pills. She owed
me."

Louise's fingers moved, so he guessed she had heard him. He
took the bottle from his shirt pocket and showed it to her. She
moaned again, this one tapering off into a noisy expulsion of air.

"Here." Craig shook out a couple of pills. "Let me get you some fresh water and you can take these."

He rushed up the stairs for the fresh water and then rushed back down, slopping water again. He held up her head so she could take the pills and drink the water, and then he lowered her to the towels.

"Have you soiled yourself yet, Louise?"

"Unh."

Craig lifted the lime green housedress and checked the large diaper he had placed on her earlier. She had peed in it, but there was no poop. Craig sighed in relief and patted her on the leg.

"Gotta go check on the birds. I'll see you tonight when I come home. Maybe you'll feel like eating something then."

Her head lolled and her lids closed. Craig sighed again and turned to go up the stairs. The birds were excessively loud today, as if they missed Louise and were trying to tell him about it. Craig fed and watered them and looked around wondering what else he should do. Then it hit him. He turned on the television and some of the noise stopped. Good. Okay. Everyone looked happy for the moment.

He went into the kitchen and made himself a pimiento loaf sandwich and ate it while standing over the sink. It had been a good day today so far. Nothing major had screwed up at the hospital and he had been successful in obtaining pain pills for Louise. He thought of the doctor he had helped last winter by visiting his house in the dead of night and unfreezing his pipes. Probably couldn't ask any favors there. Doctors were different than nurses. They didn't listen, they just talked.

It was a small thing, Craig knew, but it was virtually all he asked. The world was an unfair place when the only people who got the attention were those who either had the most money or made the most noise. A poor, simple, rational man with a few good ideas had no audience.

Craig couldn't understand people. He never had and he was sure he never would. His father had raised him okay, though he was gone a great deal of the time and never had an opinion on anything until after he had had a few beers. Craig rarely drank and *he* had opinions about everything.

He had been calm and surprisingly relaxed today, with only spurts of anxiety about Louise. He had gone out late last night for some adult diapers, and now that the pills were taken care of, he had no other pressing worry for the moment.

Long-term worries, like what he was going to eventually do with Louise, were far from his mind today. He was handling things a minute at a time, and he was doing well.

At least he thought so until he saw the news crew standing on his front porch. A short blonde pushed the bell as Craig entered the living room. He looked through the screen at the man standing behind her with a camera and nearly stumbled over his own feet.

Pieces of pimiento were stuck in his teeth as he went to open the door.

"Yes?" he said.

"I'm Kelly Cameron," said the blonde, who then told him what station she was from and introduced him to her cameraman, Pete. "We'd like to ask you about the bike found yesterday. We understand it belonged to—" Her voice trailed off as she spotted the birds. "Good lord," she said. "Look at all those bird cages."

Craig frowned at her in sudden annoyance. "You want to ask me about *what?*"

"Is it legal to have all these birds?" Kelly was asking her cameraman.

"It's legal for *me* to have them," Craig blustered. "I have a permit, signed by the lieutenant governor himself."

"What does it permit?" asked Kelly Cameron.

"It permits me to keep these birds."

"Are you a breeder?"

He dismissed the question with a wave of his hand. "What did you come here to ask me about?"

Kelly Cameron's eyes remained on the birds. "The bike you found yesterday. We understand it belonged to Cyndi Melo, the little girl who's been missing since Monday."

Craig snorted. "I didn't find any bike yesterday. Who told you I found a bike?"

"We received an anonymous phone call at the station. We've already confirmed with the police that the bike has been found. Are you telling me you weren't the party who found it?"

"That's what I'm telling you. I have to get back to work now. You people have made me late."

"May we have your name, sir?"

"Look at the mailbox." Craig came out and pulled the door closed behind him.

"Can we do a segment on your birds sometime?" Kelly asked, walking fast to keep up with him.

Craig stopped. "No. Absolutely not."

Kelly smiled. "Are you sure you have a permit to keep that many birds?"

Craig's nostrils flared. He was ready to scream. Why didn't anyone ever *listen* to him?

"Didn't I say I have a permit? Didn't you hear me say that? What's wrong with you? Get off my property now, both of you. Go bother someone else with your ignorant, stupid questions."

He slammed into his van and backed down the drive, still scowling. If he'd had a two-by-four in his hand at that moment, the perky little eyes-too-close-together Kelly Cameron and her friendly cameraman Pete might be in the same shape as his wife.

He drove slowly away from the house to make certain the news team was getting off his property as he had demanded. Pete was putting his stuff away and Kelly was climbing into the van.

Who on earth would have called and told them he had found the little girl's bike?

Craig shook his head as he realized that must have been why the cop came to his door yesterday. Mrs. Morley, across the street, must have found the bike. Or the idiot, her son Chance, had found it. That was more likely.

Perhaps the news crew had gotten the address mixed up like the cop had.

No, too much coincidence.

Someone had wanted the news crew to come to Craig's house in the middle of the day, when Craig wasn't supposed to be there, to talk to Louise. Someone had wanted the news people to come and—

Did someone suspect what had happened? Had someone in the neighborhood tried to contact Louise and failed? He didn't think she talked to anyone on a regular basis. She had been retired only a few months, so she hadn't had time to strike up any enduring relationships with any of the neighbors. She liked the eyemaker across the street, Craig knew, but the ex-cop wasn't the type to hang on the fence and jaw with the neighbors.

Craig didn't know what was going on. He guessed he would have to be more wary of his neighbors in the future.

In the news van, Kelly Cameron flipped the visor to check her makeup in the mirror. "What a jerk," she said to Pete, who nodded in agreement.

"I'm going to check on his permit. Then I'm going to check state law, and international law where those birds are concerned. There's no way a little scrap of paper signed by a lieutenant governor can bypass national law . . . is there?"

"I doubt it," said Pete. He was looking out the window around the neighborhood. "If he didn't find the bike, then who did?"

Kelly took a deep breath and opened the door of the van. "The only way to find out is to start knocking on doors and asking."

# CHAPTER

# 6

ELI OPENED THE DOOR and stood staring at the woman in the pink blazer. When she smiled at him, his jaw dropped slightly.

"Hello," she said. "Is your mother at home?"

"No," said Eli. "We're divorced. You're on TV."

"Yes, I am. How about your father? May we speak with him?"

Eli deliberated; then he said, "My dad isn't here right now. What's this about?"

She smiled again. "It's about a bike found yesterday. We're trying to—"

"You mean Cyndi Melo's bike?"

Kelly Cameron's brows lifted slightly. "You found it?"

"Not really," Eli said honestly. "But I recognized it."

"You recognized it? What do you mean?"

"I mean Chance found it and was riding it around. My dad saw him riding it and asked me to go over and look at it. It was Cyndi's bike. She was in my class at school."

Kelly Cameron was blinking rapidly and scrambling for a pen and pad. "Who is Chance?"

"He's our neighbor. Well, he doesn't live right next door to us, but he lives a house over, that way." Eli pointed past the Conlan house.

"He found the bike where? Can you tell us?"

48

"He told me he found it at the walking bridge, a couple of blocks over. The cops came and took it yesterday."

Pete signaled to Kelly and she stepped back to speak with him. Eli saw her shake her head and he heard her say, "We can't."

At that moment, Eli heard Zane enter through the pantry. Eli said, "If my dad says it's okay, will you guys put me on TV?"

Kelly looked at him. "I thought you said your dad wasn't here?"

"He just came in the back door. You want me to go ask him?"

"Let us talk to him," said Kelly.

"Okay, I'll go get him."

"We'll wait right—"

Kelly never finished what she was going to say. The police cars that rolled to a stop in front of the house down the street claimed her full attention. Pete was already walking in that direction, and Kelly jumped off the porch to go after him.

Eli came back in time to see the police bring Chance out the door and lead him down the drive to put him in the backseat of a police car. Chance's hands were cuffed.

"Dad!" Eli shouted. "They're taking him! They're taking Chance!"

Zane appeared behind him and stared. Pete the cameraman was filming away as Kelly Cameron attempted to interview a frantic Mrs. Morley. Zane strode across the lawns, Eli right behind him.

"Where are they taking him, Dad? He must've done something to her if they're taking him, right?"

"You don't know that, Eli, so just shut up."

Mrs. Morley held out her hand in a plea for help when she saw Zane coming. Zane scowled at the news reporter and the cameraman and Eli saw his father take Mrs. Morley by the arm and pull her into the house away from Kelly Cameron's insistent questions. When Kelly looked at him, Eli shrugged and followed his dad in the door.

"Why did they take him?" Zane was asking Mrs. Morley.

Her face was wet with tears. She shook her white head. "Because of something that happened a long, long time ago. Chance was fifteen and crazy with hormones. Once they calmed down, he was all right, has been ever since. He wouldn't hurt anyone on purpose. Sometimes he forgets how much bigger he—"

"Mrs. Morley, what are you talking about?" Zane interrupted.

She was staring past him, staring at the newswoman outside, who hadn't budged. "There was a young girl who lived next door to us. She was a horrible little child. She used to make fun of Chance and tease him something awful. One day she teased Chance until he got mad and pushed her, like he pushed Eli yesterday. He pushed her off a bridge near our house. She fell over and cracked her skull on the way down. That was over twenty years ago."

Zane looked at the floor and took a deep breath.

"This doesn't look good, Mrs. Morley."

"I know it doesn't," she said, and she began to sob.

Eli grew somber as he watched her. He said, "Chance'll be afraid, won't he?"

"Lord, yes," said Mrs. Morley into her hands. "The poor thing was just terrified. Zane, what am I going to do?"

Zane looked outside. "Go back out and talk to them if you can. Tell them about Chance. The more people know about him, the more they'll sympathize. Don't let her lead you anywhere with her questions."

"Lead me, did you say?"

"She'll ask you if he knew Cyndi Melo, or if he's ever been in any trouble. Tell them what a sweet boy he is. In other words, don't answer any questions directly. I'll call a friend down at the station and find out what they're going to charge him with, if anything."

Eli watched his father lead Mrs. Morley outside once more. Kelly Cameron's cheery smile became a look of genuine concern when she saw the older woman's tears. She looked at Zane and said, "Should we go ahead with this? Is she all right?"

"She's all right," said Eli, before his father could open his mouth. Pete winked at Eli and positioned his camera on Mrs. Morley. Eli backed up with his father to listen. When the interview was over, Zane put his arm around Mrs. Morley and led her into the house. Eli stayed outside. Kelly smiled at him and pointed to his bandage.

"What happened to your arm?"

"I fell down on my bike."

"Ouch. How'd you do that?"

"Chance pushed me."

Kelly stopped and looked at Pete. Pete looked at Kelly. "He pushed you?" said Kelly.

"Yeah. I was trying to get Cyndi's bike away from him."

Kelly signaled Pete. Pete trained the camera on Eli.

"Your name is . . . ?"

"Eli Campbell."

"How old are you?"

"Twelve. That's how many stitches I got in my arm."

"How did you get those stitches?"

"I told you. I fell down on my bike when Chance pushed me. Hey, am I on TV right now?"

"Not right now, no. Has Chance ever hurt you before?"

"Me? No."

"Why did he push you down?"

"Like I said, I was trying to get Cyndi's bike from him."

"You knew it was her bike. You recognized it."

Eli was becoming annoyed. They had already been through all of this. "Yeah. I go to school with Cyndi."

Zane came outside and lifted his brows when he saw the camera on Eli. Eli grinned at him. "I'm gonna be on TV."

"Is that okay?" Kelly was smiling her best smile and looking cute and perky.

Zane looked at Eli's hopeful face, then gave a short nod.

"Thanks," said Kelly. "We appreciate it."

\* \* \*

Mark Vaughn frowned to himself when he saw the news crew at the Morley house. Val had said they would be back and she was right. He drove the red Pontiac past his house, past the Peterwell house, and then cruised a couple blocks over to park the car. He was at the corner and walking across the road before he realized he had parked the car on Laurel, the street where the missing little girl had lived. Tucked in his shirt was his tiny bag of tools. He wore wire-rimmed glasses, and on his lip was a fake reddish gold moustache. His hair was oiled and combed straight back. No one would recognize him.

The news crew had departed and the Campbells were on their way back to their house when Mark rounded the corner. A red Pontiac just like the one he had driven zipped down the street and Mark wondered who had sold it to them. Then he cursed and mentally kicked himself when he realized he had forgotten to put a dealer tag on the Pontiac. It was his own lot, inherited from his father, and he was always forgetting simple stuff like that. It was no wonder Val stayed mad at him half the time.

What she didn't understand was that a talent like Mark's was hard to give up, even if he had inherited a car lot from his old man. With the lot had come responsibility and hard work and all that mature adult bullshit that Mark had no business inheriting—he was a burglar and a damned good one. It gave him a rush like nothing else in his life, not cocaine, not speed, not even the birth of his baby daughter could equal the surge that came with breaking and entering.

Burglary was nowhere on his rap sheet, however. The crime he had been convicted of was assault and battery, which was a joke, considering that Mark had been in the next room while his partner was in there beating the crap out of his girlfriend and raping her daughter. The law treated Mark as if he was right there in on it and sentenced him five-to-fifteen. He did three-and-a-half and walked. His partner was now in Leavenworth, a big-time loser.

Valerie was a secretary who worked for his dad in the front

office. When the old man died, Mark became her boss. Soon he became her boyfriend, then her husband. Three years later they had a daughter. Valerie's influence on him was good, Mark always liked to think. It was only lately, since the birth of their daughter, that Mark had been longing for his old friends and old way of life. This parenting shit was just too serious for him. Valerie had gotten so weird about everything and never wanted to have fun anymore. Everything was Melissa.

Mark loved his daughter, he thought she was great, but he wanted things to be the way they used to be. He wanted Valerie to stop riding him and start smiling again. He wanted her to stop reminding him of his mother.

Valerie told him he was being childish.

He walked along his own street in his water department uniform, checking meters as he went and looking to see if anyone was watching him. He saw no one. It was hot outside and his neighbors had returned inside their air-conditioned homes. When he reached the Peterwell lawn he checked the meter, then he went up and knocked on the door. He stood and waited several minutes, listening for sounds inside the house. He had tried calling every fifteen minutes for two hours that day. He thought he was safe in assuming no one was home.

When there was no answer at the front, he stood back and scratched his head for effect. Next, he walked around to the rear of the house.

The locks on the back door were so easy Mark felt almost disappointed. Anyway, they would lock perfectly again on the way out, with no trace of forced entry. Peterwell wouldn't know what had hit him.

Mark's nose wrinkled as he walked through the kitchen into the living room—he never realized birdshit could smell so bad. There were bird cages with birds everywhere, in every corner of the room, lining the ceiling and covering the walls.

The noise when Mark entered the living room was deafening,

as if the birds recognized an intruder. They jumped about in their cages, their clawed feet scratching and scrabbling for purchase. Mark approached the biggest cage he saw and reached for the hook on the door. Craig Peterwell was going to come home and find every bird out of its cage, shit on the floor, maybe a few birds flying around in the trees outside.

He began to chuckle to himself as he flipped open cage doors and urged the birds to come out. He stopped at the cage of a particularly appealing blue parrot.

"Well, ain't you a beauty?" he said to it. The parrot cocked its head at him. Mark smiled and opened the cage door. The parrot lunged and attacked, gouging flesh from Mark's hand with its sharp beak. Mark yelped in pain and jerked his hand away. Then he shoved it right back in the cage and grabbed the parrot by the neck. The blue head bobbed wildly as the parrot began to screech.

Mark gave the head a vicious twist and dropped the dead bird to the floor. Still breathing heavily, endless nights of squawking running through his brain, he moved to the next cage and removed the shrieking bird inside. When his rage subsided, five birds lay dead on the carpet at his feet.

There was a momentary pause in the screaming and screeching, as if each of the other birds in the room was afraid to be next. During the pause Mark heard another noise. It sounded like it came from the basement. He sucked in his breath and froze. Was someone home?

Soon he heard it again: a noise like someone moaning. Mark let out his breath slowly and crept toward the entrance to the basement. Smaller noises, grunts and whimpers, reached him as he stood motionless at the top of the stairs. Another pitiful moan that threatened to become a wail caused his brow to pucker.

Slowly, carefully, Mark inched down the stairs. When he was at the bottom, he stood just beyond the door and waited to hear something else. When it came it sounded just like one of the birds upstairs: a long, high-pitched, agonized shriek.

Mark twisted the knob and opened the door.

When he saw her he couldn't help the whispered curse that escaped his lips. She looked awful. She looked gross.

She looked like a human sausage.

Mark's first thought was to rush in and kneel down beside her to see if he could do anything to help. Then he thought of calling an ambulance and getting her to the hospital right away.

He dragged his eyes away from her horribly swollen form and was on his way up the stairs to find a phone when it hit him. There were five dead birds upstairs, and plenty of live ones flying around the living room. How was he going to explain that?

He was still on parole. He had six more months to go.

"Man, oh man," he whispered, and he eased himself down on the steps to think for a minute.

He couldn't call an ambulance and stick around. He could go home and put in an anonymous call to the—no, not home. Valerie would be there and she would hear every word.

What the hell had happened? he wondered. Had the old woman fallen down the stairs?

No, he thought. You didn't break both legs and both arms and drag yourself onto a pile of sheets and towels by falling down the stairs.

Peterwell? Had Peterwell done that to her? Mark wondered. The crazy bastard. He must be even crazier than Mark had imagined to leave the old woman just lying there.

Mark thought hard for another minute before deciding to drive to the nearest convenience store and call the cops from a pay phone. He got to his feet and climbed up the stairs. The place was a mess. Dead birds all over the floor, live birds perched on furniture and curtain rods. Mark stepped over the blood and birdshit and carefully let himself out the back door. He paused and stood there with the door open, knowing he should go back and let her know help was coming. Give her some hope. Three years ago he wouldn't have done it, but it was something that would make Valerie proud of him if she knew.

He went back inside and slipped down the basement steps

again. He opened the door at the bottom of the steps and approached the still moaning and whimpering old woman on the bundle of towels and sheets. He knelt beside her head and said, "Listen, I'm going to call the police. They'll send someone out to get you. Shouldn't be long."

Her eyes looked at him, but Mark wasn't sure she saw him. Her fingers twitched, as if she were trying to grasp his hand.

Mark briefly touched her flesh, as much as he could bear to touch it, then he turned to start up the stairs again.

Craig Peterwell was blocking the exit. In his hand was a huge pipe wrench. He popped Mark in the head with the wrench, just enough to send him to the floor with weak knees and blurred vision. Peterwell's nostrils flared red as he bent over. He ripped off Mark's fake moustache and glasses and said, "Was it you? Did you do that to my birds?"

Mark focused on Peterwell. He said, "Did you do that to your wife?"

The wrench came at him like a baseball bat, and sharp, sickening pain sent Mark sprawling onto the cold, damp basement floor at Mrs. Peterwell's feet.

# CHAPTER

## 7

ON THE FIVE O'CLOCK news that evening Zane watched his younger son virtually seal Chance Morley's fate. Eli stood with tears in his eyes as he saw the way his conversation with Kelly Cameron had been edited to make it seem as if he were accusing Chance of willfully and deliberately harming him. Eli was not crying for what he had done to Chance, but because of the disappointment he saw on the face of his father. When the report ended, Eli opened his mouth to speak, but Zane held up a hand. He didn't want to hear anything from Eli at the moment. When he had calmed himself, Zane walked out the door and down the drive. He had no idea what he would say to Mrs. Morley. All he could do was apologize.

He went to her home and pushed her doorbell. After fifteen seconds he pushed it again.

"She's not here," a voice said, and he turned to see Mr. Conlan's nurse, Abra, addressing him from the Conlan porch. "She asked me to tell you she'd be staying with her sister while she tries to find legal help for Chance."

"When did she leave?" Zane asked.

"Sorry?" said Abra. "I didn't understand."

She stepped off the porch and crossed the yard. Zane repeated himself as clearly as he could.

"She left just before you came over," Abra said as she approached him. "The news report upset her."

"I'm sure it did," said Zane. "I came to apologize for Eli."

"Apologize? Yes, I'm sure Eli is sorry."

"I'm not so sure he is." Zane looked at his house and decided to make a stab at trying to explain. "For all his Peeping Tom antics, Eli isn't completely clear on why a grown man would want to kidnap a young girl his age. He's confused, and he's ready to blame someone like Chance, who Eli figures couldn't possibly know any better."

Abra smiled at him. "I understood every word that time."

Zane looked at her. "You did."

"Yes. I agree with you. I find it hard to understand myself, so imagine how it must seem to Eli."

Abra was difficult for Zane to figure out. He wanted to believe she was being more friendly than polite, but her signals were impossible to read. He decided her medical background was responsible for her lack of expression when he spoke. She looked anything but sorry for him. She didn't even look at his mouth like most people; she looked at his eyes.

Zane realized he had been staring at her when he saw her smile again. He found himself inhaling deeper than usual, drawing the scent of her to him. She wore a white sleeveless blouse and a simple skirt. Her shapely legs were bare, her feet were in sandals.

He said, "I'm sorry. I don't know how to do this anymore."

"Do what?"

"Talk."

She frowned. "You're doing just fine." Her mouth was open to say more, but a sudden avian cacophony from across the street claimed her attention. Zane looked to see Craig Peterwell walk out of his house and slam the door behind him. In his hands was a large pipe wrench. His expression when he saw Zane and Abra was one of suspicion. Zane lifted a hand to wave, but Peterwell ignored him and hopped in his van.

"The bird collector?" said Abra.

Zane nodded.

"Thomas told me I might recognize him from Riverpark, but I don't recall seeing him before. I've been tempted to go over and look in his windows. The only parrots and cockatoos I've seen were in the zoo."

"I wouldn't advise it," said Zane. "He's funny about things like that. He scared the hell out of Eli and his friends when he caught them looking in the window."

Abra crossed her arms over her chest and said, "Every neighborhood has a mean old boogeyman who loves to frighten children and be hated by all the neighbors. My neighborhood had Mr. Crane, an old taxidermist."

Zane's mouth curved. "He scared kids with his stuffed animals?"

"He claimed he had a stuffed woman in his house. His late wife. We were always trying to peek in and see her."

Zane smiled. "That's something worth seeing."

Abra looked at him and said, "You speak much better when you're relaxed."

"So I've been told."

"I should go in now," she said. "It was nice talking to you."

"Wait," said Zane. "Was Mr. Crane telling the truth? Did he have a stuffed woman in his house?"

"Yes," Abra said over her shoulder as she turned to go. "He was arrested for violating state funeral laws."

Zane smiled as he watched her walk away from him.

"See you later."

She waved to him and walked across the lawn to the Conlan porch. Zane watched her until she went inside the house. He liked her. Not only was she pretty, she was bright.

At home he found a message from his patient on the answering machine in his office. The forecast was for a clear, sunny day tomorrow. Did he want to work on a Saturday?

Zane called the woman and told her to come in. Eli was still in his room, and Holt was on his phone. Zane stripped off his shirt and went out to the garden to do some weeding. He couldn't stop thinking about the nurse. He thought about the frank appreciation in her eyes when she looked at him, and the smile in her eyes. The story about the taxidermist was a good one. He enjoyed women with a sense of humor.

As a detective he had encountered women on a daily basis, most of them overly friendly with him, some extremely cold. He couldn't remember feeling so comfortable with a woman in such a short time. Especially since his injury. She had a way of making the disability seem less than it actually was, or at least not as noticeable, and he felt grateful.

He looked up at the Conlan house when he had the feeling he was being watched by someone, but there was no one there.

The day before, when he caught her watching him, Zane felt strange. Unconsciously he had tensed his pectorals and sucked in his stomach. He was in good form, with plenty of definition in his arms and chest from working out in the basement with Holt during the week. When he realized what he was doing, he felt ridiculous, but at the same time he experienced a small surge of male pride. He looked good without his shirt and he knew it.

Staying in shape was compensation for his impairment. Part of him he couldn't do anything about, but the rest of him he could, so he was dedicated to his workouts, and he made certain Eli and Holt were just as active.

He felt someone looking at him again and he glanced once more at the Conlan house. Still no one there.

"Hey," said Holt, and Zane felt himself jump.

"Dammit. Don't sneak up like that."

"Once a cop, always a cop," said Holt. "Can I borrow the car tonight?"

"You borrowed it Monday night."

"So?"

"So the rule is once a week. You've already had your day this week."

"It's Friday night, Dad. The weekend. Monday was like a whole week ago."

Zane said, "Still the same week."

"We wanna go to The Palace."

"What's on?"

"Lots of shows."

"No particular movie?"

"Nah. Mike wants to play some video games, meet some girls."

"So go. Be back by midnight."

"Can I have the car?"

"No."

"How are we supposed to get there?"

"I'll take you."

"Forget it. We'll walk."

Zane doubted it. And he was right. Holt went inside to make a phone call, and he was back again in less than five minutes.

"Will you take us over there?"

"Yep."

"And pick us up?"

"If I pick you up, it's going to be at ten o'clock. My patient's coming in early tomorrow and I need to get a good night's rest."

Holt disappeared again to make another phone call. When he returned, he said, "Mike's big brother is going to pick us up if you drop us off."

"Fine. Now, what are you going to do about Eli?"

Holt stopped and stared. "Eli?"

"You're watching him this summer. For money, remember?"

"But not at night," Holt protested, and he was ready to go on when he saw the smile on his father's face. "This is a joke . . . right?"

"Right."

Holt looked heavenward and turned to trudge back into the house. Zane happened to look at the Conlan house again and saw Abra at her bedroom window looking out at him. The expression on her face was difficult to read. She appeared to be deep in thought.

Zane exhaled and experienced something that felt like longing. Just looking at her made him want to know the feel of a woman against him again, the touch of hands on his body, the meeting of flesh. He swallowed as his skin flushed and left him perspiring more heavily than before. He wondered if she knew the effect she had on him. The fantasies she was giving birth to, simply by talking to him and by being so nice.

Abra backed away from the window and felt the lump in her throat slowly begin to dissolve. She had to stop doing this. She had to stop thinking about him and running to the window to look for him like some love-starved novice in a nunnery. She was too old for such nonsense.

She strode into the hall to check on Thomas and found him watching a talk show. She asked if she could get him anything, and he responded by holding a finger to his mouth. She left the room and on a whim she went into Clyde Conlan's office to call her mother.

Her mother's secretary informed Abra that her mother was with a patient. She wouldn't be long. Abra gave her number and hung up. She looked at the top of the desk and put her hands down on the surface. It was empty. Not even a paperweight graced the top of Clyde's desk. He reminded her of a career military man with his penchant for order. She had expected him to call before now, to find out how things were going, but he hadn't. She guessed that meant he trusted her.

Idly she opened drawers and poked through the contents while she waited. When the phone rang she lifted the receiver from the cradle. "Hello?"

"Abra?" said her mother.

"How are you, Mother?"

"What is it, Abra? What's wrong? Joan said you sounded upset."

"She did? I didn't mean to. I just wanted to talk to you. I haven't called since I've been with Mr. Conlan."

"No, you haven't. How are things going? Do you get along with your patient?"

"Yes, very well." Abra put a hand to her forehead. "Mother, there's a man here in the neighborhood. I've seen him only a few times, but I can't stop thinking about him. I've become obsessed with seeing him. I can't walk by a window without looking for him. I've never behaved this way, and—"

"Abra, I don't have time for this right now," said her mother. "Please don't call me in the middle of a work day unless it's extremely important, or in the nature of an emergency."

"Yes, of course. I'm sorry. It's been so long since I've talked to you, and I felt the sudden urge to make contact."

"Completely understandable. You're in a new situation and looking for reassurance. It happens."

"About this man, Mother. He has a speech problem."

"A what?"

"He's an ex-police detective. He was shot in the face."

"He told you this?"

"Mr. Conlan told me. Zane doesn't say much of anything. That's his name, Zane."

Her mother paused. "He probably doesn't like to hear himself speak. That happens. Abra, I've—"

"I think he's divorced. He has two teenage sons, one who likes to peek in windows at me."

"Is he on disability?"

"He makes artificial eyes and other prosthetics for a living."

Her mother said, "He sounds like a man with drive. If you take an interest, for goodness' sake try to follow through this time. Now, unless there's anything else, I really must go. Call me at home later if you must. Goodbye."

Abra closed her eyes and listened to the dial tone in her ear after her mother hung up.

Abra had often heard people talk about how cold her mother was, and instinctively Abra had defended her, believing no one knew the real woman. In the years following the death of her father, Abra gradually lost touch with the mother she loved and soon found herself agreeing with the assessment of those familiar with only the surface of Lee Ahrens. She was a brilliant, noted psychiatrist. And a bitch.

Her remark about 'following through this time' struck Abra. She had no idea how to follow through with Zane Campbell. She had done all she believed was necessary and made her interest and attraction known, and she hadn't the slightest idea what action to take next.

Why she always picked people who had no interest in her, she would never know. The people who *were* interested in her did nothing for Abra. She tried to make them her friends, which only made things worse and wound up making her feel awful about herself when they rejected her friendship. She had no idea how to make a man she was attracted to take an interest in her. Her mother hadn't been the most inspiring role model, and most female friends had long ago grown exasperated by her refusal to be set up or to go out on just a casual, friendly date. Abra saw no sense in wasting someone's time when there was no true interest, and she didn't want her own time wasted in such a manner.

Her attitude made her less than popular at Riverpark. Most of the other single nurses would go out with anyone simply for the sake of going out, and Abra's reluctance singled her out as someone who thought she was too good for the rest of them. That and the fact that she was the daughter of Lee Ahrens had dashed all hopes of winning any congeniality awards at the hospital.

With a sigh she replaced the phone and rose from the desk to walk out and check on Thomas again. He was dozing, his hand still wrapped around his TV remote. She walked into the hall and opened the cabinet to remove his next round of medication.

She was fairly certain Thomas Conlan would die soon. His symptoms were unusual, and he seemed to be losing ground on an hourly rather than a daily basis. She would not say so, of course. She would give him hope until the day he died. She would refuse to let hope die in him.

And that was why it was best if she simply forgot all about this Zane Campbell business and concentrated on her job. She couldn't allow someone with no understanding of disease, someone in obviously optimum health, to interfere with her purpose and sway her from her aim of providing aid and comfort to someone with no other source. There simply weren't enough people in the world who cared.

# CHAPTER

# 8

CRAIG PETERWELL STOOD UNCOMFORTABLY in the doctor's office and looked around himself with dismay. Dr. Ahrens saw his expression and smiled.

"Not what you expected, Mr. Peterwell?"

"It looks like someone's living room," he said.

"Without the television. Why don't you sit down and tell me a little about yourself."

"You don't even have a desk?"

"It's in the other room. Come and sit down. May I call you Craig?"

He nodded. "I went to my doctor for a headache and told him all my symptoms and he sent me to you. There's a mistake been made somewhere. I don't need a psychiatrist."

Dr. Ahrens looked at a chart in her hands and said, "You appear to be dealing with an unusual amount of stress, Craig. I may be able to help you there, and to determine if your headaches mean anything."

"You think the stress is causing my headaches?" he said. "I'm thinking it's the other way around."

"Please sit down, Craig. We'll talk for a few minutes and find out more about you, all right?"

Craig shrugged and finally moved to the sofa to sit down. "What do you want to know about me?"

She sat down on the other end of the sofa and said, "I thought I'd let you relax first. Visiting a psychiatrist can be pretty unsettling the first time. Just tell me about yourself."

Craig spread his hands. "There's not much to know. I work in maintenance at Riverpark and go home at night just like everyone else."

Dr. Ahrens nodded. "Do you enjoy your work?"

"Most of the time, no. Sometimes, yeah. I got a lot of freedom in my position. I can pretty much come and go as I please. I don't usually leave work during the day, but I left this afternoon to go home and check on my wife."

"Is she ill?"

"Not exactly. I can tell you anything, right? I can tell you and you can't tell anyone. Anyway, I never hit her in my life, but the other day I hit her really hard a couple of times and now she's all black-and-blue. Then, today, I find my neighbor in my house and I hauled off and hit him, just smacked the holy hell out of him. I don't know what's wrong with me lately. Must be the stress you talked about."

"Is he going to press charges?" Dr. Ahrens asked.

"Who? My neighbor? No."

"Why do you think you hit him?"

"Because he asked me if I had done that to my wife."

"You mean the bruises?"

"Yeah. I never really hit anybody before. Ever. I've always thought about it, you know, like everyone thinks about it. But I've never gone ahead with it, until now."

"Is your wife upset with you?"

"You could say that, yeah. She's not saying a whole lot to me."

"Why do you think you hit your wife? What prompted the impulse?"

Craig exhaled noisily. "Her not listening to me. She never listens to me. It makes me crazy like nothing else can when people don't pay attention to what I'm saying. The guys under me at work, they don't pay attention and they screw up more work by not listening to me. When I tell them how to do something the right way, I expect them to listen. But do they listen? No, they don't. They do it the way they think it should be done first, then when they find out it's wrong, they come back and ask me what went wrong. I say, did you do it the way I told you, and they say, yeah, and then when I look and see they didn't, I get mad and want to brain the idiots.''

"But you don't."

"No—I'd get fired, and if that isn't a passle of pig poop. *I'd* be the guy fired for *them* not listening."

Dr. Ahrens was nodding in commiseration. "Is there a point in your life, Craig, when you think people stopped listening to you?"

Craig frowned at her. "Is there a . . . oh, okay, I see what you mean." He stopped to think about it. Then he said, "Louise used to listen to me before we got married. The guys at work have never listened to me. They're too stupid, and one of 'em barely speaks English."

"You feel like Louise stopped listening to you after you got married?"

"After a while, yeah. I'd say something and she'd nod and keep doing whatever she was doing, without even looking up. Then she sold her pet shop and started sitting at home watching soap operas. She retired."

"Which upset you more, Craig, the fact that she sold her shop or the fact that she retired?"

He stared at the doctor. "Who cares if she retired?"

"You didn't want her to sell the shop?"

"I loved that place. It was a great place. I met her there, when I went in to buy birds from her. She had the best collection of birds in the city. I figured she was like me, a big bird lover. I was wrong. She's more of a lap pet person, if you know what I mean. Something she can touch and pet and pick up. We can't have anything like that because of the birds. The birds wouldn't like it."

"You've always had birds?" asked the doctor.

"Always. Different kinds. A long, long time ago, back when I was a kid, I used to catch crows and keep 'em."

"You lived on a farm?"

"No, I lived in a one-bedroom house with my dad. There was a big field behind us and I built a cage out there."

"What happened to your mother?"

"She drowned when I was two."

"Did you have a good relationship with your father?"

"I guess. He was always trying to get me to do things with him. Dad worked on offshore oil rigs for weeks at a time. This was in Texas. When he was gone I lived with our neighbors. The dad used to smack his little girls around, and when he did that I went back to the crows, because they were so loud they drowned out everything."

"He beat his daughters?"

Craig frowned. "Yeah. Well, he hit them, anyway."

"Sounds pretty bad. Did you tell your dad about it?"

"Yeah, but he'd just laugh and say they probably deserved to have their butts whipped."

"You didn't think so?"

"I didn't know. They got on my nerves a lot."

"The girls did?"

"Yeah." Craig lifted his head suddenly and looked gratefully at her. "I haven't talked to anyone about this stuff for a long time."

Dr. Ahrens said, "I'm glad you feel like you can talk to me. Do you want to go on?"

"Yeah, just for a minute, then I'll get out of here. What I was wondering just now is what you think I should do about my wife."

"Do you love her?"

"I don't know. I don't think so. Not anymore. Not since she put all the money from her pet shop in her name. That really hurt me."

"You think she should have shared it with you?"

"I think she could have put it in both our names. It bothered me to know she didn't trust me."

Dr. Ahrens folded her hands in her lap. "What do you want to do about your wife, Craig?"

"I'd like to forget her. Just move out."

"Why can't you do that?"

"Because I hit her and I feel awful about it."

"What does she want? Do you know?"

"No."

"Can you ask her?"

"I guess."

Dr. Ahrens was silent a moment. "Craig, why don't you make an appointment with my secretary so you can come talk to me again. Will you do that?"

"Yeah, I guess. Sure."

Dr. Ahrens stood. "Well, thank you for coming to see me today, Craig. You have my number if you need to reach me."

"Thanks." Craig rose from the couch, shook the doctor's cool hand, and then shuffled out the door. He actually felt better. Somebody had listened to him.

Mark awakened in time to throw up and avoid choking on his own vomit. The pain in his head was so intense it made the nausea seem never-ending, and with each throb came the urge to heave. He struggled to place his hands on either side of him and found they were chained together. His feet were chained as well. He opened his mouth and screamed in anguish around his hitching throat. He couldn't believe this was happening to him. He couldn't believe he was a captive in a damp basement, his limbs chained and vomit dripping from his chin, while next to him lay the human sausage lady.

Worse yet, he felt something crawling up his back toward his neck. The basement was not sealed. There were pill bugs in all the corners, egg sacks on the ceiling and a cricket chirping somewhere nearby. Mark didn't want to think about what might be on his back. He thought of rolling over and crushing whatever it was, but if it was a spider, then he might get bitten, and in his own basement he had found more than one brown recluse spider—the spider you didn't want to bite you. He gritted his teeth and forced his mind away from the thing on his back. He craned his hurting head to look at Mrs. Peterwell.

Her eyes were open and staring at him. Her expression was horrified.

"Mrs. Peterwell," Mark gasped. "Can you move?"

"Unh," she said.

"I can't move my arms or legs," Mark told her. "He's got chains on me. Can you see them?"

"Unh."

"Can you help me?"

Her eyes filled with tears and her jaws worked in a monumental effort to speak. "Pain," she managed, and then she repeated herself.

"I know," Mark whispered. He knew. One side of his face felt caked with something that he knew must be blood. His left eye twitched with each excruciating throb of pain. He couldn't see his watch, but from the dimming light he knew Valerie would be worrying about him by now. They had argued again that morning, about sex, but she knew he wouldn't be deliberately late because of that.

He hoped she did, anyway.

What would she do? he wondered. How long would she wait before making some phone calls? Knowing Val, not long. She had probably called work already. They would tell her he had left that afternoon, though his car was still at work. Nobody would know where he went or how he had left, since all the dealer's tags were accounted for.

Goddammit.

The new red Pontiac would be towed off Laurel Street and the police would have no idea where it came from or how it had

gotten there. The car had come in from the factory that morning. There was nothing anywhere on the Pontiac to identify that
it belonged to Mark's dealership. No one would think to count
the new cars to see if one was missing unless the police called,
and God knew how long that would be.

It appeared that in planning the strike on Peterwell and his
birds, Mark had outsmarted himself.

Only one thing gave him hope. If Peterwell had planned to
kill him, he would already be dead. He looked at Mrs. Peterwell . . .

. . . and thought death might possibly be preferable to life in
her condition. He didn't want Peterwell to come home and start
breaking his arms and legs with that fucking pipe wrench. The
pain in his head was bad enough; he couldn't imagine lying there
hour after hour with everything broken and his body in agony.

Though it brought the nausea back to do so, Mark tried to
twist his torso around so he could work himself into a sitting
position. It took what seemed like hours, and was made even
more unnerving by the thing on Mark's back. He turned one way
and the thing crawled the other way. It wasn't going anywhere.
It liked the sweaty shirt of the water department uniform plastered to Mark's back. He stopped several times and tried to will
the thing off, but to no result.

He tried to make a psychic link with Val while he struggled.
He pictured her face in his mind and thought one word over
and over: *birds.*

She would probably go out and rent the Hitchcock film that
evening.

When he finally managed to pull himself up, the pain in his
head and the rush of blood nearly made him black out again.
He dipped back and then fell forward again until the tingling
darkness receded and he could hold his head up without wanting
to puke. He took deep breaths and looked at Mrs. Peterwell
again. He thought he smelled something.

*God, no,* he silently moaned. *Don't let her be lying there shitting all over herself. I couldn't take that. For crissakes, she looks like my grandma.*

Her eyes were squeezed shut, as if she were too embarrassed and humiliated to look at him. Mark attempted to scoot himself out of her sight. She'd probably feel better if she didn't have to look at him.

As he reached the spot he wanted, he heard a commotion upstairs. The birds were raising hell again.

He heard a door close.

Steps on the boards above them.

Peterwell was home.

Mark had some quick decisions to make. Did he put on his car dealer's voice and try to bull and bluster his way out of this, or did he play helpless and hope for mercy?

He thought of the birds he had killed upstairs and decided that for now the helpless bit might be his best move.

Mark hated to do it, but he tumbled himself over again to lie on his side as before. When he heard footsteps coming down the stairs, he began to moan.

He heard movement in the room and peered through his lashes to see Peterwell lifting his wife's hem. The old woman wore an adult diaper under the lime green dress.

Mark's breathing shifted as he realized how long the broken old lady must have been there. More than a day, anyway.

Shit, this is just great, he thought. How long am I going to be here? What the hell was Peterwell thinking?

Peterwell finished changing his wife's soiled diaper and came to jab Mark with his foot. "I know you're awake, so you can open your eyes."

Mark moaned and opened his eyes. "My head," he whispered.

Peterwell snorted. "What did you expect, snooping around in a man's house? You're lucky I didn't have a gun, Mister Glasses and Moustache."

Mark's muscles tensed, and an immediate retort sprang to his

lips, but he forced himself to swallow it. The pipe wrench probably wasn't too far away.

"What are you going to do?" he asked.

"With you? I don't know, I'm still thinking. I thought I'd feed
you a dead bird a day until you'd eaten all you killed. Then I
thought the last two or three might be pretty rotten by the time
you got to them, and it would probably make you sick to eat
them, so I took them to the big incinerator at work."

"A guy I work with knows I'm here," said Mark.

"Nope. I already checked. They don't know where you went
or when you're coming back. Neither does your wife."

"You talked to her?"

"I called the house and told her I was from the dealers' auc-
tion. I said I'd already checked at work and they suggested I call
your home. They said you took off sometimes to go home and
check on your new baby." Peterwell paused. "I haven't been able
to figure out how you got here, but I'm sure it'll come to me."

"I drove a new car right off the factory truck," Mark told him.
"I slapped a dealer's tag on it and parked it around the corner.
When no one shows up to claim it, the police will tow it. They'll
find out it belonged to me. Valerie will know where I am, because
we fought about it this morning. I told her I was going to do
something about your birds and she told me not to. When I don't
come home tonight, she'll know something went wrong."

Peterwell smiled. "She won't call the police, though, will she?
Not with you on parole. Oh, don't look so surprised, I know a
prison tattoo when I see one. A few phone calls told me all I
needed to know about my fine neighbors. She's scared to death
you'll go back to prison, isn't she? If she comes here, I'll deal
with her."

The smugness of the statement made Mark's stomach churn.
Val wouldn't come, thank God, but just the idea of Peterwell
touching his wife made Mark's teeth grind.

"You should have listened to Valerie this morning, Mr.
Vaughn. I've told you and told you that I have a *permit* to keep

these birds, and just because you don't like the noise doesn't mean you have a right to come in and start killing them. You have no idea what those birds were worth to me, Mr. Vaughn."

"I do now," said Mark. "I know what kind of time you're going to get, and I know how you'll do it. You'll be the sniveling punk of the cell block."

He tensed himself for a kick, but Peterwell only shrugged and walked away from him. He went to his wife and took a bottle of pills from his pocket. He shook out two or three, then lifted his wife's head and placed them in her mouth. He gave her a drink of water from the glass beside her head and then disappeared back up the stairs. The birds started raising hell again, and Mark heard Peterwell talking to them as he banged pots and pans in the kitchen.

The smell of frying meat soon reached Mark's nose, causing his stomach to roll in violent protest. The pain was still too much. The reality of his situation was too much. He hung his head and fought to keep from soiling himself.

# CHAPTER

# 9

ZANE INJECTED MODELING COMPOUND into the empty eye socket of his patient and smiled comfortingly at her.

She took a deep breath and said, "Feels strange."

"Try not to move your face too much," Zane requested. "Have you ever had an impression made at the dentist's office?"

"What? An impression? Yes."

"This is similar. It sets up like rubber. I'll use the impression to make a wax eye in the shape of your socket. I'll then use the wax eye for the final mold."

"And the color will be just right?"

"It usually is."

She looked at his face. "You have oddly colored eyes yourself. What color are your parents' eyes?"

"Both my parents have hazel eyes," Zane told her. "My father has brown flecks in his, and my mother has yellow flecks in hers."

"I'd never get this eye if it weren't for you," said the patient. "You don't know how grateful I am. Most folks don't mean to be rude, but it's awful when they stare."

"My father had an artificial eye," Zane said. "I used to beat up kids who made fun of him."

The woman chuckled. "Can't do that now, can you?"

76

He smiled. "You mean because of my speech? I've been tempted a few times."

When the compound was set he walked the woman to a room off his office and showed her a stack of books and magazines to look at while he made the wax eye.

The rest of the day went by quickly, with Zane working on the iris and pupil, the final mold, and finally the painting of the eye, with the patient facing a north window.

By five o'clock that evening she was looking at herself in the mirror and marveling at her new appearance. Her natural eye reddened and became moist with tears. She reached for Zane's hand and squeezed it hard.

"I can't thank you enough. I never dreamed I would look like this. I look so *nor*mal. You got the color just perfect."

"I'm glad you're happy with it."

"I am. Everything looks so real, even the little squiggly red lines."

"Red thread made to resemble blood vessels."

"And it's shiny, too, so it looks even more real."

"Polish on the plastic."

She gushed on for another five minutes before she swept out of the office. Zane closed the door behind her and sat exhausted in his chair. He had a headache, but otherwise he felt pretty good. He enjoyed helping people improve their appearance, and ultimately, their self-esteem. The patient looked like a new woman, and it was clear she felt like one.

After checking his watch he picked up the phone on his desk and punched in a number. Holt and Eli had gone with their mother that morning and wouldn't be back until late Sunday night. Zane listened to the silence of his house in one ear and the ringing of the phone in the other. Finally it was picked up.

"Detective Ptacek."

"Hello, John. It's Zane."

"Who? Zane?"

"Yeah. What's going on?"

"Not much. How are things with you? You making lots of eyes these days?"

"Enough. I was calling about my neighbor. His name is Chance Morley. They picked him up in connection with Cyndi Melo, the missing little girl."

"Oh, yeah, the retarded guy."

"Have they charged him yet?"

"No. They released him to his mother today. They didn't have enough to hold him. The bike had enough mud and guck on it to back up his story about finding it under the bridge. And the other little girl was a long time ago. Then when your kid called up and told how the news got it wrong, that he played with Chance all the time and he never hurt anybody ever, the guys let him go."

"Eli called?" said Zane.

"Yeah, he called this morning. He's not there with you?"

"No, he's with his mom." Zane smiled to himself. The wicked Eli had a conscience after all.

"I just heard another weird thing," Ptacek continued. "Parked out in front of Cyndi Melo's house this morning was a brand new car. Is that weird, or what? Really spooked the parents. Was the guy who took their daughter giving them a trade?"

"Were the keys inside?"

"One in the glovebox. No tag on the car. Nothing to say whether it belonged to anybody. We're running the serial number now to find out where it came from. Should find out in the next couple days or so."

"That long?"

"Yeah. Everyone's sick up here with a damn virus. It's awful."

"They're bad in the summertime," said Zane.

"Huh?"

"I said I'll talk to you again sometime. Thanks, John."

"Don't mention it."

Zane hung up the phone and walked into the kitchen. He ate

a tomato out of the refrigerator while he stood looking at the Conlan house from his pantry window.

Before he could talk himself out of it, he took off his white coat and headed across the lawn.

A voice hailed him halfway between the houses. He looked to see Valerie Vaughn calling to him from across the street. She was beckoning to him with a wave. Zane frowned and walked across the street. He had talked to Valerie on several occasions, but they didn't know each other well.

"Mr. Campbell," she said as he approached. "I have to ask your advice. My husband didn't come home last night. No one knows where he went yesterday, and no one knows where he is today. How do I go about filing a missing persons report?"

Zane looked at the baby girl she was holding on her hip. "He's been gone since yesterday morning?"

"Yesterday afternoon. He left work in the afternoon and no one has seen him since."

"Was he driving?"

She looked at him funny for a moment, then she seemed to understand. "No. His car is still at work. Someone must have picked him up."

"Has he ever done this before?"

"No. Never. He always comes home after work."

"What about arguments? Did you have a fight?"

She rolled her eyes. "What difference does that make? I'm telling you he always comes home after work whether we fight or not."

"I'm only asking what the police will ask," Zane told her. "You can go in and request to file, but they may ask you to wait."

"Why?"

"Sometimes a new father skips out for a day or two. I'm not saying that's the case here, but it happens."

"Thank you, Mr. Campbell," said Valerie, her dainty nostrils flaring. "I'll let you get back to whatever you were doing."

Abra was coming from Zane's backyard when he saw her crossing the lawn. She stopped and used a hand to push back the falling wisps of hair that had escaped from her bun. Perspiration dotted her forehead, and the front of her blouse was spotted with tomato soup.

"I was looking for you," she said.

He smiled. "Were you?"

"Mr. Conlan tried to get out of bed before dinner and he's fallen. I tried to get him up myself, but he's fighting me." She led the way to the house and Zane stepped inside. He followed her back to the bedroom and found a sobbing Thomas Conlan lying on the floor in pajama bottoms that were soaked with urine.

"Hello, Thomas," Zane said as he entered the room. "Can I help you get back in bed?"

Thomas put his hands over his face. "I wanted to go pee by myself. I didn't want the damned bedpan, and I don't want a catheter. I wanted to walk in the bathroom and stand up and pee by myself, just like I've been doing every day for the last fifty-five years of my life. I needed to do it just one more time . . ." He broke off into uncontrollable sobs.

Zane looked at Abra, but she was already on the floor beside her patient. Her arms went around him, and her eyes were moist with tears as she began to rock his thin, frail body back and forth. She began to murmur to him, soothing words that meant nothing, but eventually served to calm the man. He laid his head against her breast and looked at Zane with reddened eyes.

"You can help me get back in bed now. I'm sorry I fought you, Abra. I'm sorry I hit you."

"It's all right, Thomas."

"I haven't been myself lately. I keep getting further and further away from myself."

"You're still Thomas."

"You won't leave me?"

"I won't leave you."

"I'd hate it if Clyde had to hire someone else. We'd never find another nurse like you."

Abra saw Zane frown as he moved to help her lift the pitifully thin man. Working together, they carefully placed Thomas on the mattress and changed his pajamas. When they were finished, he fell back against the pillows in exhaustion and closed his eyes almost immediately. By the time Abra finished clearing away the mess he had made of dinner, Thomas was asleep.

Zane followed her into the kitchen. "He looks terrible."

Abra nodded, but didn't look at him as she dumped the dishes in the sink.

"Is he dying?"

"Yes."

"He seemed just fine only a month ago."

"Disease works in strange ways, Mr. Campbell. Some people live for years with a virus, others don't."

Zane put his hands in his pockets. "Call me Zane, okay?"

"Excuse me?" She still didn't turn around.

"I told you to call me Zane. Have you worked with lots of terminal patients?"

"My father did. He gave an experimental vaccine to a patient who begged him, and it killed the man. His family sued and my father lost his license to practice medicine."

"Because he gave the patient the vaccine?"

"Because he acted irresponsibly and should have known better."

She glanced at him and saw him staring pensively at her. She turned away again.

"What does your father do now?" Zane asked.

"Nothing. He's dead."

"Oh, I'm sorry."

"That's okay. He died of a heart attack four years ago."

"You're very open about the trouble. Did he face a lot of criticism?"

Abra smiled. "Not as much as you would think. He was a scapegoat of sorts."

"You mean other doctors have committed similar acts and never faced retribution?"

"Doctors almost never get caught, Zane. Can I have some more tomatoes?"

Zane nodded. "You want some zucchini?"

"I'm sorry?"

"Zucchini. Squash."

"All right. Shall I come and get it?"

"No, I'll get it." He paused, then, "Unless you want to come along."

She lifted a hand. "Sure. I've never been in a real garden before."

"Never?" Zane asked. "Where did you grow up?"

"In the city."

"This is the city."

"Downtown, in a penthouse apartment."

Zane lifted both brows and looked at her. "Your family lived in a penthouse?"

"My mother does." Abra exhaled through her nose. "We weren't really rich, so please don't look at me that way. My mother's father owned the building and gave the penthouse to her. She owns the building now and gave me a ground floor apartment to live in. I can't have any animals and anyone who comes to see me is grilled by the doorman, who answers to my mother, so I practically never have company."

Zane headed for the back door and gestured for her to follow him. "So you grew up with a doctor and became a nurse. What does your mother do?"

"My mother?" Abra hesitated, but kept on walking. "She's a doctor also. A psychiatrist. She has an office a half mile away from here."

Zane stopped and looked at her. "A psychiatrist? I suppose you have a brother who's a research scientist and a sister who's a concert pianist, right?"

"No."

Zane started walking again, regretting his sarcastic tone, and she walked with him across the lawn and into the garden.

"Do you have any brothers or sisters?" he asked.

"No, do you?"

"No. Well, I had a sister, but she died in a plane crash about ten years ago."

"Older? Younger?"

"Older."

"Your parents?"

"They travel around. Right now they're in Zapata, Texas. We see them once or twice a year."

They stopped beside the tall stalks of corn and Abra clasped her hands together. "Thank you for helping me with Thomas," she said. "For not being afraid."

The corner of Zane's mouth curved. "Glad I could help. Are you seeing anyone right now, Abra?"

She looked confused, so he repeated himself.

"Me? Am I seeing anyone? No, not right now," Abra answered. She spotted the zucchini and ducked away from him. Her cheeks were pink, he noticed.

"I want that one," she said. "Can I pick that one?"

Zane looked and then nodded. "Pick all you like." He decided to change the subject. "Is your mother still practicing full-time?"

"Yes. Is that cantaloupe over there?"

"You want one?"

"I'm taking all your food."

"There'll be more to come. You said she has an office nearby?"

"Just five minutes away, at Lakepoint."

"Do you see her often?"

"No. Not really."

Zane felt awkward for having embarrassed her. He no longer knew what to talk about with her or what to say.

She stopped picking and looked at him. "Should I stop?"

"Not at all. Do you want a sack for that stuff?"

"Have you got one?"

"I'll get it."

When he came back from the pantry he avoided looking at her, and he saw her look down at herself as a result. Her cheeks turned pink again. Her hair was in disarray, her blouse was soiled, and her hands were grimy with dirt from the garden.

Zane walked over and handed her the sack. As she took it from him he smiled at her and saw her eyelashes flutter. She swallowed and put down the sack to fill it with the vegetables she had picked.

"I took some yellow squash, too," she pointed out.

"Okay."

When she looked up again, he grinned.

"What?" she said.

"For never having been in a garden you certainly know how to pick. You'd better get these home. Put some of it in the fridge."

"Thanks." Abra took the vegetables and turned away from him. She walked only a few yards and then glanced over her shoulder at him.

Zane lifted his hand in a small wave. She quickened her pace.

When Abra entered the house, the phone was ringing. She put the sack of vegetables on the counter and lifted the receiver on the kitchen wall. "Hello?"

"Miss Ahrens?" said a male voice. "For a moment I was afraid something had happened. This is Clyde Conlan."

"Hello, Mr. Conlan. I was outside getting some vegetables. How are you?"

"Very well, thank you. How is Thomas?"

"He's sleeping at the moment. We had a rough afternoon."
She went on to tell him what had happened earlier.

"I'm sorry I wasn't there to help you," he said in a stiff tone.
"I didn't foresee anything like this happening. You say it was Mr.
Campbell who helped you?"

Abra cleared her throat. "Yes. He was very kind. Will you be
coming home soon?"

"Any day now. I've almost wrapped things up here. I'll call
and let you know when I'm coming in. Take care, and say hello
to Thomas for me."

"I will. Goodbye, Mr. Conlan."

"Goodbye, Miss Ahrens. And one more thing: please do what
you can to limit exposure to others. It really is very important at
this stage. I'm sure you understand."

Abra said she did understand, and she hoped to avoid any
more such occurrences for all their sakes.

"I'm counting on you," said the chief of staff, and then he
hung up, leaving Abra to stare at the phone with the beginnings
of a frown on her face.

# CHAPTER

# 10

WHEN CRAIG FOUND HIMSELF taking clothes from drawers and putting them on top of the dresser, he had to stop and ask himself just exactly what he was doing. He wasn't sure. Some inner instinct for flight had gripped him and moved him as if by hidden strings, lifting this arm and that one and moving them without instruction from his conscious mind.

He sat down on the bed and looked at the mess around him. The bed itself was unmade, the sheets in a tangle. His dirty clothes lay on the floor across the room, and a plate containing part of last night's sandwich was on the table by the bed, the bread hard, the bologna curled. Things were back to the way they had been before he married Louise. He liked things better the other way, but he wasn't sufficiently motivated to clean up the mess himself, so things would stay this way as long as Louise was hurt.

And it didn't look like Louise would be getting better any time soon. Just moments ago, Mr. Mark Vaughn had informed him that Mrs. Peterwell might be turning gangrenous.

That was just swell. Craig was so happy to hear that. Really. It made him so happy he couldn't resist whacking Mr. Mark Vaughn across the face with one of his trusty two-by-fours. The blow had broken Vaughn's nose and spewed blood everywhere, turning Craig's stomach.

Though Craig worked in a hospital, he detested the sight and smell of blood. After his father's triple bypass Craig went to visit the old man in the ICU unit of the hospital. His father's sunken chest looked like one long railroad track of staples. While Craig was standing by the bed his father went into a coughing fit and began to pop his staples, one after another, opening himself up like a man unzipping his coat. Craig saw the blood and passed out right there in the hospital room. The nurses had to step on top of him to get to the man in the bed. His father died later that day, and Craig had avoided contact with patients ever since.

When Mark Vaughn began to spew blood, Craig dropped his two-by-four and hurried up the stairs. That's when the automatic motions of packing had begun. When the unconscious took over and said, *Go.*

But he knew he couldn't. He knew a group of people identifiable only as "they" would come looking for him. And "they" would probably find him. He wasn't smart enough to disappear. He didn't know how to make a new identity for himself, how to drop out of this life and into another one. He had his birds to worry about, for one thing. He couldn't take all of them with him, and he couldn't leave them without food and water for the several days or perhaps even weeks it would take for someone to discover he was gone and the house was deserted except for the two dead people in the basement.

Craig paused there. Maybe they wouldn't be dead. Maybe Louise would start eating and Mark Vaughn would keep his mouth shut long enough to take some food and water. Craig had left a bowl of water near him last night, thinking he could suck it up if he wanted it. Vaughn had started screaming his head off, making a racket that Craig knew he couldn't pass off as the birds. He shoved a rag in Vaughn's mouth and taped it in place and that was that.

He blinked suddenly as he wondered if Mark Vaughn could breathe with a broken nose.

Craig left the bedroom and hurried back down the stairs.

Mark Vaughn was lying on his side, curled in the fetal position, fighting for air. Craig rushed over to him and ignored the hitch in his throat at the smell of the blood to rip the tape from Vaughn's mouth and remove the rag from his mouth. Vaughn sucked in air in huge gasps, until the color of his face began to look less blue. Craig couldn't believe it when the man began to cry. Loud, braying sobs racked Vaughn's body as he lay chained on the basement floor. Tears and snot streamed down his face and mingled with the blood from his nose. Craig sat down to watch him.

He found it hard to believe that a man who had been to prison would cry like that.

Soon Craig scooted forward and reached out to touch Vaughn on the shoulder. "Hey, it's okay. You're gonna be all right now. I'm sorry about the nose thing, okay? I forgot you were gagged when I hit you. I didn't mean to scare you like that. You probably thought you were going to die, didn't you? You're okay now. Come on, big guy."

Craig stopped when he realized he was stroking the other man's arm. Men didn't do things like that.

Surprisingly, Vaughn's sobs dwindled down to snuffles. He asked if he could blow his nose, and Craig held out his dirty handkerchief. Vaughn cried out in agony as he cleared his nasal passages, and Craig's mouth twisted at all the blood that came out in the hanky. He dropped it as quickly as he could.

"You feeling better now?"

Vaughn nodded.

"You want something to eat?"

"No."

Unable to help himself, Craig patted him on the shoulder again. "You're okay. I need to give Louise some pills, then I'll fix something and leave it down here for you in case you get hungry."

"Wait," Vaughn said in a thick voice. "I have to ask you

something. I was . . . I was crying because I thought I was going to die and never see my baby girl again. Am I going to see her again?"

Craig looked dumbly at him. "I can't bring her here."

"No, no, please God no, don't bring her here," Vaughn said quickly. "I meant, are you ever going to let me go?"

"I don't know," Craig said in a flat voice. "Don't ask me again."

"What would you do if you were in my position?" Vaughn persisted. "It's all I can think about. It's all your wife can think about, when she's not drugged to the gills."

Craig exhaled through his nose. "What did you think about while you were in prison?"

"Getting out."

"Every day?"

"Every fucking day."

"Watch your language in front of my wife."

Craig didn't know if she could hear them or not—her eyes weren't even open—but he still felt duty bound in that respect.

"My arms and legs are numb," Vaughn told him. "I can't feel anything. In prison at least you're allowed freedom of movement."

"You're not in prison," Craig reminded him. "And you know good and well that I can't afford to take the chains off. You just shut up now before I remember my dead birds and get mad again. I don't want to get mad again. I don't want to hurt you anymore."

"I don't want to get hurt," said Vaughn. "Can you come and look at my back? Something's been crawling on me off and on since I've been down here. It's right between my shoulder blades."

Craig walked around him to have a look. He cursed through his teeth then and backed up. "Stay right there," he told Vaughn. "Don't move. I'll go get something to take care of it."

"What is it?" Vaughn asked.

"You don't want to know."

Craig hurried upstairs to find his can of bug killer. He couldn't believe a spider that big was in his basement. He hoped there weren't any more of them. A vision of the huge brown spider walking across Louise's face gripped him and made him shudder suddenly.

He had to get her out of there. He really did. He had to do something. He couldn't leave her on the basement floor. He would get her up somehow and move her to the bedroom they used for a guest room in the back of the house. There were no spiders in there, and it would be easier for him to attend her if she was on a bed and not on the floor.

Mark Vaughn would have to stay in the basement for the time being, until Craig decided what to do with him.

Dr. Ahrens might be able to help him with that one, Craig decided as he carried the can of bug killer down the stairs.

Vaughn looked up and said, "You can't spray that on me."

"Would you rather have the spider on you?"

"Spider. Oh, fuck."

Craig tightened his lips. "I told you to watch your mouth. You wouldn't want me to put the gag and the tape back on, would you?"

Vaughn shook his head. "Get it off me."

"I will." Craig stepped around behind him and pointed the nozzle of the can. When the spray hit the spider, the spider began to run. It crawled up Vaughn's neck and into his hair. Craig told Vaughn to close his eyes and kept on spraying. Vaughn shuddered violently and squeezed his eyes shut. The spider ran down his neck again and sought shelter in the collar of Vaughn's shirt.

"Get it off!" Vaughn yelled.

Craig leaned down with his can and saturated the inside of Vaughn's collar with bug killer.

Vaughn was hyperventilating and ready to pass out from the fumes. "What are you doing?" he gasped. "Just kill the sonofabitch."

Craig's face was turning red. He was mad at the spider for not dying and mad for using half a can of bug killer to try and kill it. He switched the can around in his hand and swung it hard against Vaughn's neck, where the spider was hiding in the collar. There was a crunching sound, a sickly sensation, and then Craig pulled back Vaughn's collar to look. The spider's legs were still moving. Craig used the bottom of the can to flick the spider onto the floor, where he moved to quickly stomp it.

Vaughn's face was white. His lips moved, but Craig didn't hear anything.

Still mad, Craig went up the stairs to spend the next fifteen minutes trying to wash the smell of bug spray from his hands. When he had calmed down, he prepared some food and took it downstairs to leave where Vaughn and Louise could reach it if they wanted. He fed Louise more pills and turned to look at Vaughn. His skin was splotchy now, red in places as if he were suffering an allergic reaction to the bug killer. In a croaking voice he asked Craig for some water.

"Please," he whispered.

Craig got him some water. He held it up for him to drink and watched as Vaughn gulped nearly the whole glass.

"More?" Craig asked.

"No. Could you wash some of that stuff off me?"

Craig frowned. "Wash you?"

"My neck. The bug spray. Could you wash some of it off?"

Craig picked up a towel from the pile beneath Louise and twisted the dial on the washer to get it wet with water. He twisted the knob back and knelt down beside Vaughn to swipe quickly and roughly at the skin of his neck. When he was finished, Vaughn thanked him.

That made Craig feel good. It was a genuinely sincere expression of gratitude, something Craig didn't hear often. He liked the sound of it. He ran the towel over Vaughn's hair and across his back, and Vaughn thanked him again.

He wasn't going to yell anymore, obviously. With the broken

nose and the bug spray, he could barely talk. Craig went upstairs to eat a sandwich and see to his birds.


Mark Vaughn listened to Craig Peterwell mount the stairs and swore an oath to himself to rip the crazy bastard's dirty, yellowish-white head off his neck the moment he was physically able. If he ever regained the use of his arms and legs, he was going to find the nearest shank and gut the idiot like a fish. Who else but an idiot would waste half a can of bug spray to kill one spider? A spider he could have knocked off to begin with and crushed with his foot.

Peterwell was a coward, Mark decided. He never used his fist to hit, he always had something to hit with. A coward with a dual personality. One side of him was hard and ruthless, and the other side was concerned and even conscientious about the welfare of his victims. Mark had seen the pity and remorse in Peterwell's eyes when he cried. Peterwell wasn't a complete monster. He could still be reasoned with.

Mark had also seen the appreciative expression on Peterwell's face when he so kindly thanked him for wiping the bug spray off his back. Mark thought he might be on to something there. If he could get Peterwell talking, if he could make him feel he could take Mark into his confidence, then a way out might be in sight. Everyone's favorite subject was himself, and if Peterwell wanted to talk about himself, well then, Mark was there to listen.

The problem was his wife, Louise. Peterwell didn't like to look at her, Mark could tell. He suspected it made old Craig feel just a tad bit guilty when Mark pointed out the greenish cast of his wife's lower left leg earlier that evening.

The woman would probably die. The swelling of her limbs was too awful, too far gone. What would happen when she did die was anyone's guess. Would Peterwell take off for parts unknown, or would he figure he had nothing to lose by killing Mark and sinking both bodies to the bottom of some sand pit?

What a cheerful thought, Mark told himself. Why don't you figure all this out for him? Then you'll be sure to miss your little girl's graduation day.

Maybe the bug spray had affected his brain.

At least the fat, hairy spider was off his back. Mark could see it if he craned his head. It was big. It made him shudder again to think of it crawling around on him.

He hoped there wasn't a sack of eggs somewhere on his shirt.

A snuffling sound made him look at Louise. Her eyes were open. Her face and hair were plastered with perspiration. The poor thing looked like she was burning up with fever. Mark wished he could help her. He wished there was some way to end her suffering. He hawked some of the blood from his raw throat and moved around so she could see him.

"I hope those pills work for you," he rasped in a voice hoarse from the chemicals. "I hope they do something for your pain. Your husband is one sick sonofabitch. But you already know that, don't you?"

Her mouth opened and released a breath of air. She said one word that sounded like "die."

"I'd help you do that if I could," Mark told her. "But I—"

She made a noise of impatience and her eyes went to the tiny basement window. A finger lifted. "*Dryah . . .*"

Mark stared at her as he tried to figure out her meaning.

Finally it struck him. She wasn't saying "die" and pointing outside as if to heaven. She was saying "dryer" and pointing to the hose and the dryer vent.

"Dryer," Mark said aloud, and the woman closed her eyes and dropped her finger.

Dryer. Could he get to the dryer vent? How would he get if off the dryer? How would he yell once he got it off?

It was a damned good idea, providing there was anyone standing near enough outside to hear him.

# CHAPTER
# 11

MRS. MORLEY AND HER son Chance came home Sunday morning after spending the night at her sister's home near the court-house. Chance was restless and fitful, alternately depressed about what had happened and jubilant to be away from all those men who were so mean to him. His mother had always told him there were people who feared what they didn't understand, and it was their fear that made them mean, but Chance didn't think it was fear that made these men mean. He thought they liked being mean. On their own they weren't bad, but whenever two or more of them got together it was awful.

His mother had cried when she found out he was placed with all the other men, and not in a cell by himself. They told her it was because the jail was too crowded, and she got mad and said the damned jail was just built because the old one was over-crowded, and how could the new jail already be overcrowded?

They did what most men did when a woman like his mother asked questions: they looked at each other and shook their heads and pushed air out their noses with a knowing smirk. They didn't know Chance and didn't care to know him. They had a job to do and that was that.

Chance's mother told his aunt that if she were younger, smarter, and had more money, she might think about bringing suit against someone.

Chance didn't know what that was exactly. He imagined his mother sewing a suit and holding it up against one of those people in the jail. He didn't like the idea and he told her so. She smiled at him and gave him a hug.

Now he was ready to get out of the house and go outside for a while. When he told his mother, she looked doubtful a moment, then nodded for him to go on. He wanted to go for a walk, but he couldn't go to the bridge where he found the bike. Chance's mother had told him never to go near there again. People had the wrong idea about him, and it wouldn't do if they saw him down there messing around. Chance didn't know why people had the wrong idea about him. He still didn't know what he had done to make them send him to jail with those mean men. They asked his mother a lot of questions about a girl he knew a long time ago, but Chance could barely remember her. He didn't remember things the way other people did.

He left the house and walked down the drive to stand at the street and think about where he wanted to go. When he couldn't make up his mind, he simply started walking. He reached Eli's house and stopped at the curb. He thought Eli might be mad at him, but he wasn't sure. His mother told him he had hurt Eli by pushing him down and that Eli had to get stitches in his arm. Stitches were serious business, Chance knew. Someone was hurt bad when they got stitches. He didn't mean to hurt Eli and make him get stitches, but he never got a chance to tell him he was sorry. He hoped Eli was okay.

After several minutes of indecision, he went up to Eli's house and knocked on the door. The dad answered. The man who couldn't talk good. Chance asked for Eli, and the dad said the boys were with their mother for the weekend. Chance smiled at him. He had understood every word. Then the dad asked him something and Chance frowned helplessly.

"Huh?"

"Are you doing okay?" the dad asked slowly.

"Oh, yeah. Yeah, I'm doing okay. I'm gonna go now, Mr. Campbell."

The dad nodded and said for Chance to tell his mother something for him. Chance didn't get what he was supposed to tell her, but he said he would. He went back down the drive to the street and stood there once more, wondering what to do. He guessed he would just walk.

When he walked by the Vaughn house, he saw Mrs. Vaughn loading her baby into the car in the driveway. He waved to her and she raised her brows as if she was surprised to see him. She smiled and waved back, then she stopped smiling and threw her purse in the car and climbed into the driver's seat. Chance watched her back down the drive in the car and race down the street. He thought she was pretty. She was always nice to him, and she usually talked to him.

Except for today. But she had been going somewhere.

Chance wandered idly down the street and turned around to come back before he got to the busy street. Dogs barked at him and people peered out windows, but no one came and spoke to him. He reached familiar houses again and was walking in front of the Peterwell place when he heard the birds.

His mother warned him never to go and peek in weird Mr. Peterwell's windows, because it made him mad. But Mr. Peterwell's van wasn't out front, and if he wasn't there, then he couldn't get mad. Chance looked all around and then crept up the drive toward the house. If someone saw him, he would say he just wanted to tell Mrs. Peterwell he was home again. She was nice to him, too. Once she had given him a turtle from her pet shop.

The turtle died, but she said that was all right. She said turtles did that sometimes.

Chance reached the porch and looked around again before moving to the window and cupping his hands around his face. The birds were so pretty. So many bright colors, all of them put together in such a nice way. They looked like birds wearing rainbows. And the noise they made; screeching and screaming and shrieking like in the King Kong movies, only ten times louder. Chance smiled as he watched and listened.

He moved to another window on the other side of the porch and was about to peer through the glass when he heard something that caused him to halt all movement. He stopped breathing to listen and soon he heard it again.

It was a voice asking for help. Someone who sounded really far away.

Chance stared through the glass. He swallowed. He opened his mouth and said, "Hello?"

The voice came again, not from the glass, but from somewhere nearby.

"Help us! If you can hear me, send someone to help us! He's got us in the basement! We can't get out!"

Chance was still staring through the glass when Craig Peterwell drove up in his van. The face under the whitish-yellow hair was bright red as Peterwell climbed from behind the wheel.

"What are you doing here?" he demanded to know. "What are you doing in my yard?"

"I wasn't doing anything," Chance told him, and he turned to run. He stumbled over his own feet and fell down in the grass. He picked himself up and ran as if the man were chasing him. He looked back to see the angry Peterwell stalk up to the porch and shove his key in the lock.

Chance ran all the way up to his door and threw it open. He rushed inside to find his mother. She was making rolls in the kitchen. Chance went to her and said, "I didn't do anything to Mr. Peterwell's house. I was just standing in his yard listening to the birds."

Mrs. Morley's face creased with worry as she turned to him. "Chance, you didn't go in his yard? I've asked you not to go in that man's yard."

"There was a voice," Chance told her. "All the birds were talking and screaming and then there was this voice asking for help. It came from the house. It said to send someone to help because they were in the basement and they couldn't get out."

"Was it Mrs. Peterwell, Chance?"

"No, Momma, it was a man. It was a man's voice."

"Where did it come from?"

"I couldn't tell. I was looking, but Mr. Peterwell came home and I ran away."

"Where were you standing when you heard it?"

"On the other side of the porch, away from the picture window."

Mrs. Morley nodded. "That's Mrs. Peterwell's room, honey. What you heard was probably her television. She's a big fan of old movies. After she retired I visited her and she said she watched them all day."

"And soap operas," Chance murmured. "She watches them, too."

"That's right, and the way those things are turning out, I wouldn't be surprised if it was a soap opera you heard. She's got to keep the television turned up loud to hear it over all those birds. Don't worry yourself about it, Chance. And stay out of that man's yard. I won't tell you again."

Chance lowered his head and looked at the bread dough she was working. "Maybe it was the birds, Momma. Maybe they learned how to talk and was asking somebody to set them free. Maybe they're tired of being caged up in that mean old man's house."

His mother looked at him. "Maybe you imagined that voice, Chance. Coming from where you've been, stranger things have happened."

Chance shook his head. "I didn't imagine it. It was the birds. They want someone to let them out."


Valerie Vaughn left the police station in tears. A prickly, growling officer had just suggested that in view of her husband Mark's arrest record and past association with known criminals, desertion seemed likely. When Valerie told him that was not a possibility, he turned away with an air of indifference that said he had already made up his mind about the situation.

When she asked about filing the missing persons report, he told her to give it until Monday. Then he went on with his work and ignored her.

Valerie's nostrils had flared as she stared at his shining bald head.

She carried her daughter Melissa back out to the car and bundled her into her car seat, all the while thinking of the scathing letter she would send to the local newspaper's opinion page. When she saw the desk cop come running out to the parking lot after her, she felt a spurt of adrenalin and something like fear take hold of her. He was holding a finger out, pointing at her as he ran toward her.

"You," he said. "Wait."

Valerie took a deep breath and closed the car door. She glanced at Melissa, round-eyed as she sat in her car seat. The cop approached.

"Your husband's name is Mark Vaughn. Is that the Mark Vaughn who owns Vaughn Pontiac?"

"Yes. Why?"

"Come on back inside, ma'am. We have some questions for you."

"What? Why? Do you know something?"

"Please come inside. Bring your baby."

Valerie frowned and removed Melissa once more from the back seat. She followed the officer into the building and down the hall to an office where two men were seated behind desks. They looked up and smiled when she came in. She placed Melissa's carrier on an empty desk top and waited for one of them to speak.

"Mrs. Vaughn," said the first man, "I'm Bill Weld, and this is George Savaglio. We're working on the Cyndi Melo case."

"The missing little girl?" said Valerie. "What have I got to do with that?"

"Not you, ma'am," said Bill Weld. "Your husband."

George Savaglio stood. "Yesterday morning a brand new Pontiac was found in front of the Melo house on Laurel Street. It came from your husband's dealership."

"My husband has been missing since Friday afternoon," Valerie said. "Was there a key in the car?"

"We found one in the glove compartment," Savaglio answered. "We think he left the car there on purpose."

"Why?" Valerie didn't understand.

The two men looked at each other. Bill Weld held up a file he was holding. "We've been talking to the man who was convicted along with your husband back in 1986. He's claimed all along that it was actually Mark Vaughn who raped his girlfriend's daughter that night. This man freely admits to holding his girlfriend and hitting her when she tried to intervene, but he said Vaughn raped the child."

Valerie stared at the men before her. She began to shake her head. "That man is a pathological liar and you know it. I know what you're doing. You're trying to say Mark took the Melo girl. You think he did something with her, and you think he's gone because he's guilty."

"Why else would he dump a brand new car in front of her parents' house and then leave?"

"I don't know. But I know he didn't do a thing to Cyndi Melo. Mark couldn't. He's a good, loving man. He hates men who molest children."

"Every con on the inside has to say that if he wants to stay alive, Mrs. Vaughn."

"Mark is different," Valerie insisted. "Prison didn't ruin him the way it ruins others. He stayed warm inside. He kept his dignity and—"

"Mrs. Vaughn, we need to ask about the last time you saw him. I assume it was Friday morning?"

Valerie's lips quivered. "That's right."

"Did he mention anything that might be of help to us? Did he say anything that sounded strange to you?"

"No." Valerie shook her head. She looked at her hands then. "We were arguing about sex."

"Sex?" Weld repeated.

"Yes." She looked at Melissa. "If either of you are married men, then I'm sure you've been there. Since having Melissa I haven't been as ... eager ... as Mark would like me to be. He realizes that it takes time, but it's still hard for him to understand."

Weld and Savaglio looked at each other.

"Was it a violent argument?" Weld asked.

"No, for heaven's sakes." Valerie scowled at the man. "It was an argument between married people. We've had arguments before. Mark has never been violent. Not once. I keep telling you he's a gentle man. He respects women."

Savaglio sighed. "If he respects you so much, why hasn't he called to let you know where he is?"

Valerie wished she knew the answer. She said nothing at all, merely looked at her hands again.

"All right," said Savaglio. "We'll be in touch with you if we hear anything, Mrs. Vaughn."

"That man who told you Mark raped a girl is lying," Valerie said. "You know it and I know it. He tried this during the jury trial and he's trying it now. He's hoping to get a sentence reduction by framing Mark."

"Maybe so," said Weld. "Thanks for coming in and talking to us."

Valerie's chin lifted in frustration as she stood and stared at the two men. The officer who had escorted her in was waiting to escort her out. Valerie snatched Melissa in her carrier and strode from the room.

In the parking lot once more she thought of going through the phone book and looking for a good lawyer. They weren't going to get away with this. They weren't going to frame her husband for the disappearance of a neighborhood girl on the say-so of a convicted hot-house felon. They weren't going to make her doubt the man she married and the love he had for her. They . . .

She paused to sob after buckling in Melissa and slamming the door. She climbed in the driver's seat and leaned her head against the steering wheel.

She *was* having doubts. The car in front of the house. Mark's disappearing act. The story about the little girl's rape. Mark had always sworn to her that he was in the next room while the rape was happening. But how could someone be in the next room and not hear what was going on? How could he have heard and allowed it to happen?

Valerie squeezed her eyes shut and felt hot tears course down her cheeks. She had always known there was a wildness in Mark, an unwillingness to conform that made him appealing in the beginning. Now she knew it was simply juvenile behavior on his part. He didn't want to grow up and become a mature man with responsibilities. He didn't want to settle down and become a re-spected businessman in the community. He wanted to have fun. Having fun was more important to Mark than taking pride in his accomplishments or being well thought of. Having fun was ev-erything.

Since having Melissa, Valerie guessed she had become too much of a drag for him. She had seen the signs but had foolishly believed all the difficulties would pass. Valerie stared at her baby in the rearview mirror. Then she looked at her own reflection.

If Mark Vaughn really had left her, she was going to kill him.

# CHAPTER

## 12

ZANE FINISHED MOWING THE lawn and asked himself why he had done it. Holt and Eli usually alternated on the mowing. That's what boys did. They learned responsibility by mowing the lawn. Why he had gone out and worked himself into a lather was beyond him. He put the mower in the shed in back and came out to see Abra in her window. He guessed the reason wasn't beyond him, after all. He had been hoping to see her. He waved to her, and she gave him only a short nod before moving away from the glass. Zane shook his head. Okay. So he had embarrassed both of them the day before by asking her if she was seeing anyone. What he didn't get was why she was still standing in the window and looking at him if she had no interest in going out with a guy who couldn't talk right.

Zane went to sleep the evening before thinking about kissing her. He hadn't kissed a woman in a long time. He couldn't even think about kissing his wife after being shot. The pity in her eyes had sickened him. Friends on the force had warned him it would; they had told him about the anger, frustration and helplessness he would feel.

What they hadn't told him was how to deal with all those things and still keep his marriage together.

The divorce wasn't entirely his fault. His wife had been ultra-sensitive and ready to land with both feet on every syllable out of his mouth, tortured though they were. Zane went off to train at the Dean McGee Eye Institute in Oklahoma City. For two and a half years he commuted to Wichita on the weekends, leaving his wife and sons at home alone during the week. He always figured she met her present husband during that time. Zane never accused her of anything. He felt he had no right to accuse.

Now for the first time in two years he was having romantic thoughts about a woman again. Romantic and sexual. And it wasn't because she didn't feel sorry for him; it was because she seemed so open and accessible. So real and honest. And pretty.

Zane went inside the house and showered. When he was finished he put on clean clothes and headed to the kitchen to make a list for the grocery store. Midway through the list he wondered if he should ask Abra if they needed anything. Groceries were delivered to the Conlan house, he knew, but only on Tuesdays. She might like something from the store before then. And he might get a better handle on what her problem was if he could talk to her.

He finished his list and stuck his keys in his pocket. He locked the doors behind him and stepped outside to walk across the yard and ring the Conlans' bell. Abra's blue eyes registered surprise when she opened the door. Zane smiled warmly at her and watched her lower her gaze as if in discomfort.

He said, "I saw you at the window earlier. Is everything okay?"

"Yes," she said. "Everything's fine. Thomas is dozing."

"I'm on my way to the store," Zane told her. "I wondered if there was anything I could get for you while I'm there."

She looked away from him and fingered the door. "That's very kind of you, but once Thomas wakes up, I need to run out myself, if I can ask you to watch him?"

Zane saw the sudden high color in her cheeks and took a wild guess.

"I can buy those for you," he said.

"Excuse me?"

"I used to buy them for my wife."

Her face grew even pinker. "I wouldn't ask you to—"

"What brand do you use?"

"Kotex. Regular."

Zane was charmed by the fact that she was embarrassed. He wouldn't have thought it of her, being a nurse. He gave a nod and said, "Anything else?"

She was staring at him in a funny way. She said, "No, not that I can think of."

He turned and walked down the steps. He glanced over his shoulder to find her still standing at the door and staring at him. He stopped. "Did you think of something else?"

She seemed disconcerted. "What? No. Nothing."

"See you later," he said.

"Yes." She closed the door.

Zane's brows knitted as he walked across the yard. Maybe she did have a boyfriend somewhere, he thought. Maybe she had just broken up with one, or was hoping to get back together, or whatever. But a woman with a serious relationship didn't lock herself into a job where she couldn't leave long enough to go and buy feminine napkins.

Maybe that was it. Maybe she was feeling trapped and regretting her decision to live with the Conlans. Things would change for her once Clyde returned from his business trip. She had to know that.

Zane was about to get into his car when he saw Valerie Vaughn pull into her drive. Hers was the only car in the drive, so Mark Vaughn had obviously not returned. Zane shut the Buick's door and walked across the street. Valerie's face was red, her eyes slightly swollen. She wiped at her cheeks when she saw Zane.

"Is there anything I can help you with?" he asked.

"Help? Is that what you said?"

"Yes."

"I don't know. I don't know what you could do, Mr. Campbell, unless you still have friends in the police department."

"A few," said Zane. "What do you need?"

She took the baby from the car and stood looking at him with a dazed expression. "I don't know what I need. I need help, but I don't know what kind."

Zane moved to the porch and held out his hand for her keys. She gave them to him and he opened the door. Valerie carried the baby inside and removed her from the carrier. She sat down in a rocker placed near the sofa in the living room and began to rock her daughter. Zane stood just inside the door and waited.

Finally, Valerie began to talk. She told him what the police had asked her, and what they suspected of Mark. When she told him about the Pontiac, Zane lifted his head. He said, "Don't all new cars come with two keys?"

"Usually, yes."

"Then why leave only one?"

Valerie had no idea.

"If the car was meant as a gift, I'd think he would leave both keys," said Zane, and Valerie looked gratefully at him.

"Why not call and tell your friends that?"

"Weld and Savaglio are not my friends. Neither are they the best detectives you could ask for."

"Were you a detective?"

"For nine years."

"In what division?"

"Several. I was in the narcotics division when I was shot."

"Oh." Valerie looked down at her sleeping baby. "I'm sorry for bringing it up."

"It's all right. I have to go now, Mrs Vaughn. Try not to worry. Without the missing little girl they can't pin anything on your husband."

"What husband?" Valerie murmured.

"Call me if you need anything," Zane said. Then he let himself out the door.

Interesting about Mark Vaughn's criminal record. Zane had tagged him the moment he saw the crude tattoos on his hands, but he had figured Vaughn for a burglar rather than a rapist.

Vaughn fit the burglar profile: cocky, believing he was smarter than everyone else, good with his hands. Zane had once seen him open his front door without a key when his wife locked them out of the house. He didn't see Mark Vaughn as a rapist. But stranger things had happened.

Zane walked back to his car and climbed behind the wheel. Better get to the store and get those Kotex.

Abra sat with Thomas and watched Stewart Granger's nostrils flare on the television screen.

"Philip Fury," said Thomas. "Fictional characters have the best names, don't they? Why don't real people ever have names like that? Scarlett O'Hara. Romeo Montague."

"Blanche DuBois," said Abra.

"Holden Caulfield," said Thomas with a chuckle.

"Victor Von Frankenstein."

"Hercule Poirot. My God, we're good at this, aren't we?" He punched the mute button when a commercial came on. "Who was that at the door a while ago?"

"Zane Campbell. He was going to the store and asked if I needed anything."

Thomas smiled. "His parents did something right when they raised that boy."

"He is thoughtful," Abra agreed.

"Don't ask me why Clyde doesn't seem to care for him. But then Clyde has always been a suspicious type. He can't imagine a man who does things for people just because he wants to. Clyde thinks there's always a motive.

"Of course Clyde is right," Thomas went on. "We have motives that may not be obvious even to ourselves, but they're still there. If I didn't know Zane Campbell, I'd say he was coming to see you. But since I do know him to be thoughtful and kind, I'd say he was being thoughtful and kind *and* coming to see you."

Abra sighed. "Please drop it, Thomas."

"Zane is a handsome man. And you're no slouch, Abra."

"Gee, thanks."

"When was the last tumble you took?"

"Tumble?"

"Sex. When was the last time you had sex?"

"Thomas, I don't talk—"

"Oh, for crissakes, Abra."

Abra sighed and screwed up her mouth while she thought, and Thomas made a horrified face. "Has it been that long?"

"Longer," said Abra. "I've never been what you would call generous with my favors."

Thomas shook his head. "How old are you?"

"Twenty-eight."

"How many serious relationships have you had?"

"By serious, you mean sexual?"

"Yes."

She squinted, and Thomas stared at her. "You're not a virgin, are you?"

"No, no. At the age of nineteen I had backseat sex with a boy I never saw again. I was celibate all through nursing school, and then after graduation I had a brief affair with a doctor."

"What happened?"

"I wasn't his first, only, or last nurse."

"Understandable," said Thomas. "And then?"

"And then nothing. I don't need a man to feel complete, Thomas. I'm happy with who I am."

"You sound like Clyde. What did you think of him?"

"Clyde? Well, he's older."

"I'll have you know my brother was considered extremely handsome in his day."

"I'm sure he was."

"If he put his mind to it, he'd still be a force to be reckoned with."

Abra smiled. "I think you're better looking."

"Please," Thomas snorted. "You and my Aunt Iris. Clyde had the worst crush on her when we were children. But I was her favorite. Clyde hated me for it."

"This is the aunt you mentioned before?"

"My father's sister. Such a pretty thing. The exact opposite of my father in every way. He was large and dark, and she was small and white and soft. She had the sweetest laugh, carefree as a child's, and the most winning way with my father. He was different when she was around. Needless to say, my mother hated her."

"Was she married?" Abra asked.

"No. She never did. She was one of those spinster schoolteachers you hear about, who love children all their lives but never get married and have one of their own."

"What happened to her? Is she still alive?"

"No, no. She took ill one summer and Dad moved her into our house against our mother's wishes. Her kidneys were failing and she wasn't with us long, but the time she was there gave me and Clyde much to speculate about as we watched her with our father."

Abra looked at him with interest. "About what did you speculate?"

"The two of them. We thought they might have been sweethearts."

"Your father and his sister."

"Yes. They were very close. They'd hug each other, touch one another constantly, and kiss more than my father kissed his own wife."

"Did you ever ask about it?" Abra inquired.

Thomas looked at her. "Don't be silly. Such things weren't discussed in private, much less openly. My father would have beat us both soundly if he knew what we were thinking."

"Even if it was true?"

"Even if it was true. Farm families were more isolated than

they are now. There was no one to flirt with, or to tease and tickle and test yourself with but your siblings. What went on was much more common than anyone realizes.''

"What went on? You mean incest?''

"Of course.''

"Do you think your mother knew?''

"She had to. Aunt Iris never married, and wherever we moved, she moved to be near us. Iris kept her distance much of the time, but at family gatherings you could hear my mother bitch and moan the moment Iris walked in the house.''

"You think they were carrying on the whole time your father was married? That's why Iris didn't marry?''

Thomas shrugged and lifted his brows. "Who can say? Don't mention any of this to Clyde, by the way. He still believes such things shouldn't be discussed openly. He's more like my father than he knows.''

Abra eyed him. "Who are you like, Thomas?''

He smiled. "Aunt Iris.''

Abra checked her watch. "Time for your medication. Don't go away.''

As she went to fetch the medication, Abra heard the doorbell ring. She went to the door and opened it. Clyde Conlan stood on the porch, papers jammed in his teeth and hands searching his pockets. He smiled at Abra. "Can't seem to find my keys,'' he said around the papers. "Could you open the door, please?''

"Certainly.'' Abra stepped to the side and opened the door wide, allowing him to carry his suitcase in. "Did you try to call?''

"What? Oh, no, I completely forgot. Didn't even think of it until I was on my way home from the airport. How is Thomas? Is he awake?''

"Yes, he is. I was about to give him his medication. You can say hello while I prepare it.''

"All right, I will.'' Clyde left the big suitcase sitting in the foyer and walked down the hall to Thomas's bedroom. Abra followed him as far as the medicine cabinet and prepared Thomas's medication. She carried a tray in to Thomas's room and was surprised when Clyde took it from her at the door. "I'll give it to him. Why don't you sit outside for a while? I'm sure you're ready to go crazy being stuck inside."

"I was prepared to be stuck longer," Abra told him. "You said you wouldn't return for ten days or so."

Clyde lifted a hand. "I can never say for certain how long I'll be gone. Ten days always seems like a good number to tell people when they ask how long I'll be gone. I can usually accomplish a great deal before then, and it always makes people think highly of me when I do." He finished by chuckling and gave a shooing motion with his hand. "Go on now. We'll be fine."

"All right," Abra said cautiously. "Goodbye," she called to Thomas. "I'll see you later."

"Don't get burned," Thomas called in reply.

Abra smiled and went to her room to change clothes. By the time she was ready and on her way out to the back, Zane Campbell was walking up the steps with a small sack in his hand.

"For milady," he said.

Abra's cheeks heated again. "I can't thank you enough. As it turns out, Clyde has just arrived home and gone in to sit with his brother. I'm sorry to have put you to the trouble."

"No trouble at all," Zane told her. "What are you going to do?" He was looking with undisguised admiration at her swimsuit top and shorts.

"Do? Well, I thought—"

"Go to a movie with me," Zane suggested. "We can pick a show over at The Palace. A buck fifty a head."

He was smiling at her again, and Abra's heart felt as if it would burst in her chest.

"I'll even spring for popcorn," he added.

Abra's mouth went dry. She tried to smile and form words, but nothing would come out.

Zane said, "It's been years since I've done this. Am I going about it wrong?"

"No," she managed finally. "You're doing it right."

Zane looked at her. He stood still. "Have I gone and overestimated my appeal?"

Abra shook her head. "I want to go with you, Zane, but I can't. Not right now. Thank you for asking me."

She tried to move past him and he took hold of her arm. "Abra, talk to me. You made me think my problem didn't matter."

"The way you talk doesn't matter. I can't leave the house. I agreed to stay. I have a job to do here, a patient to think about. I can't run off with you or anyone else, not even to go to a movie. Do you understand?"

Zane's eyes were unreadable as he released her. He took her face in both hands and lowered his mouth to touch hers. Abra sucked in her breath and felt her body stiffen as his lips clung gently to hers in a brief kiss. By the time he lifted his head she was on fire. Without a word he stepped off the porch and walked away from her. Abra stared after him, her breath coming in gasps.

He certainly kissed better than he talked.

# CHAPTER

## 13

CRAIG CARRIED THE DRYER hose up the stairs and out to the garbage can before he left the house on Monday morning. One nervous look from Louise had given away the disconnected hose shoved behind the dryer. When Craig saw it he couldn't help but admire Mark Vaughn's thinking. How he had removed the clamp without using his hands was something to wonder about. Craig pictured him using his teeth to rip the hose away; and then the painstaking movements necessary to get the hose into position so he could yell into it. Amazing.

And foolish. Craig had thrashed Vaughn with the hose before carrying it out of the basement. Louise watched with dull eyes, her fingers bending and unbending.

The green color of her leg was worse, and Craig was damned if he knew what to do about it. At work that day he planned to acquire a gurney with casters so he could move her out of the basement and into the back bedroom. He would strap her tightly to the gurney and use a pulley system to get her up the stairs. Then he would engage the wheels and roll her down the hall. He hoped to get her up without too much pain, but just in case, he had procured another bottle of pills from another nurse who owed him a personal favor. There was no danger of the nurses talking to each other, since they worked on separate floors. The way Craig figured, he could get a bottle of pills for just about every floor in the hospital. There had been a lot of personal favors granted over the years.

The question of what to do with Mark Vaughn still nagged at him, but he hadn't lost any sleep over it. Vaughn had stumbled into something he shouldn't have, and now he was paying for it, plain and simple.

Craig went to work, got mad at his idiot crew only two or three times that day, and slipped a gurney into his van with no problem. At quitting time he hopped into the van and drove to the east side office of Dr. Lee Ahrens.

Her smile appeared genuine when she greeted him. "I'm glad you came to see me again, Craig."

"I am too," he said. "I felt a lot better after the last time I talked to you. I thought we should talk some more."

"All right. That's fine, Craig. Sit down and tell me what you'd like to talk about today."

"My anger again," he said quickly. "How it's getting the best of me lately."

"You mean you're losing control more often, or you're only just noticing how often you become angry?"

"Whatever. Listen, Saturday night there was this spider in my basement. It was a *big* spider. I wasted half a can of bug spray trying to kill the thing, and it made me so mad I finally just took the can and whacked the spider with it."

Dr. Ahrens was smiling. "Did you kill it?"

"Eventually, yeah."

"Sounds like you solved that problem all right. What was it that made you angry, Craig?"

"That I didn't think of the simpler thing to do right away, instead of wasting the bug killer."

"Let me make you feel better right now by telling you countless men and women across America have done the same thing. And not just with bug spray. Women use whatever's handy to them, be it hairspray or Windex."

"And they waste it like that, just spraying and spraying and not killing anything?"

The doctor nodded. "Strange as it sounds, yes."

"Why do we do that?" Craig asked her. "Do you know?"

"It's probably an aversion that dates back thousands of years, when spiders and snakes meant sickness and death to us. A gene memory of sorts. We all know the simpler way to kill an insect, but to avoid actually touching the thing to kill it, and to stay out of its reach, we grope for alternate methods, usually snatching up something we can use as a weapon."

"Yeah," Craig said, shaking his head. "I think that may be it."

"What else did you want to talk about?" asked Dr. Ahrens.

"Gangrene," said Craig. "Do you know anything about gangrene?"

"What causes it, you mean?"

"No, what people do for it once it sets in."

Dr. Ahrens looked him over. "Do you think you have gangrene, Craig?"

"Me? No. I, uh, saw a lady at the hospital before I came over and I was wondering what they do about it."

"In cases of gangrene, amputation is usually necessary."

"Amputation? You mean cut it off?"

"That's right. Did you know this woman, Craig?"

"No. Look, I've also got this other problem. See, I'm keeping something I shouldn't be keeping down in my basement. If anybody finds out, I'll be in big trouble, and I don't want to get in trouble, so I haven't done anything about it yet."

"Are you saying what you have is illegal?"

"Maybe."

"You don't know?"

"Well, yeah, I do, I guess. But I'm taking really good care of it, so—"

"Is it a bird, Craig?" Dr. Ahrens interrupted gently. "Is it some rare bird you're not allowed to keep in this country?"

Craig closed his mouth. "I'm not saying. I want to know what I should do with him. Our neighborhood is one of those where everybody knows everybody else and everybody keeps an eye on each other, and so if someone finds out I'm keeping him, I'll get in trouble."

"I see," said Dr. Ahrens. "Well, if it's bothering you, you need to find a solution. If there's some way you can turn the negative feelings about this into something positive, then I urge you to do so. No sense in weighing yourself down with guilt, Craig."

He looked at her. He hadn't really understood any of that, but she had such a look of gentle concern and kindness that he didn't want to embarrass her by asking her to repeat herself.

She smiled again and said, "Let's talk some more about when you were growing up."

"Is this therapy?"

"No, Craig, we're still just talking. All right?"

"Okay. What about when I was growing up?"

"How did you feel about your father? Were you proud of him? Afraid of him? Happy to spend time with him?"

Craig lifted a shoulder. "Mostly I missed him. He worked off-shore a lot. When he was home we did okay. He got mad at me, but he always had good reason to get mad at me. He—"

"Excuse me for interrupting, Craig. When you say he had good reason, can you explain that to me?"

"Well, it was usually my fault. I'd either say something stupid or do something wrong when he was trying to teach me and he'd get upset. I do the same thing. I never had any kids because I knew that part would drive me crazy, the trying to teach them something and them just staring at you with a blank look and going, huh? You know damn good and well you've explained what you mean as clear as you know how and still they give you that look. Jesus, that would make me nuts. Like those scatter-brained idiots at work."

"Did it make your father nuts?" Dr. Ahrens asked.

"Yeah, didn't I say so? He'd smack me upside of the head

and hold my face so I could read his lips while he said it to me one more time. I usually got it that time, and if I didn't, I made sure I pretended I did."

Dr. Ahrens nodded. "Did you learn your trade from him?"

"What, you mean fixing things? No, he never taught me. The guy I told you about, the people I lived with when my dad was gone? He's the one who showed me how to fix stuff."

"The man with the daughters?"

"Yeah, him. He didn't have anyone to teach, so he taught me."

"Did you admire him? Respect him?"

Craig gave a grudging nod. "I guess I did. I didn't understand him sometimes, but I respected him."

"Like when he beat his daughters?"

"Right."

"When was the last time you saw him?"

"Who? The guy I lived with? Oh, it must have been about twenty-five years ago. I had just gotten out of the army and went back to see old faces. There was no one left but the father, and he asked me what I learned in the army. I told him all the courses I took, and showed him my certificates, and he just laughed at me. I got mad and left."

"His wife and daughters were gone?"

"He said they'd all run off on him."

"What about your father? When was the last time you saw him?"

Craig's gaze lowered. "In the hospital, the day he died. Triple bypass, and all that mess."

"Did you remember to ask your wife what she wanted, Craig? The last time you were here we talked about what you wanted to do, and you were going to ask her what she wanted to do."

Craig looked at the doctor. "She's still not talking to me. I'm being good and doing everything I can for her, but she's not communicating at all. I'm going to move her into the back bedroom tonight."

"Separate beds might be the best thing right now," Dr. Ahrens agreed. "It'll give both of you time to think about where you want to go from here."

"You're right," said Craig. "I really need to think about that."


Mark lay in the basement and thought of every hostage story he had ever read or heard about.

This was different, he told himself. Most hostages weren't chained up and left to piss all over themselves. He had to take a shit so bad his bowels were cramping and making him even more miserable than he already was. But he wasn't going to do it in his pants like his four-month-old daughter. He would not. There had to be a way to reason with Peterwell tonight when he came home.

Wasn't anyone looking for him yet? What the hell was Valerie doing? Sitting on her butt and talking to her mother on the phone?

He gritted his teeth against the pain and unreasonable anger and attempted to sit up. He felt nauseous most of the time now, so it was nothing when his gorge rose and he vomited. Mark still smelled bug spray every time he inhaled, so his throat went on hitching for several moments after his stomach was empty. He was losing weight, he knew, but not enough to free himself of the chains.

It was difficult to keep the self-pity at bay; the *Why me?* bullshit and the general whining about his situation. Mrs. Peterwell knew all about the *Why me?* stuff. She was living pure agony. The terrible green bruising in her leg that Mark had called gangrene to frighten Peterwell was as dark as it was going to get. It would probably start to change color anytime now. Or so Mark thought. For all he knew it really was gangrene.

Not that it appeared to matter, since Peterwell had done nothing for his wife but shove pills down her throat and leave plates of food that went uneaten. Mark didn't know what Peterwell was thinking of, or what his logic was in regard to his wife's situation. Or his own, for that matter.

When the man came home from work toting a gurney with casters on the bottom, Mark could only wonder at Peterwell's latest brainstorm. The gurney was placed on the floor next to Louise, who proceeded to shriek in pain and beg for mercy when her husband attempted to move her on top of the thing. Mark could barely watch as a red-faced Peterwell strained and tugged and pulled his wife's upper torso into place. When he picked up her legs, she emitted a long, tortured screech that hurt Mark's ears. Then Louise fainted.

"Where are you taking her?" Mark asked. He hadn't bothered to fall over as he usually did. He didn't have the strength. He didn't think Peterwell even noticed.

"Upstairs," huffed Peterwell. "There's a bedroom in the back. Gotta get her away from the spiders."

"What about me?"

Peterwell stopped what he was doing and looked at Mark. "What about you?"

"Are you going to leave me down here with the spiders? I have to go to the bathroom pretty bad. Am I going to get a diaper, too?"

"I'll bring a can down later and help you," said Peterwell. "As for the spiders, well, you're a man. You can take it."

Mark opened his mouth to say something else, but he closed it when he smelled something peculiar. He opened his nostrils wide and said, "Is something burning?"

"Yeah," said Peterwell as he strapped his unconscious wife to the gurney. "I started a fire in the fireplace."

Mark frowned. A fire in the middle of summer? "Why?" he asked.

Peterwell didn't answer him.

"Why?" Mark asked again. His voice was better now, stronger. Tomorrow he thought he would start yelling again while Peterwell was at work.

"Never mind," said Peterwell. He turned to Mark then. "I'm supposed to start feeling positive about you. Don't ask me how."

"Who told you that?"

"A doctor. A very good doctor, recommended highly by everyone at the hospital."

"You mean a psychiatrist?"

"Go ahead and call her a shrink if you want. I don't care. She's a nice lady. She's got great legs. A pretty smile, too. I like her a lot."

"How long you been seeing her?"

"Not long."

"You tell her about us?"

Peterwell looked at him. "In a roundabout way. Why?"

"Even if you told her everything, she can't call the cops on you. It's a rule doctors like her have. She can't testify against you or say anything to anyone."

Mark hoped he sounded convincing. Peterwell's look became a stare. "Don't you think I know that?" he said.

"Sure, everyone does. A guy I know raped someone and told his shrink he did it, but his shrink refused to testify on the grounds that it would be a breach of confidentiality."

"So, what you're saying is that even if I tell her about you, she can't say anything to the police?"

"Sorry to say."

Peterwell turned suspicious. "You're lying to me. You want to trick me into telling her about you."

"I wish I was. The thing is, she's sworn to help you no matter what you've done. That agreement keeps her mouth shut about anything you tell her."

Peterwell had to think. After a moment he began fiddling with the straps on his wife. Mark watched him and said, "Louise needs help, Craig."

"I know," he said. "I'm going to help her."

# CHAPTER
# 14

ABRA LAY IN BED with a frown on her face. Down the hall she could hear Thomas's television, which he never turned off, and the male voices of the brothers, deep in early morning conversation. If she concentrated and listened, she could hear them quite clearly. She could hear because Clyde Conlan would not go near his brother and both were forced to speak loudly to make themselves heard. This was knowledge that troubled Abra. Clyde Conlan was chief of staff at a busy hospital and he knew very well that the HIV virus was not transmittable through touch, or even close physical contact such as hugging. Yet he stood at least six feet away from the bed and never went any closer. His behavior was ridiculous, and Abra intended to ask Thomas about it that day.

Then she thought of the picture in Clyde Conlan's bedroom, the two young boys with the two stern-looking adults, and wondered if she had to ask at all. Obviously, there was not a great deal of affection in the family, not counting the rumored affection between the father and his sister, Iris.

Abra smiled to herself. Then she felt guilty and pinched herself for it. Then, for the hundredth time since it had happened, she thought about Zane Campbell kissing her.

She felt like a fool for the scene with him on the porch and the way she behaved. She had made herself sound like some cross-bearing martyr crusading for the terminally ill. Every word she said was the truth, but it all sounded so silly she cringed to think of it. She couldn't imagine what he must think of her. Worse, she couldn't imagine why she was still experiencing altered breathing, sweaty palms and sharply sweet pangs in her middle when she thought of his kiss. She wished she could stop thinking about it. She was too embarrassed to look him in the eye anytime soon, but at the same time she was desperate to see him again.

Abra threw first one leg out of bed and then another. Movement was the only way to take her mind off her thoughts. Her alarm read a quarter to seven, so she had time to take a shower and dress before seeing about Thomas. Clyde had surprised her by rising as early as five o'clock each morning and finishing breakfast almost before Abra was out of bed. She would see him only in passing as he rushed by her to leave the house and go to the hospital. She had no idea he was such a dedicated chief of staff. He did make a point of speaking to Thomas often, something both Thomas and Abra appreciated.

Thomas himself was deteriorating rapidly, and Abra was as attentive to him as physically possible. Having dealt with several AIDS patients, she was surprised at the timetable the disease followed in Thomas, but he told her he had been ill often that year, suffering everything from a bout with pneumonia to bronchitis during the spring. It was the trip to Russia that did it, he claimed. He had gone in search of a mantel believed to have belonged to the family of Stalin and had spent months eating fish and drinking vodka, all to the detriment of his health.

Had he made the acquisition? Abra wanted to know.

Of course, he had told her, and waved his veined hand as if it were nothing to him.

The Conlan brothers were both dedicated, each in their own way, Abra ascertained.

One other thing she noticed, and that she found strange in some way, was Clyde's studied attempts to avoid her. Not that

Abra craved his attention in any way; she did not. But a female alone in a house with two men could usually find herself being looked at by at least one of them. Nothing overt, but a spontaneous glance by a male looking at a female. There was none of this from Clyde. He looked not at her legs, not at her breasts, not at her backside or any of the other places normal men discreetly eye a woman. It made Abra wonder if he weren't more like Thomas than even he knew.

Abra showered and dressed and entered the kitchen to find Clyde leaving through the back door. Before Abra could open her mouth to wish him good morning, he turned and said, "Thomas and I need to visit an old friend today, Abra. "We'll be gone a good part of the day, so you'll need to prepare Thomas's medication for the next eight hours. I know I should have told you yesterday, but my friend called last evening after you went to bed."

"You're taking Thomas?" Abra stammered.

"Oh, yes. There won't be any problem. I'm perfectly capable."

"I wasn't suggesting otherwise, Mr. Conlan. But an extended journey in a car will cause him to suffer."

"A visit to an old friend will do him good," Clyde countered.

"Pardon me for asking, but does this friend live far?"

"No," said Clyde. "Have him ready to go in an hour, please. I'm going to stop in at the hospital and then come right back."

"I'm sorry if I seem to pry. Does Thomas know?"

"Of course. I told him last night." He looked at her then. "I'm going to need you to stay here and wait for us, in case there's an emergency of some kind."

"All day?"

"Is that a problem for you?"

Abra backed up and shook her head. "Of course not. I'll be here if you need me."

"Thank you. I knew I could count on you. As I said, have him ready to go in an hour."

"That sounds fine." Abra still wasn't certain Thomas was up

124 S.K. Epperson

to the trip. Spending time in the car would be torture for him. But Clyde appeared determined, and in this household Clyde was obviously the boss, so she didn't argue further.

At times such as this one, Abra's reduced position grated on her. As a nurse, she was accustomed to giving the orders and used to having them obeyed. Following the orders of doctors who were accustomed to the same thing was difficult. It was the only part of what she did that she disliked. But, she reminded herself, she had no choice. If she wanted to keep working, she would have to deal with bossy bosses.

Several times she thought of going to work for a lab facility and continuing in that direction, but she would miss the one-on-one contact with the patients. It was the getting to know people and aiding them in dealing with their physical and emotional problems that Abra needed. The patients she worked with didn't care that she disliked taking orders from arrogant doctors; they were happy to have her beside them in their time of need.

She sighed to herself and decided to ask her mother to come for lunch that day. It would be good to talk to someone, even if it was her.

Zane woke up thinking about the new car Mark Vaughn had ostensibly left as a gift for the Melo family on Laurel Street. It was all too simple in Zane's thinking. Savaglio and Weld were looking for easy answers and snatching at anything that came up. If it were Zane, he would be wondering why the man had taken no clothes with him. Why he had removed no cash from his account. What was he traveling on? He had asked these questions of Mrs. Vaughn the evening before and learned the answers, after which Valerie Vaughn asked him why none of the detectives at the police station had asked the same questions.

"I couldn't tell you," Zane had said.

Then he asked the big question. The one that made Valerie Vaughn's face turn pink and caused her to look at the floor.

"Mark hasn't broken into a house in years," she said.

"So he was into burglary?"

"Yes. That's what he told me. But he's been straight for a long time."

"Did you tell this to the police?"

"No. Why would I?"

Why indeed. They were looking at Mark for rape and kidnapping, not burglary. But Zane was thinking how many burglars parked their cars or vans a street or two away from their intended house when they went to break in. What if Mark had done that? What if he was ripping off people in the neighborhood and driving the cars from his dealership to do it? Maybe something had happened to him while he was breaking into someone's house. Maybe something serious.

He mentioned none of what he was thinking to Valerie, but he did put in a call first thing that morning to find out how many homes had been burgled in the immediate or surrounding area within the last year. Statistics said most burglars worked within two miles of their home, so if Vaughn, or someone, was working houses, the records would show it.

The other thing he couldn't seem to get out of his mind was those fifteen seconds with Abra on the front porch of the Conlan house. He had known her only a matter of days, not long enough to be thinking about her the way he was thinking about her. He was crazy for opening himself up the way he had. She sounded sincere enough when she said the way he talked wasn't the problem, but Zane knew better. The idea of going to a movie with him, out into public where other people might hear him and see her with him was obviously too much for her.

He didn't know why he was so disappointed. The kiss he couldn't help. He had to do that.

When he saw the Conlans leave together that morning in Clyde's car, he was curious. He wondered what Abra would be doing that day. He had a patient coming in around nine o'clock, so he would be tied up until sometime after lunch. His patient was a two-year-old boy who was going to need artificial eyes in increasing size every four or five months to keep the bone and tissue developing as they would with a normal eye. Since it was a first visit, there would be much work to do, with forms to sign and instructions to deliver. Zane would have a busy morning.

Two hours after his patient arrived Zane took a break and walked by the main window in the living room in time to see a woman in a silver Jaguar roll down the street and pull into the Conlan driveway.

Zane exhaled and continued on his way to the kitchen, where Holt and Eli were creating sandwiches for lunch. Holt asked his dad if he wanted a sandwich and Zane told him no. Holt shook his head.

"We're gonna lift tonight, Dad. You need to eat."

"I'll eat something later. I thought you guys were going to the pool today?"

"Too hot," said Eli. "I was sleepy right after I woke up this morning."

Zane knew how he felt. The sweltering rays of the sun seemed to reach right through the roof of the house and cause yawns and sluggish behavior in not just Eli, but in Holt and Zane as well. The dog days seemed to last longer every year.

After drinking a glass of cold water and eating a couple of crackers, Zane left the kitchen and passed through the living room again on his way to his office. His steps faltered when he heard what sounded like a human screech. He strode to the window and looked outside. Nothing. He looked across the street at the Peterwell house and gave his head a small shake before continuing down the hall.

Damned birds.


Abra greeted her mother at the door and was reminded of the stiff Clyde Conlan when the air beside her cheek was bussed. Abra tried to smile.

"How are you, Mother?"

"I'm fine, Abra. And I'm hungry. To tell the truth, I was ready for lunch an hour ago."

"I've whipped up a spinach quiche," Abra said as she led her mother into the dining room. "I'm so glad you agreed to come."

"I needed to get away. It's been one of those days when no one wants to concentrate and pay attention to what you're telling them. I'm beginning to know how my six o'clock patient feels when he complains no one ever listens to him. I feel the same."

Abra played hostess and seated her mother before moving to serve the quiche. "Would you like some wine?"

"Just half a glass, please."

Abra poured and searched for something to start a conversation. "Who is your six o'clock? Interesting?"

"Fairly interesting. He has a history of what could be termed emotional abuse, if not physical, at the hands of his father and possibly a neighbor. He's easily frustrated and becomes irrational when people don't listen to him."

"Guess you'd better listen then," Abra said, and she smiled.

Her mother's answering smile was brief. "He told me he's already struck his wife for not listening to him. A niggling something tells me there's more than meets the eye with this one. His mental processes go suspiciously awry at times, so much so that he appears not only irrational, but borders on unstable if he thinks someone is going to disagree with him."

Abra made a face. "Be careful with him, Mother."

"I will. How about you? Still ogling your handsome neighbor?"

"No, not today, anyway." Abra paused; then she blurted, "He kissed me."

"Why?" her mother asked, her tone matter-of-fact.

Abra sat back and picked up her wine glass. "I don't know. Do you suppose he likes me?"

Her mother looked at her over a bite of quiche. "Don't be facetious, Abra; it doesn't suit you."

"I thought you'd be happy."

"That depends. How do you feel about him? And before you respond, please take into consideration the length of time the two of you have actually known each other."

"I knew you would say that." Abra gulped at her wine. "The attraction is definitely physical and I'll be the first to admit it. It doesn't happen that often for me, you know."

"I know," said her mother. "What else is there?"

"What do you mean?"

"I mean do you like him? Enjoy his company? Does he make you laugh?"

"He kissed me," Abra repeated. "He kissed me right after I told him I couldn't go to the movies with him. He thinks I turned him down because of the way he talks. I don't know what to say to make him think any differently. I was hoping you could help me."

Lee Ahrens took another bite of quiche and had a sip of wine before she answered. Finally, she said, "Tell him you were born with Venus in Virgo and as a result you're incredibly picky where men are concerned."

Abra stared at her mother. "Was that a joke?"

"What did you expect?"

"A little interest. A little concern."

"Why? Because you're my daughter?" Her mother smiled and put down her fork. "Abra, do you have any idea how many times a day I do this?"

"What? Eat?"

"No. Smile and listen to someone ask me what to do."

Abra felt her mouth tighten. "You're right, Mother. I'm sorry. I don't know what I was thinking. Can I get you some more quiche?"

"No, thank you. I need to be going. I'm glad you called, Abra. Lunch was very good. Let's do it again soon."

There was nothing to do but sit and watch as Lee Ahrens rose from the table, dabbed at her mouth, and excused herself to visit the restroom. Abra picked at the quiche on her own plate until her mother emerged again. She walked her to the door, and her mother gave her arm a brief pat.

"Let me know how you're doing, will you?"

"Of course," said Abra. "Goodbye."

"Goodbye, dear."

Abra watched until her mother was in her Jaguar and backing down the drive.

She wondered if her mother knew Clyde Conlan. If not, she definitely had to introduce them.

# CHAPTER
# 15

CRAIG RECOILED IN HORROR when he saw that the axe had merely dented the bone in Louise's leg rather than severed it. The blood gushed, covering Craig and everything in sight. He stared at the dull edge of the axe and got sick at the sight of the blood soaking the sheets and comforter of the bed. Louise herself was white and still as she succumbed to shock. Craig looked helplessly at her and dropped the axe to grab a tie from his closet in the bedroom. He hadn't remembered to put the tourniquet on first. He rushed to do that now, before she lost every drop of blood.

He put the tie around her leg and pulled it tight before tying a knot. It slowed the bleeding somewhat, but not completely. Still gagging, Craig went to the bathroom for a towel. He came back and wrapped it around her leg, just below the tourniquet. He had been a fool to think he could take off her leg with just one chop. He couldn't believe he hadn't thought to sharpen the axe. Or put on the tourniquet.

What was wrong with him? Why couldn't he seem to think straight lately? Why was he messing things up all the time?

He stood panting beside the bed and realized that Vaughn was yelling at him from the basement. He wanted to know what was going on. Why Louise had screamed like that. Sweat poured down Craig's face as he wondered what to tell him. Vomit crept up his throat once more. More than ever, he wanted to hop in his van, load up his birds, and leave. He could drive straight north and be in Canada within a day.

No. Anyone crossing the border with birds would be stopped.

Could he leave them? Could he leave his precious parrots and go far away from this house, his job and his life?

The birds in the living room began to squawk, almost as if reading Craig's thoughts. He sat down at the foot of the blood-soaked bed and stared at his wife. "I'm sorry, Louise. I really am. I wasn't thinking. I was trying to help you and I screwed up. I thought it would be easy to take off your leg below the knee. I had no idea the bones would be so hard. I could give you some more pills, but you might overdose."

He knew he should go and sharpen the axe blade and try again, but the thought of raising the axe over his head one more time threatened to make the vomit spill over. He couldn't do it.

Maybe all the blood that ran out took the poison with it. Maybe the green would go away now.

Craig told himself he should wait and see. Just keep her in the bed and do his best to keep her from bleeding anymore, and go on as before.

That decided, Craig checked the towel. Soaked. He retrieved another one and wrapped this towel even tighter around the gaping wound. Then he went downstairs to see about Vaughn.

"What are you doing?" Vaughn asked immediately, his voice scared. "Why did she scream like that?"

Craig inhaled and put his hands on his hips. He still felt sick. "I tried to amputate her leg to take care of the gangrene."

Vaughn's eyes rounded. His mouth opened and began to move, but no sound came forth.

"I didn't do it right," Craig admitted. "I forgot to put the tourniquet on first. And the axe blade was dull. That thing has been in the garage forever."

Vaughn was apoplectic.

"I can't believe I didn't think about those things, but I haven't exactly been on my toes lately. There's nothing to worry about.

Louise is in shock, but I think she'll be okay. I'm pretty sure I got the bleeding stopped. The bed is a mess, though, so I need to change the sheets sometime. Not right now. I don't feel well. I need to sit down for a while and think. My head hurts." Craig started out of the basement, then he stopped and turned. "Don't yell anymore," he said to Vaughn. "If you do, I'll come and show you what a dull axe blade feels like."

Without even looking at Vaughn's expression he turned and walked up the stairs. The squawking birds squawked even louder when they saw him. Craig sat down in the chair beside the television and allowed their noise to cover him.

Just like when he was a kid, and the father was yelling and the little girls were screaming while his hands slapped and punched and his feet kicked in their heavy black boots. They were the boots he got in the army. He wore them all the time. He told Craig a girl tried to steal them from him in Italy, but he was too quick for her. He knocked the piss out of her and then took what he wanted. He said that's what a man did. The rest of the world was too goddamned civilized. If a man was big enough to kick the shit out of a guy with a lot of money, then he ought to be able to do it and take what he wanted. Why should the weak men, the scrawny men, have all the power? The men with the muscles to take what they wanted were the rightful kings.

The man had a problem. Craig knew that even as a child. But at the same time, a lot of what he said made sense. You couldn't help but stop and think about the points he was making, because there was some tiny bit of truth in his rantings. It was only when taken as a whole that the color of his comments began to slide toward the dark end of the scale. Craig had been forced to listen for hours at a time, held prisoner by the fact that he was a young male in the house of a man's man with no sons.

The birds were his only refuge. When the neighbor's hand rose (it rarely descended on Craig), it was time to go and let the cries be drowned by the voices of the sky.

Those voices were different now. They were louder, more strident, more demanding. Craig listened just the same. He listened until he became the sound, and then he wasn't anything else.


Mark was hyperventilating. His breathing was fast and shallow, and he was close to passing out. He kept seeing the falling axe in his mind and he heard Louise's ululating screech over and over again.

It was his fault. It was his fault Peterwell had tried to cut off her leg. He told him it was gangrene, and Peterwell believed him.

"Oh, God, oh, God," Mark murmured. "Oh, dear God, I'm so sorry. Louise, my God, I had no idea he would do this."

Mark started crying. He kept picturing the blood on the bed upstairs. The forgotten tourniquet.

How could anyone be so stupid? How could anyone be so incredibly ignorant?

He wasn't dealing with a rational man here. Mark had to remember that. No matter how sane and logical he might sound, Craig Peterwell was shopping without money and looking through windows at the real world.

But to try and cut off his wife's leg?

Oh, man.

Mark had been too horrified to ask how successful he had been. If he had cut bone or splintered it.

Maybe they could save the leg if it wasn't too bad, providing Louise didn't die from loss of blood first. And providing anyone came to the rescue within the next fucking year or so.

Mark had been close to the edge for hours. He couldn't feel his arms or legs and he was constantly dizzy. His circulation was in serious danger, and unless Craig Peterwell wanted to put that axe to use chopping up body parts and hauling them out in trash bags, he would have to remove the chains sometime soon.

Mark's shock had been too great to ask when Peterwell was down earlier, but the next time Mark saw him, he was going to ask him to take off the chains. If Peterwell said no, then Mark was going to ask Peterwell to kill him. He couldn't go on like this anymore. He couldn't stay in the basement and retain his sanity. Louise had helped when she was there. She was someone in trouble just like him, a person in jeopardy of losing her life. Now that she was gone, Mark lived for those moments when he heard Peterwell coming down the stairs. Otherwise, he was utterly alone.

Every hour he swore to himself and to God above that if he escaped this situation, he would never, *ever* commit another sin as long as he lived. He would be good to his wife and daughter, he would go to church on Sundays and become a model citizen. He would vote in all the elections, make better deals on the cars he sold, and not cheat on his taxes. He would be a new man, if God allowed it.

He swore to give up the occasional drugs and cigarettes, stop sneaking peeks at his secretary in the bathroom at work, and give yearly money to Jerry's kids.

There was just one thing. He wanted to do something about Craig Peterwell. Not because he hated him, though he did hate him, but because a man like Peterwell had no business walking around living and breathing with the rest of them. He didn't play by the rules designed to allow human beings to live comfortably with one another, and because he didn't, because he was crazy and would probably be sent to a state hospital and then be released in ten years, something needed to be done.

Mark was a rule breaker himself. He knew that. But the rules he broke were the ones people expected to be broken. The rules no one really cared too much about. Loss of a CD player or a thirteen-inch color television was babyshit compared to loss of a limb.

The way he looked at it, Craig Peterwell had stepped over a line, and for the first time in his life, Mark wanted to take responsibility and do something for his fellow man: he wanted to remove Craig Peterwell from existence.

He felt God would understand.

*   *   *

Peterwell didn't come down to see him again that night. Not even to bring him food. Mark dozed in spurts, his mind turning, and when he heard Peterwell leave for work the next morning he came to a decision. He was going to try and leave the basement. If he could make it over to the dryer and back, then he could try to make it up the stairs. He was weaker now, and his muscles were uncooperative, but if he didn't try, he would go insane.

It had taken him almost an hour to get to the dryer, but he had eight hours to work with today. He didn't think about what he would do once he was upstairs. He didn't think about what he *could* do. He just knew he had to try and get up there.

The thought of the dull axe blade galvanized him. He tried shimmying first on his stomach, and went nowhere fast. Next he tried walking on his knees. Finally he fell down on his side and tried flopping himself.

Exhausted, he stopped. The stairs were still twelve feet away. But he had made progress.

When he could breathe he started again, shimmying, flopping, and attempting to use his knees and chin to move himself along. He was encouraged by the amount of space he had covered, and he went on until exhaustion claimed him once more. He continued like this, gaining ground with each effort, urging himself on with the picture of him shitting in the coffee can Peterwell had placed beneath him. It was enough to move him to the base of the stairs. There he stopped, weakened beyond reason, and fell into a short doze.

Fifteen minutes later his eyes opened and he looked around himself in a panic, wondering how much time he had left. The light appeared the same to him, but he had never been one to notice such things, so it could be five o'clock outside and he wouldn't know it. He attempted to get up on his knees to try and crawl up, using his chin for leverage. It was then that he heard the noise in the basement. The tiny tapping on the glass. *Tap tap tap.*

Mark froze and wondered if he was truly going insane. Several seconds later he heard it again. *Tap tap tap.*

Someone was out there.

*Oh, God,* Mark moaned to himself. Someone was out there looking in, and here he was at the bottom of the stairs where no one could see him. Who was it? The meter reader? A neighbor?

"Help!" he shouted. "Help! Somebody come and help me!"

Mark's ears strained when he stopped, and he thought he heard a voice outside, but he also thought he might have imagined it because he wanted it so badly.

He began to scream again, making himself hoarse. In the rooms above him, the birds set up a deafening din, swallowing up the sound of his cries. Tears began to stream down his face as Mark realized no one would hear him above the bird noise. He gritted his teeth and slammed his head against the stair. How did they get such volume with those tiny little lungs?

He used the anger to move himself. He poured his rage into his movements and made it up three stairs in almost one motion. Fueled by his progress, he gave a kamikaze yell and moved up three more stairs, using his knees and scraping his chin raw. He was starting to bleed on the carpeted steps.

Mark didn't care. He was moving and he wasn't stopping. He was doing it. He was making it up the stairs and he wasn't going to quit until he was at the top.

Twenty minutes later, a heaving, triumphant Mark lay on his belly at the top of the stairs and wondered what to do next.

Then the light in the room darkened. He saw it darken and knew it wasn't the sun going down. Someone had just stepped in front of the window. Mark twisted his head and saw someone looking through the glass, trying to see past the sheers. It was Chance Morley.

Before Mark could open his mouth, Chance disappeared.

"Goddammit."

Not that Chance could have helped him. But maybe he would go home to get his mother.

Mark was lifting his head for another look around when he heard the glass on the kitchen door break. He couldn't believe his ears when he heard the door open. Before he could get twisted around, he saw Chance Morley come striding through the dining room.

When Chance saw Mark he stopped. His eyes rounded and he turned as if to run, but Mark shouted at him, "No, Chance, don't go! Stay! I need your help."

Chance stopped. He stepped cautiously forward and said, "I didn't do nothing bad. I just came to let the birds go."

Mark smiled weakly. "I won't tell anyone, Chance. I need you to let *me* go."

Chance blinked and looked at the chains holding Mark.

"How would I do that?"

"Can you go get my wife? Valerie?"

Chance shook his head. "She ain't home. I saw her leave this morning with the baby and a big suitcase."

Shit, Mark thought. Running home to mother. "How about the cop across the street? Mr. Campbell? Can you go and get him?"

"No," Chance said flatly. "He'll know what I done and he'll tell my momma I came to let the birds go. She'll get really mad at me."

Mark was losing patience. "I've said I won't tell anyone you broke in here, Chance. I'll tell them you came to help me."

Chance was still doubtful and Mark was ready to panic.

"Chance, in my garage there are some bolt cutters. You know what bolt cutters look like?"

He nodded. "I think so. Big long handles, right?"

"That's right. Go get those and bring them to me. Once you get the chains off, I'll . . . I'll help you set the birds free. But we have to hurry."

Chance's face lit up. "You will? You'll let 'em go?"

"Yes. Go get the bolt cutters. If the door is locked, break the glass just like you did in the kitchen, all right?"

A fleeting look of guilt passed over Chance's face. "I wasn't supposed to do that."

"I'm giving you permission to do it at my house. Now go. And hurry back. We've got to let those birds go."

Chance's head bobbed and he backed out of the dining room and turned to exit the house at a trot. Mark watched him go and squeezed his eyes shut in earnest prayer that Chance cared enough about his mission of freeing the birds to return. He knew the retarded man was frightened, and more than a little forgetful, but he thought he had been startled enough to remember what he had seen, and if he himself didn't return, Mark hoped he would tell someone.

While he waited, Mark counted seconds into minutes and wondered what the hell was taking so long. Finally he heard footsteps returning, and he nearly burst into tears when he saw Chance come in carrying the bolt cutters. He quickly told Chance where to cut and how, and winced repeatedly as the chains fell away from his tortured body. When he was done, Chance stood back and said, "Your chin's bleeding."

"I know," said Mark.

"Can we let the birds go now?"

"Would you help me up first? I don't know if I can walk."

He couldn't. He asked Chance to help him down the hall to look in the bedroom.

"What for?"

"Mrs. Peterwell is back here. I want to check on her before we go."

"What's she doing?"

"Probably sleeping, Chance."

She wasn't sleeping, she was dead. Mark picked up her wrist and felt for a pulse. Her skin was still warm, her flesh still pliable, but she was no longer breathing and her heart had ceased to beat. He gently placed her arm back by her side. Her eyes were half-closed, her expression pained. It hurt Mark deeply to see her.

As promised, Peterwell had changed the sheets.

"Is she sleeping?" asked Chance.

Mark couldn't answer. His eyes filled with tears and he turned his head. "Help me to my house, Chance. Will you do that?"

"Can I let the birds go first?"

After a pause, Mark nodded, and as he watched Chance go for the same cages he himself had opened days before, his fevered mind began to work. He began to think of the possibilities that being "missing" offered him where Craig Peterwell was concerned. He pictured Peterwell coming home today and taking his sweet time about coming down to the basement. He pictured the man's eyes bugging out of his fat white head when he discovered Mark missing. He pictured the terror on his face, the sweat on his brow, the panicked thudding of his heart and the shit in his shorts when he found Louise dead. And Mark, crazed with pain, nearly paralyzed with stiffness, and ravenous for revenge, liked the idea.

# CHAPTER

# 16

CHANCE HAD A GREAT time setting the birds free. He didn't understand why Mr. Vaughn had been chained up, and he meant to ask, but he had to help him get home first. Mr. Vaughn didn't want anyone to see them, he said, so he made Chance look carefully around to see if anyone was watching. Chance didn't see anyone. There was a strange car at Eli's house, so that meant Eli's dad had a patient and wouldn't be looking outside. There was no one home at the Conlans', and Chance knew Mrs. Vaughn was gone. There was only Chance's mother to worry about, and Chance wasn't worried about her because she was working in her sewing room and never looked up for anything when she was doing her sewing.

He told Mr. Vaughn that everything was okay and he helped him out the back door. When they were down the steps, Mr. Vaughn said, "Wait. We need to leave the back door open so the birds can fly out. Get that brick over there, Chance. We'll prop it open."

Chance let Mr. Vaughn lean against the trunk of a maple tree while he got the brick and opened the back door. One bird, a white cockatoo, flew out immediately. Chance laughed and clapped his hands.

"That's probably the one who screamed for help. Did you see him? Look, he's in that tree over there."

140

Mr. Vaughn looked strangely at him. "The bird screamed for help?"

"He told me he was trapped and couldn't get out. He asked me to help him."

Mr. Vaughn rubbed his face and looked at the sky. Chance watched him and asked why he was chained up in Mr. Peterwell's house.

It was several moments before Mr. Vaughn answered. He felt his swollen nose and said, "We were playing a game, Chance. I got loose, so I win. Let's keep it a secret, all right? You don't tell anyone I was there, and I won't tell anyone you broke into Mr. Peterwell's house. Okay?"

Chance's nod was vigorous. "I won't tell. I won't tell anyone. And you won't tell anyone I let the birds go."

"That's right. Now, help me home, Chance, and remember, don't tell anyone you saw me. I'm not home. You haven't seen me. Got that?"

"But you just said to take you home." Chance was confused.

"I know I did, but don't tell anyone you helped me. You haven't seen me, all right? If anyone asks, you haven't seen me at all."

"Okay. I understand now. You don't want anyone to know you're home."

"Right. No one. Not even your mother, okay?"

"Okay. Mr. Vaughn, we better get going now."

Chance went to help him into the house next door. As they rounded the corner of the yard, Chance wrinkled his nose. It wasn't nice to say so, he knew, but Mr. Vaughn didn't smell very good. He smelled like pee.

They went in through the garage, where the window was broken, and Chance asked Mr. Vaughn how he was going to get in his house. Mr. Vaughn smiled at him and said, "We got locked out once and my wife bought a spare key to keep out here in a magnet box. It's on the underside of the gas grill. Can you get it for me?"

"Sure I can."

Chance got the magnet box and handed it to Mr. Vaughn, who removed the key and opened the door. Once inside the house, Mr. Vaughn collapsed on the sofa in the living room and asked Chance to get him a drink from the kitchen sink. Chance got him a drink and carried it in to him. He said, "I'm sure glad you won the game, Mr. Vaughn. I don't like Mr. Peterwell. He's mean."

"He's meaner than you know," Mr. Vaughn murmured, and he drank the whole glass of water.

"Will Mrs. Peterwell get mad because we left her back door open? The air was on, you know."

"She won't get mad, Chance."

"She didn't look too good, did she?"

"She's been sick."

"Her arms looked real big. Her legs, too."

"Mr. Peterwell needs to take better care of her, doesn't he?"

"He does." Chance then looked around. "Guess I'd better go now. We're both not going to say anything, remember?"

"I remember. Chance, tell me something. Didn't you worry about Mrs. Peterwell when you broke into the house?"

Chance looked guilty again. "I didn't see her car in the garage when I looked. I didn't know she was in the other bedroom. She told me once that was her junk room, where she keeps stuff she doesn't use anymore but might need again so she doesn't throw it away."

"Weren't you scared of being caught?"

"I did get caught," said Chance.

"Not by me. By someone else. By Mrs. Peterwell."

"Oh, no, not her. She's nice to me. And she told my momma once that she wished the birds were gone. That's why I finally decided to help. I knew she wouldn't let the birds go because of him, but that voice kept bugging me and bugging me and I even dreamed about the birds, so I knew I had to try and let them go."

"You'd better go on home now, Chance. Some of those birds are probably flying around the neighborhood, and you want to be safely in the house when Mr. Peterwell gets home."

A spurt of adrenaline at the mention of Peterwell's name got Chance moving. He said goodbye and walked out the back door and through the garage again, stepping around the broken glass and thinking he was lucky Mr. Vaughn hadn't asked him to pick it up. He looked all around as he walked home, but he didn't see any birds. Once in his house, he went to see if his mother was still sewing. She was. Chance stood in the doorway and said, "Hi, Mom."

"Hi, honey," she said with pins in her mouth.

Chance smiled to himself and clapped his hands as he went back down the hall to get himself a drink out of the kitchen. He felt like he had won the game, too.

At five minutes after six Craig settled himself into the chair in Lee Ahrens's office and returned her warm smile. He liked her more every time he saw her. She was so sweet.

"How are you today, Craig?" she asked.

"Okay," he said. "I had a rough time with Louise last night, but I feel better just seeing you."

"A rough time? You didn't hit her again, did you?"

"Not really, no. Only in a manner of speaking. But I handled it and everything's okay now. I got her moved into the back bedroom."

"Is that why you argued? Over the separate bedrooms?"

"No. We didn't exactly argue. She screamed a lot while I was moving her, but she finally stopped. She doesn't see that I'm only trying to help. I don't mean to mess up the way I do. I don't mean to forget things and hurt her and make her scream at me. All she sees is the guy who screws up."

The doctor nibbled on her pen. "I'm sure you don't mean to

forget things, Craig. What we need to find out is why you do forget them."

"Tell me about it," he said. "I can't remember my own name around these headaches I get. It's—"

"Tell me about your headaches. Front, back, sides of your head, where?"

"Mostly on my right side. Feels like it's right behind my eye. Comes on early and stays all day."

"Every day?"

"Pretty much," said Craig. "But I've had headaches for years. Only lately, it's like I'm blacking out."

"You didn't mention that to the doctor who sent you to me. How long do these blackouts usually last?"

"Not long at all. Only a second or two."

"You say you've had headaches for years. Has it always been the same headache? On the right side?"

"I don't think so. Heck, I don't know. Like I said, I can't remember things anymore."

"Any numbness anywhere? Hands, legs?"

"My left hand goes numb sometimes. Or is it my right? Sometimes a leg will feel prickly when I wake up."

Lee Ahrens nibbled on her pen some more. "Craig, why don't you humor me and see a friend of mine who's a neurologist?"

"A brain doctor?"

"Yes. Let's find out if these headaches mean anything. I know it's frightening to suggest, and you're probably jumping out of your skin right now, but it's much better to be safe under the circumstances."

Craig was staring at her. "What? It isn't stress? You think something's wrong with my brain?"

"I didn't say that. But my friend can find out for sure, so at least you won't have to worry about the headaches anymore. They may be the source of your problem."

"I thought stress was the source of my problem. Now it's the headaches that are making me mad all the time?"

"It would certainly upset me to have a headache all the time," said the doctor. "Let's do it, Craig. Let's set up an appointment and get you in to see the neurologist. He owes me a favor, so maybe he'll get you in quick."

Craig didn't know what to say. He hadn't expected anything like this. She was supposed to listen to him and make him feel better, not send him to brain doctors to cure his daily headaches.

He said, "I guess it's okay, if that's what you think we should do."

She nodded. "I do." She paused then. "Did you ever resolve your problem with the thing in the basement?"

"The thing in my . . . oh, yeah. No, I haven't. See, it keeps getting more and more complicated. Every time I try to do something to make the situation better, I make the whole thing worse. I keep getting the urge to just leave town and forget about everything. The thing is, I can't leave my birds."

Dr. Ahrens was shaking her head. "Leaving is the worst thing you could do, Craig. None of us can run away from our problems. They follow us, in some form, wherever we go, and if we allow them to, they disrupt the rest of our lives. I think I can help you if you allow me to, Craig. I'm going to try. But I want you to tell me you'll try, and that you won't run away from your troubles."

She was staring so intently at him that Craig was powerless to do anything but nod. "Okay," he said with a sigh of resignation. "I won't skip town."

"No matter what? You'll come and work it out with me?"

"No matter what."

"All right, Craig. That's good. Let me find the number of that neurologist."

"Wait a minute," he said. "About this confidential rule you people have. Does that apply to everything?"

"Yes. Everything you say to me is confidential and doesn't leave this room."

"Everything? Even the bad stuff?"

"Everything, Craig. Is there something you want to tell me?"
"No. No, I was just checking."

Later, as he opened his front door, Craig was smiling. Mark Vaughn had actually told him the truth. Craig figured he was lying to save himself, but Vaughn had been right about the confidential stuff. Craig was going to be extra nice to him tonight, maybe even give him some of the steak Craig planned to cook for himself.

The smile on his face froze when he entered the living room and saw the open cages and only a few birds in the room. One parrot looked at him and cocked its head before flying toward the kitchen. Craig made a choking noise in his throat and charged down the stairs.

When he didn't immediately see Vaughn in the basement, he stopped and stood where he was, his thoughts whirling. Vaughn had escaped. His neighbor had escaped somehow and the police would be coming for Craig any minute. He had to get out.

He raced up the stairs again and had his suitcase on the bed before he thought to check on Louise. He went down the hall and into the room and walked right up to the bed. "Louise, we have to—"

Craig paused at the sight of her yellow, half-lidded eyes. He touched her arm. It was stiff and cool. He tried to move her head. It was stiff, too.

She was dead. Her glazed eyes were never going to look at him again. Craig backed out of the room and sat down in the middle of the hall. He wanted to cry. He wanted to sit and bawl his head off because he had killed his wife. He didn't know what to do. If he left now, he would be a hunted man. They would come for him and track him down and put him in prison. He couldn't take that. He couldn't live without his birds.

While he sat with his head in his hands, the phone began to ring. Craig ignored it as long as he could, but when it rang past ten rings, he realized it was someone who knew he was home. He went to the phone in his bedroom and picked up the receiver. He said nothing, just waited.

"By now you know I'm out, Peterwell," said a familiar voice. "And you know Louise is dead. The question is, what are you going to do about it?"

"What are *you* going to do about it?" Craig countered. "If you tell anyone about me and Louise, I'll tell them you broke into my house."

"You think they'll believe an insane axe murderer?"

"You think they'll believe a convict?"

"I don't have to tell them who's calling. All I have to tell them is there's a body in your house."

Craig's nostrils flared. "Are you home?"

"Don't be stupid. Get ready, Peterwell. The cops are coming."

The dial tone sounded in his ear and Craig slammed down the phone. He was angry again. He was so angry he wanted to put his fist through something. Instead, he got moving. His brain went into overdrive and the ideas started jumping like hot hulls in a popcorn popper. He ran out to the kitchen to find a pack of Louise's cigarettes. Since retiring she had picked up the habit again, but Craig had forbidden her to smoke around the birds, so she smoked only in the kitchen. Craig found a can of lighter fluid under the sink and rushed into the back bedroom with the cigarettes, her lighter, and the can of fluid.

He spurted the fluid down the front of her lime green housedress and on the sheets around her and on the rug in front of her, so it would look like she spilled the fluid while trying to refill the army lighter given to her by her father. Then Craig lit her up and shut the bedroom door.

He waited several minutes, then opened the door again to make sure she was burning.

She was. So was everything else, the sheets, the rug, her hair. Smoke was starting to crawl toward the door.

Craig hurried to put a wet towel across the bottom of the door to keep the smoke out of the rest of the house. He didn't want the smoke alarm to go off yet. He wanted Louise to burn awhile.

There would be a valiant effort on his part to free all his birds by opening the doors to their cages and letting them go. There was nothing he could do for Louise. She was already too far gone by the time he arrived and discovered the fire. He would have no idea how the tall, highboy dresser landed on her and broke all her bones.

He waited fifteen minutes more, figuring he had plenty of time before the police sent someone to check out an anonymous call about a body in a house. Corpses didn't burn the way people thought they did. Fire needed time.

When the cans of house paint, spray paint, stain and varnish in the closet of the back bedroom began to explode, it took Craig by complete surprise. He wondered in panic if the whole house was going to go. He had forgotten all about the stuff stored back there. The old drapes and wallpaper remnants. The turpentine. All the fix-it-up stuff she had wanted to put downstairs in Craig's basement.

The fire burst through the closed door and leaped across the hall to the bathroom and the next bedroom, where Craig's suitcase lay on the bed. Craig thought of rushing in to move the suitcase, but he thought he'd better call 911 first.

The smoke alarms were going crazy as he made the call. Craig hung up as quickly as he could and ran to the bedroom to see if he could snatch some clothes. It was too late. The entire room was filled with smoke, and fire licked at him as he backed into the hall. Craig screamed in pain and ran for the living room. As he threw open the door and dashed onto the lawn, he realized he was still screaming.

The Campbells' door opened and the ex-cop came running across the street. Craig dropped to the ground and began to tear at his still smoldering hair.

"I couldn't save her! I couldn't save her! Oh, God, I couldn't save Louise!"

*  *  *

From the house next door, Mark Vaughn watched the scene with amazement and disgust. Nothing had turned out as planned. He had expected Peterwell to jump, run and squirm in agony for hours while he waited for the cops to pick him up. He wanted the man to cringe in fear for his life the way Mark had done down in his basement.

But Peterwell was smarter than he had realized. Mark wondered how he could be, since he had displayed nothing but ignorance since he had known him. There was no way Mark could have predicted the fire. He kicked himself for not going ahead and calling the police. Peterwell would have everything covered now, even the broken bones, which often snapped in bodies exposed to intense heat.

Mark moved painfully away from the window and attempted to console himself. It wasn't over. He hadn't fully recovered, and his brain cells weren't functioning properly yet. Thinking about anything seemed to take a long time. But he'd get it together soon. Then he would figure his next move. He wasn't finished with Craig Peterwell yet.

# CHAPTER

# 17

ZANE LEFT PETERWELL ON the lawn and went in the house to see if he could get to Mrs. Peterwell, but it was impossible. Everything east of the living room was on fire and burning. When the fire department arrived, the fire was on the roof and reaching for the trees. Firemen with masks demanded to know if anyone was inside, and Zane told them yes, the wife of the man on the ground was in the back bedroom. The firemen looked at each other and Zane saw their silent communication. The back bedroom was an inferno. She was gone.

The firemen departed to concentrate on stopping the fire before it demolished the entire house, and a rescue unit team came to see about Peterwell. He said he had set most of his birds free when he realized he couldn't save his wife. Zane looked at the nearby trees, but he didn't see a single bird. He moved out of the way to the curb, and his sons came across the street to stand behind him. Zane saw the porch light come on at the Conlan house. Abra stepped out and walked over, her brows raised in question as she watched the busy firemen and the burning house.

"Was anyone hurt?" she asked.

"Mrs. Peterwell is still inside," Zane told her, and he saw her pupils enlarge slightly. "Mr. Peterwell was burned, but not badly. He doesn't know what happened."

As Zane finished speaking, a news vehicle arrived with Kelly

Cameron in the passenger's seat. Zane looked at Eli and gave him a warning look. Eli looked at his feet.

"Hello again," said Kelly Cameron as she approached Zane and the others. She looked over her shoulder, to where her cameraman was filming the fire. "Does anyone know how it started?"

Zane and the boys only looked at her. Abra shrugged.

"This is the guy with the birds, right? Was there anyone inside?"

Zane felt Abra look at him. He said nothing. The television reporter eyed the group of them and snorted. "Thanks, people. I'm just trying to do my job."

As she departed, Chance Morley and his mother joined the others at the curb. Chance's eyes were huge. Zane noticed that he seemed nervous. He kept looking at the trees.

"Mrs. Peterwell was inside, wasn't she?" said Mrs. Morley in a sad voice.

"Yes," said Zane.

"Where is Mr. Peterwell?"

Eli pointed. "He's over there with the rescue people."

"Is he burned?"

"Dad said not bad."

Some neighbors from a block over came to watch, and Zane told the boys it was time to go. They turned reluctantly and Zane found himself face to face with Abra. He met her glance and then moved around her. She touched him lightly on the arm. "You're burned."

He stopped in surprise and looked at himself.

She pointed to a large reddening area on his left arm.

"It's already blistering. Did you go inside?"

"Just for a second."

"I can take care of it for you if you like. I have a bag at the Conlans'."

He hesitated; then he realized Holt and Eli were watching him. He told them to go on home. He would be there in a minute.

Eli grinned.

Zane wanted to smack him. He followed Abra to the Conlan house and walked in behind her. She led him to the kitchen and asked him to wait while she got what she needed. He sat down at the small dinette in the breakfast nook and looked at his arm. It was blistering. Strange that he hadn't realized he was burned.

He thought about Mrs. Peterwell in the burning house, and his expression made Abra pause as she walked into the room. She said, "Most burn victims are dead from the fumes before the fire ever touches them."

Zane looked at her in surprise and she pulled a chair over to sit down beside him. In her hands she had salve, gauze and tape. Without saying anything further she began to work, and within minutes she had him fixed up, with a warning to keep the burn moist, change the bandages often and give the wound a chance to breathe.

Zane watched her as she worked and when she finished he was almost sorry, in spite of the pain she caused. He had enjoyed having her touch him. She read this in his eyes and her breathing changed slightly. Zane turned his head away.

"Abra, I'm sorry for putting you in the embarrassing position of having to turn me down for a date. I wasn't thinking when I asked you. Don't hold it against me."

Abra looked at him. "I'm not sure I got all that. Did you just apologize for asking me to go to the movies?"

"No, I apologized for putting you in the position of having to turn me down."

"It's the same thing, Zane. I told you it had nothing to do with the way you talk."

"Any woman would have to think twice about going out with me, and I understand that. It's embarrassing for *me* when people can't understand what I'm saying, so I can only imagine what it would feel like to someone else. Eli likes to talk for me, and Holt will do the same thing in front of his friends. I'd hate to embarrass you."

Abra's sigh was resigned. "Embarrassment is something you learn to live with as a nurse. I'm probably immune to any more embarrassment at this point."

They were close, sitting just inches apart from each other at the table. Zane saw her looking at the small round bullet scar in his cheek, next to his mouth. She looked at his lips then, and next she looked into his eyes.

"How did you get shot?"

"Chasing an armed man across a parking lot."

"You don't seem like the type," she said. "You seem so unlike a policeman."

Zane's smile was crooked. "I'm not a policeman. Not anymore."

"You mean you were different at one time?"

He nodded. "Like night and day. When I was a cop I was moody as hell."

Abra eyed him. "It's still in there. It's still inside you. I can see it."

"Maybe the good part. Not the bad. Being shot and left with a permanent impairment has a way of changing your attitude."

She looked at her hands. "I tend to get moody myself at times."

"I can see that."

Abra frowned, and Zane smiled at her. "Those of us who serve the public sometimes suffer from all the inane smiling and aimless chitchat. Right?"

She made a noise of agreement and Zane reached out to squeeze the hand that rested on her thigh. They gazed at each other until he remembered himself. He let go of her hand and pushed back his chair. "Thanks for the bandaging, Abra. Come over when you want something from the garden."

"I will," she said.

As he left the house, Zane cursed her for being so nice to him. He'd rather she be distant and bitchy toward him. It might be easier to stop thinking about her if she were. He still wasn't buying the dedication to her patient bit. No one was that dedicated. The problem had to be his cursed mouth.

The firemen were still battling to put out the blaze at the Peterwell house. Zane watched from the yard for a moment before going in the house. Kelly Cameron and her cameraman were still hovering, still trying to find out what was going on from the person in charge, who was still involved in managing the fire. Holt and Eli were at the window, looking across the street. Zane let them watch. It wasn't every day there was such a spectacle to witness. It wasn't every day one of your neighbors perished in a fire. He thought of sweet old Mrs. Peterwell, and when he couldn't stop thinking of her, he went in his office and closed the door.

Abra, too, stood at her window and watched the firemen put out the fire. She didn't know Mrs. Peterwell, and though the loss of human life always disturbed her, she found herself even more disturbed by Zane Campbell. For a moment, just before he left, she would have sworn he was going to kiss her again, and even though he hadn't, her nerves were still jangled by the possibility. Abra had wanted him to do it. She wanted to kiss him again and feel what she had felt the first time. She couldn't help it; everything in her was changing and he was responsible.

Him and Clyde Conlan.

Over the next week, Abra was to find herself with even less human contact, as Clyde decided on the spur of the moment to spend several days of "vacation" at home. His explanation to Abra was: "He doesn't have much longer. I want to be with Thomas as much as possible."

She understood, but she also felt left out when Clyde took Thomas's medicine and closed the door on her, barring her from entering the room.

When Zane was outside she left the house to speak to him. He was always glad to see her and willing to stop what he was doing to chat. She didn't know if it was her or him, but she thought he was speaking clearer all the time. She understood more of what he said and had to ask him to repeat himself less often. She found herself spending time near the windows again, hoping to see him emerge from the house so she could go and be near him. He didn't touch her, but she found herself wishing he would, so she could touch him.

The day Clyde Conlan emerged from Thomas's room and saw her outside with Zane, he opened the back door and spoke harshly to her. Abra blinked in surprise at his tone and walked quickly to the porch to see what was wrong.

"Is it Thomas? What's wrong?"

"Nothing is wrong with Thomas. I don't want you out here talking to the neighbors. Is that clear?"

Abra frowned. "Don't talk to the neighbors? You must be joking, surely."

Her employer's dark eyes turned almost black. "Miss Ahrens, I would hardly joke about something as serious as the care of my brother. You were brought here to look after him, not familiarize yourself with the neighborhood. If you find it impossible to stay in the house, tell me this minute and I will find a replacement."

"There is no need to find a replacement," said Abra between her teeth. "I was merely talking to Mr. Campbell. I've hardly spoken to any of the other neighbors."

Clyde Conlan glanced surreptitiously around himself before saying, "There has always been speculation about my brother and myself, and I will not have my hired nurse standing around out here to fuel it. When you took the position you agreed acquiescence with my wishes, and it is my most fervent wish, Miss Ahrens, that you come in the house this minute and stop making me look like a complete and utter fool."

Abra sucked in her breath and held it while she stared at her employer and blinked. Not even her own father had spoken to her in such a manner. She felt like a naughty, disobedient child.

The feeling got worse when Clyde hissed at her and briefly stomped one foot. Still blinking, she hurried up the steps and into the house.

For the next several days Abra stayed in the house and didn't go near the windows. Zane came over several times, but Clyde told him Abra was busy and sent him away. Finally, late one night, Zane called and Abra answered the phone. They discussed the weather and politics and other trifling details; then Abra asked about his divorce, thinking it might be something he didn't want to talk about. It turned out to be a subject he was more than willing to discuss. With a dry tone he told her he had been a real bastard after being shot. Abra felt that was commendable of him. Most men would not have taken sole blame.

They talked about many things, including the fate of Louise Peterwell, who had been totally incinerated in the heat of the fire created by the combustibles in the back bedroom. Craig Peterwell stayed in a hotel for several days, but was back at home again, living in the undamaged part of his house with sheets of plastic separating him from the charred half. There had been only a brief investigation into the cause and the results were inconclusive.

Mark Vaughn had returned home, Zane informed her, though Abra was unaware of the business with the Vaughns. The police picked him up a day after he returned, and according to Zane's detective friend, John Ptacek, he told them a wild story about having been kidnapped by a nameless acquaintance of his former partner who was in Leavenworth. The man forced him to drive the Pontiac to the Melo house and leave it in an effort to frame him, and then took Vaughn in another car out to western Kansas, where he was chained up and left in the middle of a field to die.

"He even had the chain marks to prove it," Zane told her. "Vaughn said he managed to free himself and hitch back to Wichita. When the cops asked him for the name of someone he had ridden with, Vaughn couldn't tell them. He said he hadn't asked."

"Why would they attempt to frame him for the Melo girl?" asked Abra.

"To reduce the sentence of his partner in Leavenworth, convicted in 1986 of raping a young girl about the same age."

"By leaving the car in front of the Melo house, he wanted people to think Vaughn took their little girl?"

"So the story goes."

Abra was appalled, but fascinated just the same. She could tell Zane still found such events gripping. It was in the way he held his breath when he spoke, the tremor in his voice when he related the details.

"Is Vaughn back at home now?"

"They couldn't hold him, same as Chance. He's back with his wife and baby girl."

Abra was glad to hear it. She thought they were probably relieved in a way that the birds next door were gone. For two or three nights after the fire, Kelly Cameron did segments on the news about what to do with tropical birds if any were caught in the area. She also embarrassed the lieutenant governor by asking him about the permit for the birds supposedly given to Craig Peterwell. The man cleared his throat and mumbled something about the permit being for only a couple of birds before shoving the microphone away. Since the birds were no longer in Craig's possession, he would not be prosecuted.

The neighborhood was much quieter without the birds. Abra's mother called to see if she wanted to meet somewhere for lunch, but Abra told her it wasn't a good idea at the time because of the condition of her patient. Clyde Conlan stood behind her during the length of the conversation, his eyes boring into her back.

Clyde did make her curious one evening when he caught her watching Zane through the window in the kitchen. He looked to see what had captured her interest and stood gazing abstractedly out the window himself. Suddenly, he said, "The day Mr. Campbell helped you with Thomas, was he working in the garden when you went out to get him?''

"No. He was in the front yard. Why?''

"So he wasn't wearing his garden gloves? Like the ones he's wearing now.''

"No.'' Abra looked at Clyde. "Why?''

"Just curious.''

Abra refused to let it go. "May I ask why?''

Clyde looked annoyed and ready to snap at her for her insistence. Then he shrugged. "I was wondering what kind of man he was. I suppose as he's in a related medical field, he's aware of communicable diseases.''

"Mr. Conlan,'' said Abra. "This is something I've been meaning to ask you about. You know and I know that HIV is communicated through body fluids. The day Thomas fell to the floor I assure you he did not bleed or ejaculate anywhere near me or Mr. Campbell. Why you feel you have to stand at least six feet away from your dying brother—''

"He was wearing pajamas, you say?'' interrupted Clyde.

"Yes,'' said Abra, near exasperation.

"Were any of his sores open? Were they oozing through the fabric?''

"No, it was a fresh shirt. It was his bottoms that were soiled.''

"Excuse me, Abra.'' The man walked out and left her standing there, mouth open to continue. She breathed deeply, forcing the air through her nostrils, and decided she definitely disliked the weird jerk.

Taking his strange questions into consideration, his avoidance of both Abra and his brother no longer had the same meaning to her as before. Abra could only assume Clyde believed the few suppurating sores on Thomas's back were capable of transmitting the virus, thus explaining his avid interest and odd behavior. Abra herself had avoided contact with the sores and washed her hands dozens of times a day out of sheer habit. The sores were unusual and therefore worthy of surveillance. But not once had she found herself wondering if they placed her in any kind of danger.

Late that night she heard a tapping at her window, and the blood in her veins froze. She rose from her bed and peered cautiously outside. Zane gave her a small wave, and she exhaled in relief. Abra crept down the hall to the back door and stepped outside. Zane was still by her window and she went to stand beside him.

It surprised her when he said nothing. After summoning her, she expected him to say something. She looked at his face, but his expression was difficult to read in the darkness.

He saw the look and said, "Don't worry, I won't try anything."

Abra managed a smile. "I'm not worried. I was just wondering why you called me out here."

"I haven't seen you in a while. I wondered if you were being held against your will."

"I'm beginning to wonder the same thing."

"Meaning?"

"Clyde Conlan is an absolute jerk."

"Playing hardass?"

Abra searched his face in the dimness of the porch light. "I don't know what he's playing, but I do know he wants me to stay away from you."

"From me?" Zane said in surprise. "What did I do?"

"Distracted me from my duties, I suppose," said Abra.

Zane smiled. "That's good to hear. I think."

"You'd better go, before the chief hears us talking and trips the alarm system. I wouldn't put it past him."

"Can I call you?" asked Zane.

"He's always listening," she said in frustration.

"When is he going back to work?"

"Probably not until Thomas dies."

"When will that happen?"

"I can't say."

"Abra . . ."

"I'm sorry, Zane. This is my livelihood, you know."

"I know. Okay. Well, I guess I'll let you get back to bed."

He leaned toward her, but a sound behind her in the house caused her to lean violently away.

Zane stood very still. Then he turned abruptly and walked off across the lawn.

Abra started to follow him and explain, but as she opened her mouth she heard a noise next door from the Morley place. There was a cough, and then she heard a whispering voice. Abra held her breath and listened. Two voices, one of them fierce. The other person was unmistakably Chance, who forgot to whisper until the other person shushed him. Abra couldn't hear what was being said. Frowning, she moved closer. She still couldn't see anyone, but she could make out some of the words.

". . . to tell me this? Don't you think I know how you feel? I liked her, too. Trust me, Chance, you had nothing to do with that fire. It happened on the same day we were there is all."

"There was just eighteen people at her funeral," Chance whispered sorrowfully. "My momma cried about that."

"Is this all you wanted to talk about? You scared my wife when you pounded on the door like that."

"I'm sorry. I didn't mean to scare her. I just keep thinking about the birds. The lady on the news said Mr. Peterwell let them out of the house. Why would he—"

"Chance, you have to let it go, all right? I'm sure the birds are happy now. Stop worrying about all this stuff, okay? Just forget it."

"We're still not saying anything, are we?"

"That's right. You're okay and I'm okay."

"Okay. Good. I'll go in and go to bed now."

"All right. See you later."

Abra stayed perfectly still while Mark Vaughn walked away from the trees beside the Morley house and came within a single green bough of where she was crouched behind a thick cedar. He had a pronounced limp, and there was pain in his movements, but she couldn't see his expression. His conversation with Chance was confusing to Abra. She tried to remember as much as she could as she went inside the house. It was something she thought she should pass on to Zane. Particularly the part about them being in the house the day of the fire.

# CHAPTER

# 18

MARK HAD TO STOP and rest on the way home. His strength had still not completely returned, and his arms and legs ached when he used them for long periods, such as the walk from his house to Chance's house. He stopped in front of Peterwell's burned abode and stared at the hated basement windows. The man had luck Mark couldn't believe. Did Mark ever have such luck? Hell, no. The minute he called his wife at her mother's house, he found out the cops were after him again, and that his asshole buddy in Leavenworth was trying to set him up for a fall. Mark took care of that problem right away with the lie about the abduction and the car. It came out so well, he used it on both Valerie and the cops. He didn't want his wife to know her husband had been chained on the basement floor beside the woman who died in the fire. Not only did it make Mark sound like a complete dickhead, it would break Valerie's tender heart to hear any of that business. It was all he could do to get her to come home to him again.

Once she saw his condition, she was convinced, and she was sweeter to him than she had ever been, kissing him all over and making love to him until he wanted to cry because it hurt so much and he couldn't stand it because he wanted it so bad even if it did hurt. He still swore she was the best thing that ever happened to him.

And if she was the best, then Craig Peterwell was the worst. Mark couldn't sleep at night for trying to think of a way to bag the lying bastard. He had blown his chance to use Louise's murder, so now he had to come up with something Peterwell couldn't burn his way out of. A thousand ideas the old Mark would have used came to him, but each of those ideas had a flaw that could be traced back to its originator.

He had seen Peterwell twice since escaping from his basement, and each time Mark had relayed a silent, chilly message to the other man: *You're dead.*

But dead was too easy. Mark wanted some grief and pain. He wanted panic and fear and agony. He wanted a big dose of good old-fashioned terror for old Petersmell.

A mosquito landed on the back of his neck and Mark swatted at it. An idea came to him then. Nothing major, nothing cataclysmic, just a regular idea, the kind the new Mark, the Mark who wanted to stay out of jail, would come up with. It was beautiful in its simplicity.

Mark smiled to himself and forced his aching muscles to get a move on again. He was getting stronger every day, but by nightfall he was exhausted. Chance had come to the door just as he was drifting off, startling Mark and causing Valerie to utter a strangled little squeak of fear.

He figured Chance was having a tough time keeping his mouth closed. Mark supposed it wouldn't hurt anything if he talked now, if he told his mother he had gone in Peterwell's house to let the birds go but had found Mark Vaughn chained up instead. But it would never come out that way with Chance, and things would become convoluted beyond belief if Chance took his story to the police and added it to the stories told by Peterwell and Mark. It was better for all concerned if Chance simply kept quiet.

Mark let himself back into the house and walked down the hall to look in on his baby daughter before he went back to bed. He couldn't believe how good it felt to hold her and kiss her.

How sweet she was just to look at. Emotion made his eyes tear up as he stood beside the crib and patted her soft little tummy.

A hand on his arm made him turn his head, and Mark saw Valerie's smile in the dim glow of the night-light. She took him by the arm and guided him back to the bedroom, where she sat him down on the bed and proceeded to kiss the tears from his face. Mark put his arms around his wife and remembered, for the first time, to thank God for letting him out of Peterwell's basement alive.

Craig Peterwell sat in a chair at the kitchen table and pushed a piece of raw hamburger through the bars at the crow he had caged that day. It was the second crow he had caught that week, using a dead cat he had found on the road and a net he rigged up to the trees. Crows loved dead cats, and there was enough left to fetch him several more birds, he believed. His appointment with Dr. Ahrens had not gone well that evening. She kept trying to get him to talk about the fire, and how he was dealing with Louise's death. Well, what could he say? He was dealing with it, for crissakes. What did she want him to do? Break down and bawl in front of her? Craig didn't do things like that, and it irritated him that she kept harping about "letting go."

He'd let go, all right. He'd let go all over her nice little living room office if she didn't start being sweet to him again.

He struck his head then, as if he could strike at the throbbing behind his eye.

Maybe she was right about the headaches causing him to think bad thoughts and become angry all the time. He didn't want to hurt Dr. Ahrens. He liked her too much. She understood about the birds, and what they meant to him. She understood about nearly everything. She had given him the names of two contractors to call about rebuilding his house. She had suggested some consignment shops downtown that sold good used clothing. She was as helpful as could be.

And Monday he was going to see the neurologist. Most people had to wait nearly six weeks, but for him it was less than two, all because the guy was a friend of Dr. Ahrens.

Craig stared at the crow in the cage, at its round eyes and glossy black feathers. It opened its sharp beak and cawed at him, causing his flesh to goosepimple. The sound took him back to long days spent in a weedy field behind his father's house, where pods of milkweed grew and filled the air with tiny little tufted parachutes of white when they opened. Craig had worn a path in the field, a path used only by him when it was time to escape or just time to play. Boys could do that; they could run off just to play and not have to tell anyone when they would be back. They could be gone for hours and not get in trouble when they came home to their neighbor's house. Girls were different. Girls had to be careful, and tell where they were all the time. Girls had to be watched while they played. Bad things happened to girls who weren't watched by their parents. Girls couldn't talk to strangers, and girls couldn't leave their yard without permission, or they got their little butts beat by their daddy.

Cyndi Melo should have had her little butt beat, Craig thought to himself. Something bad had happened to her because no one was watching and no one knew where she was going.

Craig didn't know why he should think of her just when he did. He hadn't thought about Cyndi Melo for a while.

He shook his head and stared at the crow again. The field. He had been thinking about the field behind his father's house, and the crows he kept there. More than a dozen. He collected dead animals and scavenged through nearly every trash can in town for scraps to keep the crows all fed. Once or twice he had thought of killing something himself, but Craig could never do it. His crows were important to him, but he couldn't kill anything just to feed them.

Then he reminded himself that he had killed his wife.

And burned her.

"But I didn't *mean* to kill her," he said to the crow.

The crow blinked and cawed at him.

Craig looked at the ceiling. "I swear, Louise, if you're some-place where you can hear me, I didn't mean to kill you. God, I was only trying to help you. You know that now, I'm sure. I'm sure you know how sorry I am about the way things turned out. Dr. Ahrens thinks it may be the headaches that made me break your arms and legs with that two-by-four. I think she's helping me. I really think she's—"

He stopped when he realized what he was doing. When he saw the crow cocking its head at him and turning its beak this way and that.

Louise couldn't hear him. She was dead, burned to a crisp and buried in the plot next to her mother. No one could hear him but the crow, and the crow didn't care that he hadn't meant to kill his wife when he tried to chop off her leg. Crows didn't care about things like that.

He shoved another piece of hamburger through the bars of the cage and pushed away from the table. He wandered into the living room to lie down on the sofa and look at the sheet of thick plastic that separated him from the burned remains of the rest of his house.

Craig didn't want to live there anymore. He didn't care about fixing the place, or remodeling the rooms or any of the other stuff the insurance company was bugging him about. When every-thing was done he was going to sell the house and move away.

Maybe he would even move back to Texas, back to his old hometown, where his dad and his neighbor had made their homes and raised their children. With Louise's money he could buy some new birds and find a new place. He was still in contact with the bird man from Brownsville, the oily guy who smuggled in hundreds of birds a year. Craig could quit his job at the hos-pital and move away from the neighborhood and the people who lived there. One person in particular.

When Craig's phone rang at a quarter after three that morning, he knew who it would be. He lifted up the receiver and said nothing.

Vaughn said, "I knew you wouldn't be sleeping. How could you sleep, doing what you did? You know what, neighbor? I lied about Louise having gangrene. The green was bad bruising, that's all. If you weren't so fucking stupid, you would have seen that, but no, you go and try to cut off her leg. You go and kill her just because you think the green bruising is gangrene. How stupid can you be? I figured if you thought it was gangrene, you'd get some help for her. Instead, you chop her up, and with a dull axe, at that. You are one stupid—"

Craig hung up the phone. His mouth was trembling with rage. His knuckles went white as he curled his hands into fists. He wanted to go over and hurt him. He wanted to go next door and hurt him bad. Hurt his wife, too. Even hurt his baby. He wanted to hurt them all for living with such a . . . *a liar.*

But some part of Craig knew Vaughn wasn't lying. And it was that part that set his fists to beating against the couch cushions until buttons popped out and the fabric tore. He pummeled the couch until he could hardly breathe; then he lay down, exhausted, and reached over to rattle the crow's cage so it would start cawing and drown out everything else in his head.

# CHAPTER
# 19

ON SATURDAY MORNING ZANE worked out downstairs until his muscles spasmed in protest and the weights in his hands began to quiver. Holt was quiet as he watched his father push himself. Finally he said, "What's wrong, Dad?"

"Nothing," said Zane through gritted teeth.

"You're hurting yourself."

"I'm fine."

"You always tell me not to let what's on my mind interfere with what's in my hands."

Zane ignored him and completed his reps. When he was finished, Holt said, "It's Abra. You like her."

After rubbing his face and neck with a towel, Zane sat down on the bench. "Yeah, I like her."

"She doesn't like you?"

Zane had to think about that one. He thought about whether he wanted to discuss this with his sixteen-year-old son. Holt was mature for his age, but he was still only sixteen.

"Dad?"

"I think she does like me. But I also think she doesn't want to."

"Why wouldn't she? Because of your problem?"

"She says no, but that's probably part of it."

"What's the other part?"

"I'm not sure. Something tells me she hasn't had much luck with previous relationships. Being burned a few times can make anyone overly cautious."

"Have you asked her?" Holt asked.

"About previous relationships? No. That's an area few people care to talk about, and when you do, it's best to tread lightly. I keep thinking she'll bring it up on her own."

Holt was smiling at him. "You're talking a lot better."

"Am I?"

"Yeah."

"Good."

"She have something to do with that?"

Zane nodded. "Maybe. Maybe I'm concentrating more on forming the words and worrying less about how I look when I'm saying them."

"She looks at you like she likes you."

"Does she?"

"Yeah. Like she wants to keep looking at you, but she makes herself stop in case you see her. Just like Amy used to do."

"Your old girlfriend? Whatever happened to Amy?"

"She started looking at some other guy the same way."

"She dumped you?"

"I dumped her before she could dump me. It made me feel better."

Zane smiled at his son. "I'm sure it did. Your mom teach you that?"

Holt smirked. "No. So, what are you going to do?"

"About what?"

"Abra."

Zane shrugged. "There's nothing I can do. You can't force someone to care about you."

"You're just going to leave her alone?"

"I won't avoid her, no. But I won't seek her out, either. It's the only way to stop thinking about her."

Holt nodded. Then he asked, "How did you get Mom?"

"I didn't," said Zane. "She got me."

"She came after you, huh?"

"With everything she had. It worked, too."

"Did you love her?"

"Sure. But people change, and your mom and I changed too much. You know that. Your mom's happy where she is."

"I know," said Holt. His voice lowered then. "I want you to be happy, too, Dad."

Zane stood and reached for his son to give him a brief hug. "I'm not unhappy, Holt. I don't need a woman to give my life meaning."

"But it would be nice to have sex again before you die, right, Dad?" said Eli from the stairs. "Abra's upstairs asking for you."

Holt and Zane exchanged a look. Zane put his towel around his neck and walked upstairs after Eli, who darted away when Zane tried to cuff him.

"Mom's coming to get us at ten."

"Pack a toothbrush this time."

"I will."

Abra was waiting in the foyer, her hands clasped in front of her. Her smile for Zane was cautious. She said, "May I speak to you in private?"

"If you don't mind my smell," he said. "Holt and I were—"

"I told her," said Eli.

Zane scowled at him. "Toothbrush. Pack it."

Eli rolled his eyes. "Like forgetting your toothbrush is a felony or something."

"According to your mother, it is. Excuse us, Eli." He lifted a hand to indicate the way to his office. Abra preceded him and Zane used the towel to wipe the worst of the sweat from his body as he followed her. In his office she looked around with obvious surprise and approval at his choice of furnishings. Zane smiled at her and said, "What did you expect?"

"I like it," she said.

"So do I."

She picked up one of the sample artifical eyes Zane showed to his patients. "Did you do this one?"

"Yes."

"It's perfect," said Abra.

"Thank you."

"You're really good. I mean it. This is incredible," she said as she went on examining the eye. "You do noses and ears, too?"

Zane nodded. "Occasionally."

She met his glance, and in her eyes there was a new light of respect. Zane sat down in his chair.

"You wanted to talk?"

Abra nodded and put the eye back in its case. She took a chair in front of the desk and inhaled before beginning.

"Last night after you left I heard voices nearby. Whispering. It was Chance Morley and Mark Vaughn, the man who lives next door to the Peterwells."

"What were they whispering about?"

"I'm not sure, exactly. Vaughn was asking why Chance had pounded on the door and scared his wife. Chance apologized and started talking about the number of people at Mrs. Peterwell's funeral. Before that, I heard Vaughn say something about it not being their fault the fire happened the day they were in the house."

Zane's eyebrows lifted. "They were inside Peterwell's house the day it burned?"

"That's what I understood from the conversation last night."

"What else?" asked Zane. "Was there anything else?"

"Not really. Chance was concerned about the birds, but Vaughn told him not to worry, that the birds were happy. Chance seemed to accept this, and he said something about neither one of them telling. That's all I remember."

"Where were they when this conversation took place?"

"In the cedars beside Chance's house."

"And where were you?"

"Behind a cedar on the Conlan side of the yard. They didn't see me."

"You're lucky. It sounds like this is something they wouldn't want anyone else to know." Zane thought about the way Chance had looked at the trees while the Peterwell house was burning. Had Chance done it? Had he set the birds free? And Vaughn was supposed to have been stranded in western Kansas at the time Peterwell's house burned. If he was in the house with Chance the day of the fire, then he could not have been in western Kansas with his armed, unnamed kidnapper.

"What?" said Abra. "What are you thinking?"

"That a whole lot of lying's been done. Mark Vaughn's wife told me he disappeared several days before the fire. Where was he all that time? And how did he hook up with Chance Morley?"

Abra could only shake her head. Zane looked at her suddenly. "What made you listen to them?"

She shrugged. "Curiosity. When you hear people whispering, it's only natural to be curious about what they're saying."

"So you hid behind the cedars and listened."

"I . . . yes." She looked away. "I thought you would want to know what I heard. Was I wrong?"

"No." He eyed the curve of her jaw and the slant of her mouth. "Abra Ahrens, nurse, doctor, sleuth."

Her eyes came back to him. "Did you say sleuth?"

"Not very well, I'm afraid."

Zane put his hands up to rub his eyes. Sweat streamed down his side under his arm and he took his hands away in time to find Abra's gaze following the path it took. He caught the perspiration with the towel.

"What are you going to do?" she asked.

"I don't know. Not much I can do anymore."

"You can call your friends."

"And give them what? A conversation based on hearsay?" Zane sat back in his chair. "I'll have to think about it."

Abra stood. "I'll let you get back to your workout."

Zane got up. "It's finished. Just need to shower."

"Eli said his mother was coming today."

"Yeah, she's taking them for the weekend."

Abra stared at the sample eyes in the case again. She looked at the charts and certificates on the walls. "May I see your lab?" she asked suddenly.

"Sure." Zane went into the adjoining room and turned on the light. He stood back while she walked inside and looked around, then he moved in to show her his tools and paints and polish; his molds and waxes and assorted pupils. She saw more examples of his work and picked up each piece to examine it individually. she shook her head again and turned to look at him. "These are truly incredible, Zane. It's like seeing another side of you. You can duplicate the color of any eye just by looking at the patient?"

"Generally, yes."

"How would you do your own?" she asked softly. "You have the strangest eyes I've ever seen."

Zane exhaled. "People have been telling me that all my life."

She moved closer to him and looked into his eyes. "It's true. I don't know how you would duplicate the colors, because they're always changing. They never appear the same."

She was too close to him. Zane's throat became constricted as the scent of her filled his lungs.

"Abra, what are you doing?" he asked.

"I don't know," she said. "I really don't. I can't stop thinking about you. I know I hurt you last night and I didn't want to do that. When I heard those men whispering it gave me an excuse to come and see you today."

"You acted like you didn't want me near you," Zane reminded her.

"I know I did," she said. "I didn't mean to. I heard a sound in the house and thought it was Clyde coming out."

He looked at her like he didn't believe her. "Where is Clyde right now?"

"Probably looking for me. He doesn't know I'm here."

"So you need to get back. Okay. Thanks for coming by to tell me what you heard. I don't know what you expect from me, but if the opportunity arises, I'll pass along the information."

Abra was staring in mute hurt when Eli burst into the lab and informed his father that their mother had arrived. Without looking at Abra, Zane turned and followed his son out of the lab, turning off lights as he went.

Abra followed them out to the foyer, where a slender blonde stood waiting. Abra felt her lower jaw drop as she looked at the other woman, who had the face and supple figure of a fashion model.

A curious green gaze moved over Abra as introductions were made, and Abra dutifully shook hands before excusing herself as quickly as she could.

As she was leaving she heard the woman ask Eli if he had remembered his toothbrush.

Zane's ex-wife.

In the space of an hour, Abra's entire opinion of Zane Campbell had altered. Seeing his office and the work he did made her burn with pride for him. Seeing his ex-wife made her burn with jealousy.

She felt sick.

When she reached the house she found the Conlans planning another visit to their out-of-town friend. At Clyde's request, Abra prepared two days' worth of medication for Thomas. Clyde asked again that she stay at the house, *alone*, in case they were forced to return early. Biting her lip, she agreed. After helping Thomas into the car, Abra went inside the house and called her mother.

"I saw his ex-wife today," she began by saying.

"Whose? The neighbor's?"

"Yes."

"Well?"

"She's beautiful."

"Is that all you wanted to say?"

"I had to tell someone. Someone who knows about him."

"Are you feeling threatened?"

"I'm feeling nauseous."

"Over a woman he is no longer married to, but who shared a part of his life. It's perfectly understandable."

"I feel inferior," Abra admitted.

"You sound very calm. I have to go, Abra."

Abra felt anything but calm. Her mind kept presenting her with the image of that drop of perspiration rolling down Zane's side under his arm. She didn't know why she was so focused on it. Possibly to prevent herself from focusing on anything he said.

"I'm going crazy, Mother. Everything is changing."

"Change happens. I really must go now. Call me at home later, if you must."

The phone clicked in her ear. Abra slammed down the receiver and asked herself why she had called the woman.

Because she had no one else to call. No one who knew how she felt. No one who knew her like her mother did.

What an inescapably sad comment on the life of an adult woman, she told herself.

Abra stopped there, and out of habit she walked into her bedroom and looked out the window. There was no sign of Zane in the backyard. She walked into the hall again, and as she passed Clyde's room she saw the corner of a book sticking out under the bottom of his door. She opened the door and picked up the book. It was one of a series for young adults called *Claudia's After School Club*.

Strange choice of reading material for Clyde Conlan, Abra thought, and as she had the thought, the front door opened and Clyde Conlan came hurrying into the house. He stopped when he saw the book in Abra's hands.

"That's what I need," he said. He came and held out his hand for the book.

"A little light reading?" Abra asked with a smile.

"It's for one of the daughters of the man we're visiting. Thomas counted only two gifts, and the man has two daughters and a son. I bought presents for all of them and we dropped this one. Last time I bought her the game."

"Oh, there's a game of the same name?" Abra had no idea.

"They're crazy about it. That's why I was happy to find a book she doesn't have. We're off now, Abra. Enjoy yourself while we're gone."

Before she could say another word he was off. Abra watched him hurry out the door and silently thought how buying gifts for a friend's children seemed totally out of character for the stiff Clyde Conlan. Thomas would have been the one to suggest it, Abra decided. He was the warm and funny one.

At least he was when Clyde was gone. When brother Clyde was in the house, Thomas was more reserved, less playful.

Abra was going to miss Thomas when he died. His stories and his laughter, his bluster and bull and his sudden, heartbreaking tears. There would certainly never be another Conlan like him.

# CHAPTER

## 20

MARK OPENED THE DOOR and lifted his brows in surprise when he saw Zane Campbell standing on his front porch.

"Hi," he said. "What can I do for you?"

"I'd like to come in and talk," said Zane.

"Sure." Mark pushed open the door and stepped to one side. "What about?"

Zane nodded to Valerie, and a look of guilt passed over her face. She excused herself and took the baby into the back of the house. Zane moved to sit down in a chair while Mark sat on the sofa. Mark was frowning over his wife's expression. Zane was a good-looking guy. Mark would hate to think his wife had a reason to look guilty.

"What did you want to talk about?"

Zane's look was direct. "What you and Chance Morley were doing in Craig Peterwell's house the day it burned."

Mark went still. Finally he licked his lips and said, "I don't know what you mean. I was—"

"Not in western Kansas. I know you were here all along." Zane sat forward. "Tell me what happened."

"You know so much, why don't you tell me?" Mark suggested.

"All right," said Zane. "I think you drove the new Pontiac and left it on Laurel Street so you could come back here and break into Peterwell's house. Something went wrong, and you never left. Then Chance Morley came along, and the two of you set all the birds free. Later the house burned down, with Louise Peterwell in it.''

Mark stared at him. ''Where did you come by your information?''

''Does that matter? I know you're worried about going back to prison, but you can talk to me. What happened to you while you were missing?''

Mark said, ''I was kidnapped and driven to a field in western Kansas, where I was chained up and left to die. The man was an acquaintance of the guy I went to jail with, who wanted to frame me for the missing little girl.''

Zane's nostrils flared as he exhaled. ''Both of us know that's a lie. Why didn't he kill you right there in the field?''

''Ask him,'' Mark suggested. He opened his hands to look at the reddened and bruised areas still on his arms. ''I'm not changing any part of my story. Whoever told you I was in Peterwell's house the day of the fire is mistaken.''

''I don't think so.'' Zane stood, but his eyes never left Mark's. ''Just answer me one thing, yes or no. Did you have anything to do with the fire that killed Louise Peterwell?''

Mark couldn't truthfully say no. It was his fault Craig had decided to set the blaze. His fault Craig had tried to chop off her leg. He might be as much a murderer as Craig Peterwell.

He said nothing.

Zane shook his head and walked across the room to let himself out the door. ''When you want to talk to me, you know where I live.''

''Wait,'' said Mark when his neighbor was halfway out. ''Tell me, what would change if I talked to you? Would it make Louise any less dead? Nothing is going to change, man. You should know that.''

Zane only looked at him. He let himself out and closed the door.

Mark wanted to throw something. How the hell did he know

so much? Had he somehow overheard Mark's whispered conversation with Chance? That had to be it. There was no other way he could know what he did.

Unless Chance had been talking.

Chance played with Zane's kid sometimes. Maybe he had talked.

Nah. Chance was too scared to talk. He was the one afraid of being sent back to jail with "those mean men."

But the guy *was* retarded.

Shit. Mark didn't want to think about it. He got up and went down the hall to find Valerie. She was lying on the bed, nursing the baby. She looked up when he came in the room.

"What did Campbell want?"

Mark sat down on the bed. "He wanted me to talk to him. He seems to think he knows something about where I was when I was gone. I told him he was mistaken. Did you talk to him, Val?"

"Yes," she said evenly. "I asked his advice when you didn't come home. He told me what to expect from the police, and he wasn't wrong."

"Anything else? Did you talk about anything else with him?"

Valerie's face began to color. "The next time I saw him he asked me if you were breaking into houses. I told him you hadn't done that in a long time."

"You told him—" Mark was disgusted. "Jesus Christ, Valerie. The guy is an ex-cop. You know he still has contacts on the force."

"I know. That's why I asked his advice."

Her cool, clipped words warned him he was about to upset her. The baby pulled away from her breast and gave a whimper, as if the taste of the milk had suddenly changed.

To prevent himself from blurting something stupid, Mark got up and left the room. He went out the front door and took a deep gulp of fresh air. He was going back to work Monday and he was glad of it. He had to get away from this crazy frigging neighborhood.

Out of the corner of his eye, Mark saw Craig Peterwell leave his house and approach the van in his drive. Craig didn't look so good, Mark thought. In fact, he looked awful. There were large dark rings of exhaustion under his eyes, and the skin of his face seemed to sag. Mark looked around and saw Zane Campbell standing to the side of his yard with a hose in his hand. His back was turned. Mark stepped off the porch and moved where Peterwell could see him smile.

"No gangrene, Peckerswell," he said with a smile.

It surprised Mark when Peterwell dropped his keys and lunged across the yard at him. He had time to utter a startled squawk before the barrel-chested Peterwell slammed into him and took him to the ground. Peterwell's large hands closed around his throat and Mark did his best, but his muscles were still too weak to dislodge the other man's grip. He kicked with his legs and bucked with his body in an attempt to unseat the man, but Peterwell held on with a vengeance, his bloodshot eyes boring into Mark's.

Just as the edges of Mark's vision began to dim, Peterwell received a brutal slap to the head, causing him to rear back and ease his grip. Zane Campbell stood behind him, and when Peterwell swung at him, Zane merely stepped aside and jabbed Peterwell in the nose with his fist. "Back off, dammit."

Mark scrambled away on all fours, until he could sit up and breathe. He dragged in air until the darkness went away and his vision cleared. He saw Peterwell sitting on the ground holding his nose. Zane was in front of him, his body poised and ready should Peterwell attack again.

"What the hell is going on here?" Zane asked.

Peterwell said nothing. He lurched to his feet and swayed over to his van, where he picked up his keys from the drive and then climbed behind the wheel. Mark and Zane watched him start the engine and back unsteadily down the driveway.

Zane turned to Mark. "What was all that about?"

"You tell me," said Mark. "You're my witness. I'm going to file assault charges."

Zane shook his head. "Until you decide to talk to me, I didn't see a thing."

"What?" Mark got up from the ground. "The man just attacked me."

"Did he?"

"You know goddamn good and well he—" Mark stopped. He knew the game. He had played it himself, and now it was being played against him.

"I don't have anything to say to you," Mark told him. "You wouldn't understand."

"Try me."

"Can't do it. It's definitely a gray area, something a black-and-white guy like you would have problems with."

Zane gave up. As he walked across the street he said over his shoulder, "Take some advice and stay away from Peterwell."

"Thanks for helping me out," Mark answered.

His neighbor ignored him.

Mark went around the house and into the backyard to see how his project was coming along. He checked his box and found three spiders still alive. He was disappointed in their size, but he planned to catch bigger ones. He had found some holes in the backyard that looked like spider holes, and he intended to flood the holes to make the big bastards come out. He wanted more than three spiders. He wanted the huge hairy ones that came close to tarantula size. They were harmless grass spiders, but they looked scary as hell.

He blinked suddenly as it occurred to him how well Zane Campbell had been speaking, how clearly the words had come out.

He must have been working on it, Mark thought as he dropped insects in the box for his spiders to eat. He put the lid back on the box and hoped the spiders didn't decide to eat each other.

Mark started the flooding process and spent the next hour jumping around from hole to hole in the back yard, trying to catch big spiders. When he stopped for the day, he had only two more spiders, one of them huge. He put these spiders in separate shoe boxes and slit holes in the lids. He hoped Valerie didn't walk out into the garage and open one of the boxes. She'd have a fit if she did.

When he finished, Mark realized his throat was hurting where Peterwell had attempted to throttle him. Just one more ache to thank the man for, added to the many other aches Mark was still suffering. His time in Peterwell's basement seemed unreal to him now, as if it were all a bad dream he'd had. He knew it was real every time he was able to go to the bathroom and relieve himself like a normal man, and every time he picked up a piece of food with his hands to eat it. Each time he performed some act people took for granted, Mark realized how truly lucky he was to have escaped.

His body could be littering some field for true.

He swallowed with difficulty and renewed his vow to take revenge on the man who had kept him prisoner and taken the life of his own wife. Louise would not go unavenged.


Chance came outside in time to see Mr. Peterwell leave in his van. He waited awhile, until he saw Mr. Campbell stop watering and go inside the house; then he walked down the street and up the driveway of the Peterwell house. As he slipped out back, he saw Mark Vaughn hopping around in his backyard like a big toad. He had a box in his hands and he was doing something with the lid. Chance giggled a little when he saw him, then he clamped a hand over his mouth so he wouldn't be heard. Mr. Vaughn would be mad at Chance if he knew Chance was looking in Mr. Peterwell's house.

He was going to do it, though, because Chance swore he heard birds in there again. Not the same birds, but birds just the same.

These birds sounded like something was caught in their throats while they were trying to scream.

They were screaming for help again, Chance knew. He understood bird talk now, and while they didn't always come right out and say they wanted to be free, Chance figured he knew what they wanted.

He noticed a piece of wood over the window he had broken last time. Chance sat on the back porch and waited. When he saw Mr. Vaughn go in his garage, Chance quickly stood and broke the window above the wood. He stuck his arm through and opened the door, same as last time. Chance hurried inside and looked for bright, colorful birds. When he saw the crows he stopped. They were the same cages all right, but these weren't like the other birds. Chance neared one of the cages and the bird inside squawked at him, causing Chance to jump back and crash into the television set. He hurt his leg where he ran into the corner and he gave a grunt of pain.

The bird squawked again. Chance felt his leg and reached for the cage door. The crow inside hopped around on the bar, as if eager to have the door opened. When the wire hinges swung open, the bird shot out the opening, straight for Chance's face. Chance yelped and ducked. Before he could change his mind, he hurried to open the other cages and set the rest of the crows free. None of them were leaving. They all flew around his head, cawing and squawking and diving at him as if he were the one who had imprisoned them. Chance ran out the back door, with two of the birds flying after him. He reached down to scoop up another brick to prop open the door; then he slunk around the outside of the garage again and hurried up the street toward his house.

He was getting good at this, he thought—until he ran into his mother on the front porch. She pointed at him with one crooked, gnarled finger as he approached. "You've been to Mr. Peterwell's house again. I saw you come around the garage."

Chance opened his mouth, but she didn't let him say anything.

"You realize this means you lose some privileges. No cartoons today or tomorrow. No Cocoa Krispies for a bedtime snack, and no leaving the yard for the next two days."

"Momma, I—"

"Momma, nothing. Get in this house, Chance. I don't like it when you disobey me. You've got to do what I tell you to do. These people don't understand the way you think, and they might take what you do the wrong way. God knows we've had enough of that business this summer. Let's not make matters worse by trespassing on the neighbors all the time. Do you hear me?"

"Yes, Momma." Chance trudged in the house after his mother. He hated to lose his privileges.

But the birds were free.

# CHAPTER

# 21

ZANE WENT OUT FOR dinner that evening. He sat by himself in a restaurant and read the editorial page of the newspaper while he ate. He called John Ptacek from the restaurant and arranged to meet him at a nearby bar for a drink. The divorced Ptacek was happy to see him. They talked about old times, recent cases, and how well Zane was speaking. At ten-thirty, Zane left for home.

There was a light on in the Conlan house and Zane looked long at it after he stopped the car. Then he saw a light in his rearview mirror. He turned his head to see Craig Peterwell come out his front door. He stopped in the front yard and stood looking around with his arms down, his chest heaving. He looked pissed, Zane thought. Peterwell snorted like some large white-faced Hereford bull and started next door to Vaughn's house. Zane got out of the car and hurried to cut him off.

"Stop right there, Peterwell," he said. "Let's talk about what's bothering you."

Peterwell acted like he didn't hear him. He just kept walking.

Zane stepped in front of him and Peterwell made a screaming noise through his nose as he tried to go through him. Zane held him off and Peterwell sneaked a fist into his gut, causing Zane to double over. He caught Peterwell around the waist and took him down to the ground.

"What the hell is wrong with you?" he gasped.

Peterwell responded by sinking his teeth into the skin of Zane's back.

Zane cursed and rolled, sending a hard elbow into Peterwell's nose as he did. Peterwell grabbed his nose and howled in pain while Zane sprang up and put a headlock on him from behind. The skin of his back smarted where Peterwell had bit him.

A little of the old antagonism against an assailant seeped into his veins as he held the flailing Peterwell. Zane had spent the evening drinking beer with his former partner and talking about old times, and here he was reliving it, getting bit and hit and trying to hold down an angry sonofabitch who wanted to hurt somebody. Zane tightened his hold until Peterwell's straining, clawing arms dropped to the ground. In the next second the man went limp and fell unconscious.

Zane released him in surprise. He didn't think his hold had been that tight. He put a hand to the man's throat to check for a pulse, but kept his distance in case it was a trick.

The pulse was weak, almost too weak to feel.

Zane started over to his house to call 911. Then he thought of Abra and turned instead in her direction. He ran up the steps to the door and punched the doorbell. He punched it twice more before she came to the door dressed in a robe. She looked at him in surprise. "What's wrong?"

"Craig Peterwell. He's in his yard. If you've got a medical bag, bring it."

Abra didn't hesitate. She disappeared down the hall and reappeared seconds later, bag in hand. Zane held open the door and let it close behind her as she stepped off the porch and hurried across the lawn.

Peterwell was still unconscious when they reached him. Abra instructed Zane to go ahead and call 911 while she took a look. Zane hesitated. "I'd better tell you what happened first."

She shook her head. "No time for that. Go and make the call."

"Abra, I had him in a headlock."

She looked at him and blinked. "A headlock?"

"Peterwell assaulted Vaughn this morning and I intervened. Tonight he was heading for Vaughn's house again. He bit me and I put him in a headlock."

"You cut off his air and he passed out?"

"Apparently. I didn't think I was holding him that tight."

She checked his breathing passages and pulled out a stethoscope to listen to his heart and lungs. He twitched while she was touching him, and then he opened his eyes and sat up slowly. He mumbled something and tried to scoot away from her.

"Mr. Peterwell, I have medical training," she said. "How do you feel? Are you dizzy? Nauseous?"

He shook his head and tried to get to his feet. Zane stepped up to help him and he knocked his hand away.

"Stay away from me," he said in a hoarse voice. "Don't touch me."

"You stay away from Vaughn and I'll stay away from you," said Zane.

Peterwell's eyes narrowed, as if Zane had just reminded him where he was headed before he passed out. He looked wild in the light from the porch. His white hair stood up on end and resembled tufts of strange, fuzzy clown hair.

Abra was staring at him. "Mr. Peterwell? Are you sure you're all right?"

She shone her light in his eyes and he blinked and covered his face. "Leave me alone."

"I'd like to come inside and examine you," Abra persisted.

He opened his mouth and nearly roared at her. "*Did you hear what I said?* I said leave me alone!"

Abra backed up as he lurched toward her. Zane quickly moved to stand in front of her.

"She's only trying to help you. Why are you so upset with Mark Vaughn? What did he do to you?"

"He let my bir—" Peterwell's voice jerked to a halt. He turned unsteadily and stalked back to his house. Abra started after him, but Zane put a hand on her arm to stop her.

"Better not," he said. "This guy has a problem with his temper."

"It's probably grief-related," said Abra. "I think I should—"

"Forget it," Zane said firmly. "I don't think he'll let either one of us into his house."

She exhaled through her nose and put her things back in her bag. Zane took it from her when she was finished and carried the bag back to the Conlans' for her.

"Come and let me look at that bite," she suggested once they were on the porch. Zane nodded and followed her inside. She led him to the main bathroom and turned on the light. Zane took off his shirt and grimaced at the amount of dirt and grass stains covering the back.

Abra was shaking her head. "He didn't break the skin, thank goodness."

"This is one of my good shirts," Zane grumbled.

"Does the man usually go around biting people?"

"No. But he wasn't thinking when he did it. He wasn't even seeing me, he was reacting to being intercepted."

"Sounds like the voice of experience talking. Have you been bitten before by any chance?"

"On the job. Drunks, domestic squabbles and a fifteen-year-old male prostitute on PCP who thought he was a dog."

"You still know how to handle yourself, obviously."

"It's something you never forget." He winced as she pinched at the skin around the bite.

"Sorry," she murmured. She turned him around then to look at the still red area where Peterwell had sunk his fist. "What's this?"

"He hit me before he bit me."

Abra probed the area with her fingers. "Does it hurt when I press here?"

"Not bad, no. Tender is all."

"Understandable. Did he hit you anywhere else?"

"No."

"Okay." She reached inside her bag again. "Let me have a look at your burn while you're here."

"It's doing fine. I don't even know it's there."

Abra smiled at him. "I'll bet your ex-wife knew her way around a medicine cabinet."

Zane shook his head. "She was squeamish."

"Married to a cop and squeamish?"

"You should've seen her face when I told her I wanted to make eyes for a living."

"I can imagine," Abra said with a chuckle. "Did that have anything to do with why you split up?"

"I don't think so. I don't think about it anymore. I don't think about her. She has a husband and a new baby and I'm happy she's happy."

"What about you?" Abra said, her voice sounding suddenly breathless. "What's going to make you happy?"

Zane turned to look at her. "I don't think about that, either."

She fell silent and put a fresh bandage on his burned arm. Her hands were light and quick and his flesh constantly goose-pimpled as she touched him. Zane's fingers ached to touch her.

His eyes met hers in the bathroom mirror; her pupils were large, almost covering the irises. Her mouth was open slightly, as if breathing through the nose was too difficult. Zane turned slowly to face her. His hands encircled her waist and he pulled her gently toward him. His throat and chest began to constrict as he lowered his head, and by the time he touched his mouth to hers he was barely breathing.

Her lips were soft and moist as they clung to his. He moved his mouth lightly over hers and drew her closer still to deepen the kiss. She cautiously opened her mouth to him; her arms came to rest tentatively around his neck. Zane moved his hands up her spine and over her arms to put her hands more firmly around him. He lifted her to sit on the vanity and pulled her hips to him, so he was between her legs and temptingly close to the center of her. He went on kissing her until they both were breathless and panting and unaware of anything but sensation. His hands found the opening in her robe and slipped inside to push up the long T-shirt she wore. Her hands roved over his hard chest while he tugged off her underwear and unfastened his trousers. Abra clung fiercely to him, her eyes squeezed shut as if in pain. She made a gasping noise and went rigid as he slid her hips forward and entered her in one swift motion. He stopped, his chest heaving, and waited for her to open her eyes.

"Abra?" he whispered.

Slowly she lifted her lids and looked at him. He sought her lips again and soon she moaned into his mouth while clutching at the flesh of his back and hooking her legs around him.

Zane's legs went suddenly weak, and it was all he could do to remain standing. He leaned his forehead against hers and breathed deeply to control himself. The effort was useless; he moved within her and in less than fifteen seconds she came to orgasm, taking him with her.

They were breathing hard and staring at each other, mouths inches apart, when Zane heard the front door of the house open. Abra's lips touched his, so he didn't think she heard it.

"We've got company," he said against her mouth.

She looked at him, uncomprehending.

"Someone's home."

Abra came to sudden life, shoving him away and sliding off the vanity. She searched in a panic for her underwear and hurriedly pushed closed the bathroom door.

Zane pulled up and fastened his trousers before reaching for his shirt. He put it on, but left it untucked.

Clyde Conlan's voice came through the partially open door. "Abra, are you in there?"

"Yes," she said, and opened the door. "Just fixing up the neighbor."

Clyde's eyes narrowed. His gaze flitted around the bathroom, landing on Abra's open medical bag. "What seems to be the problem, Mr. Campbell?"

Zane patted the arm of his shirt and pointed to his bandage. "Just a burn." He smiled at Abra then. "It's nice to have a nurse around."

Clyde looked as if he wanted to ask more, but he didn't bother. "Abra, Thomas has taken a bad turn. As long as you're here, Mr. Campbell, would you mind helping us get him in the house? He's completely covered, don't worry."

"I'm not."

Zane frowned and followed Clyde and the still barefoot Abra out to the driveway, where a semi-conscious Thomas sat slumped in the passenger seat of the car.

After watching Abra struggle to get her patient turned, Zane stepped forward and said, "I can get him, Abra."

"Are you sure? He looks very thin, I know, but he's still a hundred and fifty pounds."

"I'll get him." Zane moved in and placed his hands under Thomas's legs and across his back under his arms. Gently he lifted the man from the car and straightened, holding the pitifully frail Thomas in his arms. Clyde led the way into the house and Abra followed, carrying Thomas's bag of medications from the car.

In Thomas's room, Zane lowered him gently to the bed and stood back. Abra brushed past him to tend to Thomas, while Clyde hovered near the door.

Zane watched Abra's sure, confident movements and thought to himself what a good nurse she must be. After a quick check of Thomas's vital signs, she prepared and administered a syringe of something. She checked to see if he was wet; then she asked Clyde if he wanted her to move a cot into the room that night.

"For me or for you?" was Clyde's response.

"Whichever you prefer," said Abra.

"We really should let him rest," he told her. "It may distract him if someone is in the room. I know it would distract me."

Clyde looked up then and seemed surprised to see Zane still standing there. He blinked and turned to Abra.

"Would you mind escorting Mr. Campbell to the door? Thank you for your assistance, Mr. Campbell."

"It was no trouble," Zane said, and he walked into the hall, Abra right behind him.

At the door he reached for her hand and gave it a light squeeze. "What do you think?"

"He could go for another week, or slip into a coma at any time. It's difficult to say."

Zane leaned forward and kissed her, taking her by surprise. Abra cleared her throat and covered her lips with her fingers.

"Zane, I think—"

"I'm going." He gave her cheek a gentle caress and opened the door. He slipped out without another word, and without letting her say anything else. He didn't want her to ruin things by saying they shouldn't have done what they did, or maybe it was better if they didn't see each other for a while. He wanted to relive what had happened and enjoy it without any sour notes at the end.

Outside he saw that they had left Clyde's car door open. The light was on inside and Thomas's seat belt was stretched out where Clyde had pulled it to free his brother. Zane reached inside to give it a jerk and saw a tattered book lying on the floor under the passenger seat. The cover was crumpled and torn, but the words *Claudia's After School Club* were still legible.

Zane frowned and wondered whose book it was. Looked like something for teenagers. He jerked on the seat belt again and it retracted to its normal position. Zane backed out of the car and closed the door. The light inside went off.

He looked across the street at Peterwell's house and saw that it was dark. Same for the Vaughn's place. Zane looked over his shoulder once at the lights still blazing at the Conlans'; then he walked into his dark, quiet house and went to bed.

# CHAPTER

## 22

CRAIG STAYED AT HOME all day Sunday. His nose hurt where Zane Campbell had elbowed him, and his head throbbed like never before. He was alone in his house, with not a single bird to keep him company. The silence seemed deafening to him, something to be afraid of with its void of comforting noises. There was humming and buzzing and a rushing kind of noise in his head, but there were no bird sounds and no people sounds.

At ten in the morning he turned on the television just to have something to hear.

At ten-thirty he tried to call Dr. Ahrens. He got her answering machine. Craig hung up without leaving any message. He was angry. She had said to call if he needed anything, and he needed something all right, but she wasn't there to help him. Why make him think she was going to be there for him if she wasn't?

He couldn't believe his eyes when he looked out the window and saw her park in front of the Conlan house. He got up and started to the door to tell her she was in the wrong driveway; he lived across the street. He was on the porch when he saw the woman who had hovered over him the night before open the door and greet Dr. Ahrens. Craig sat down on his porch and frowned. What was going on? Was the nurse at the Conlans' related to his doctor?

Dr. Ahrens disappeared inside the front door, and at the same instant Clyde Conlan hefted a large suitcase out through the back door and put it in his car. Going on another of his trips, Craig guessed. Craig envied him. Flying away all the time.

Craig waited on the porch for half an hour. When he saw the doctor finally emerge, the younger woman walked to the car with her. A beep sounded, Craig could hear it, and the nurse walked back to the house. Dr. Ahrens got in her car and started the engine. Craig left the porch and walked to stand in the middle of the street.

He could see her frown as she slowed down the car. She leaned her head out the window and said, "Craig Peterwell?"

He nodded and walked around to the driver's side of the car. It was a nice car, he noted. A Jaguar.

She said, "Do you live around here?"

"Right there," he said and pointed to his burned and blackened house.

"Oh, yes, I didn't even notice."

"I tried to call you today," Craig told her.

"You did? What—"

"Were you visiting a friend?" he interrupted.

"No. My daughter is working for the Conlans. I decided to surprise her today and come for a visit. I had no idea you lived in the same neighborhood."

"She doesn't even look like you," he said.

"Why did you try and call today, Craig? Is something wrong?"

He nodded. "Can you come in and talk to me for a while?"

"I'm sorry," she said. "I can't do that. I'm on my way to my secretary's bridal shower. Won't you tell me what's wrong?"

"He let my birds go again," said Craig. "I was catching crows to put in all the empty cages, and he let them go."

"Who?"

"My neighbor, Mark Vaughn. And then my other neighbor came out and attacked me when I jumped Vaughn. Last night he hit me in the nose with his elbow. Does it look broken to you?"

"Not really, no. If you're worried, go to the emergency room. Have you been to see the neurologist yet?"

"I go tomorrow morning first thing. And then I come to see you tomorrow night."

She smiled at him. "All right. I'll look forward to seeing you then. Please do me a favor, Craig, and stay away from your neighbors."

Before he could open his mouth again she stepped on the gas and drove away from him. Craig watched her go and wanted to cry. He felt okay when he was around her. His head still hurt, but he felt okay. He trudged back into the house and sat down on his sofa to watch television. He got up once to eat something, and then he went back to the sofa and fell asleep.

It was six the next morning when he awakened. He looked at his watch and went to wash up in the kitchen sink. He missed showering, but the construction people weren't coming until the end of the week.

He dressed in clean clothes and made himself some cereal for breakfast. While he ate he read the paper and thought about how much he hated cartoons he couldn't understand.

At seven-thirty he left the house and drove to work. He would be there only an hour, since his appointment with the neurologist was at nine o'clock. Luckily, the office of the neurologist was just a block or two away. He would be in and out in no time.

Seven hours later Craig was the veteran of a brain scan and EEG; MRI and cerebral angiography, and the neurologist was sitting in his office and dialing up Dr. Ahrens to talk with her before he told Craig the results. Craig didn't understand why she had to know before he did, but the doctor insisted, leaving Craig to sit in the examining room just outside his office. He was nervous, made even more so by the doctor's change in demeanor throughout the day of testing. At first the man had been nonchalant, even somewhat bored, but with each test his brow had furrowed deeper and deeper, scaring the crap out of Craig.

The moment the doctor's receptionist left her desk, Craig got up and walked over to the doctor's office door to see if he could hear anything. The door was open a crack, and he saw the doctor standing by the window and looking out through the glass as he spoke.

". . . like that of a pre-pubescent, or an adolescent at best, suggesting any number of irregularities. This thing could be enormous, a once in a lifetime case study, Dr. Ahrens. I'd like for him to undergo further testing, to find out just how far the abnormalities extend . . ."

Craig tuned him out and stopped listening. The first part he didn't understand, but he did understand the words *irregularities* and *abnormalities*. And he understood something else: *This thing could be enormous.*

The headaches, the anger, the craziness, it was all due to something growing inside his brain.

A brain tumor. An enormous brain tumor.

Okay, so he had felt a little nauseous now and then, but he had blamed it on the blood at work. Or on Louise. He had no idea it was a tumor.

Or maybe it wasn't. Maybe this was some huge joke being played on him by the idiots at work. Maybe everyone was in on it. Maybe even Dr. Ahrens.

If it was, by God, he would—no, it wasn't a joke. He knew it wasn't. The doctor turned and spotted him at the door, told Dr. Ahrens he'd call her back.

Craig took deep breaths to keep himself from passing out. The doctor was off the phone and on his way out to see him, his face appropriately grim, Craig thought.

Who the hell would want such a job? he wondered. What kind of person would want to spend the day telling people they had brain tumors?

"Excuse me," Craig interrupted before the man could open his mouth. "I gotta get out of here."

The doctor reached his arms out. "Mr. Peterwell, wait. I know what you're feeling and we do need to talk."

Craig turned and hit the man as hard as he could on the jaw. The doctor fell backward over his desk, knocking his phone, files and Rolodex from the surface.

"Now you know what I'm feeling right now," said Craig, and he lumbered out of the office holding his sore fist in his other hand.

He expected to be detained on his way to the parking lot, but Craig was unhampered as he got in his van and drove out onto the street. His mind was a painful, frightened jumble of fragmented thoughts as he drove. But a curious sense of relief was still with him. It wasn't his fault he had done what he did to Louise. He had a brain tumor. It wasn't his fault he had chained up Mark Vaughn like an animal and kept him in his basement. It was the tumor. And it was the tumor that caused him to think faster than he had ever thought in his life and burn up his dead wife and half of his house.

But you couldn't do things like that and not pay for it in some way.

So he guessed he was going to die.

Craig didn't want chemotherapy. He had been around the hospital enough to know what chemotherapy could do to a person. He'd rather have surgery. Let the idiot doctor take out a quarter of his brain and get rid of it. A frontal lobotomy for all the right reasons.

Everything made sense now. There had been episodes of blankness, holes in his existence, where things had happened but he could remember only parts.

He wouldn't ask how long he had to live because he knew the doctor wouldn't know, and even if he did, he wouldn't say. The longer Craig drove, the happier he was to have hit the mealy-mouthed sonofabitch.

At six o'clock he drove to Dr. Ahrens's office and went inside to find her staring stonily at him. Craig guessed the neurologist had tattled.

"Do you feel better?" she asked.

"No," he said.

"Why did you hit him?"

"Because he said he knew how I felt. He didn't."

"So you were trying to show him?"

"Something like that, yeah."

The doctor sighed. "I spoke with him at length, and he's decided not to press charges."

"What would be the point?" said Craig with a hoarse laugh.

"Just what did he tell you?"

"Everything he told you. I was listening."

"Then you know you need to show up for more tests."

"Bull."

"Craig, you're angry right now, and probably confused. Anyone would be after going through what you've gone through. But hang in there, and don't give up on yourself or do anything drastic. We'll sort out everything and find out what it means together."

Craig began to laugh. He couldn't help it. *Don't do anything drastic* struck him as funny and he laughed until he began to choke.

"Drastic?" he said. "What would you consider drastic, Dr. Ahrens? To beat my wife with a two-by-four and break her arms and legs?"

"Your wife is dead, Craig."

"Now she is."

Craig had stopped laughing. Dr. Ahrens was staring at him.

"What are you telling me?"

"Or maybe drastic is taking a man captive and keeping him chained in the basement for a few days."

"Craig . . ."

"It could be taking an axe and trying to chop off your wife's gangrenous leg, which you later find out wasn't gangrenous at all. The man in the basement said it was, but he lied. And then he escaped, and when you came home you knew something *drastic* had to be done, so you set fire to the house and burned up your wife in it, but she didn't feel anything because she was already dead. She bled to death.''

Dr. Ahrens's chest was rising and falling at a rapid rate. "Are you telling me," she began in a whisper, "that these things actually happened?''

Craig smiled at her. "What would you do if I said yes?'' He laughed. "Boy, a person sure gets some strange ideas when he has *abnormalities*, doesn't he?'' He left his seat then and sauntered out of the office. "See you next week.''

She called after him, her voice breaking in the middle of his name, but he didn't turn around. He was tired and he wanted to go home.

As he turned the van into his driveway he took a look around the neighborhood and decided there were some things he wanted to do before his time came. Every man should have a list of final acts, he told himself.

Abra listened to Thomas tell her all the acquisitions he had wanted to make and did not. According to Thomas, the losses were almost as sweet as the victories, because the real joy was in the attempt. Clyde did not have the same love of antiques and would doubtlessly sell all Thomas's most cherished pieces in favor of purchasing additional stock in the hospital. Thomas confessed that whenever Clyde was angry with him, Thomas would offer a piece of furniture and things were instantly better.

"That doesn't say much for Clyde, does it?'' said Abra.

"No. But don't get me wrong. Just as my antiques are my babies, that hospital is and always has been Clyde's baby. It's an affront to him that someone else actually owns the place. Part of the reason we still live where we do is because of Clyde's hoarding and spending every cent available on hospital stock."

"He wants to own the hospital?"

"That, fortunately, is impossible. But he would like to become entrenched on the board of directors. He may someday be replaced as chief of staff, but as a board member he would always be involved in important decisions concerning the hospital."

Abra screwed up her mouth. "He is a bossy sort, isn't he? And sneaky." She blinked then as she realized what she had said. "I'm sorry, Thomas. I don't know why I said that. I really am sorry."

Thomas smiled at her. "You're right. He is a sneak. He always has been, forever hiding things and keeping things secret. And not just from my parents, but from me as well. I think it makes him feel superior to have his hidden things and his secrets. He knows something I don't."

"Did the two of you enjoy the visit with your friend?"

"What friend?"

"The friend he took you to visit."

"I don't have any friends at that lab. Maybe Clyde does, if you can count flunkies as friends."

"He took you to a lab? I thought you were going to someone's house. And what about the gifts he mentioned?"

Something inscrutable passed behind Thomas's eyes and he waved a hand suddenly. "I don't know what you're talking about. I'm sleepy, Abra, but I think I could eat something."

"All right, Thomas," Abra said, completely confused.

She went to the kitchen and frowned while she thought as she prepared a quick soup and sandwich. Through the window she saw Zane walk out to his garden. Her nostrils flared and she turned away from the window. Her cheeks pinkened as she experienced heat and a twinge of desire at her center. She forced herself to concentrate on what she was doing and not think about what happened in the bathroom.

What she needed to be thinking about was the lies Clyde Conlan had told her and why he told them.

She carried a tray in to Thomas and helped him eat his soup and a bite of his sandwich before he said he was full. Before she could attempt to ask him anything further, he turned on his side away from her and said he wanted to sleep. Frustrated, Abra tucked him in and carried his tray out. She went to the kitchen and prepared a sandwich for herself, but put it down when she saw Zane walking shirtless to the small shed behind his garden. Without thinking about what she was doing, Abra picked up her beeper and went outside.

It was dim in the shed, so at first she didn't see him. When her eyes adjusted she saw him standing in the back, sharpening a lawnmower blade. The noise masked Abra's approach, but he sensed her as she came in the door. He looked over his shoulder and his mouth curved into a smile when he saw her. He put down the blade and turned. Abra paused where she stood, watching him watch her. She smiled then and hurried to throw her arms around him. He caught her and held her close, and when he opened his mouth to speak she silenced him with her mouth, kissing him hungrily and straining against him with her body. He groaned as he returned her passionate kisses and used his hands to mold her shape to him. They didn't notice the pair of eyes peering in one of the shed's two windows.

Eli went racing into the house and skidded to a stop in front of the television Holt was trying to watch.

"Holt! Dad's makin' out with Abra in the shed!"

Holt sat up. "What?"

"He's *kissing* her. Man, they're really heating up. I bet they're gonna do it out there."

"Dad and Abra?"

"Yeah, come and see."

Holt sat back down. "No."

"Don't you wanna see? Damn, I didn't know Dad had it in him."

"No, I don't wanna see, and you don't either. Sit your little ass down and don't go back out there."

"You gotta be kidding me." Eli started out of the room and Holt leapt off the sofa to collar him.

"Listen to me, you little jerk. You're not going out there. Dad's crazy about her and you're not going to blow it for him."

Eli shook himself free and sat down sullenly on a chair. "I'm not gonna blow anything. Jesus, Holt, you got such an attitude about everything."

Holt sat down and eyed his little brother warily.

"Don't move."


In the shed, Zane and Abra pulled apart and drew deep, unsteady breaths. Zane said something and Abra had to make him repeat himself twice before she understood.

"Not even a chaise lounge in here."

Abra smiled. "It's probably a good thing. I wanted to—"

"I had a vasectomy after Eli was born," he said.

"You did?"

"Yeah, I thought you might be worried."

"That wasn't what I was going to say," she told him. "I was going to tell you I normally don't behave in such fashion. I'm usually more cautious and . . . reserved."

"I'm usually that way myself." Zane's mouth curved again. "I've been replaying the scene in the bathroom in my head for two days now."

"Me, too," Abra admitted.

He looked meaningfully at her. "What time does Thomas go to sleep?"

"He's already asleep. But he might wake up at any time. He often does."

Zane put both hands on her cheeks and lifted her face to look at him. "Do you want me to come over?"

"Yes," she whispered. "I do."

"What time?"

"Right now."

He smiled. "Let me go in and shower. I'll feed the boys and be over in half an hour."

"Will they be all right on their own?"

"Holt's a good kid. He'll take care of the alien child."

"The what?"

"Never mind." He gave her a lingering kiss and then steered her toward the door. "I'll see you soon."

Abra drifted across the yard and into the house. She checked on Thomas and found him sleeping soundly. She went to her room and looked in the mirror at her face and body. Zane was coming, and she didn't give a damn about what Clyde Conlan would say if he knew. If he hadn't lied to her, then things might be different and she might care more about upholding his asinine rules. She doubted it, of course, thinking about Zane, but she might.

The ring of the phone snatched her out of her reverie, and the sound of her mother's voice made her blink. This was the second time her mother had made an effort at contact and it was a pleasant surprise for Abra.

"What is it, Mother?"

"Just a warning of sorts. A very disturbed patient of mine lives across the street from you. His name is Craig Peterwell. Today he found out he has a brain tumor. I was just putting it together that he said he was attacked by one of his neighbors last night. Would that be anyone you know?"

"It would," Abra breathed. "Zane scuffled with him."

"Be careful. I think Peterwell is dangerous right now, and probably will continue to be. He assaulted a doctor today and said much to me that made me doubt his stability. Stay clear of him, Abra, and tell your friend to do the same."

"A brain tumor, Mother?"

"Among other abnormalities."

Abra inhaled deeply. "Thank you for calling, Mother."

"Be careful, Abra."

"I will." Abra said goodbye and hung up to wait for Zane.

# CHAPTER

## 23

ZANE STAYED OUTSIDE LONG enough to make the evidence of his arousal less apparent, but when he entered the house he encountered a slyly smiling Eli, who said, "I saw you."

"You saw me what?"

"With Abra in the shed."

"What do you think you saw?"

"You guys kissing."

"Right," said Zane. "We were kissing."

"You looked like you were ready to tear her clothes off."

Zane frowned at him. "I didn't."

"I know, but it looked like you wanted to. I never saw you kiss Mom like that, ever. You're going over there to sleep with her, right?"

Beyond Eli, Zane saw Holt sitting on the couch and shaking his head.

"Why would you say something like that, Eli?"

"Well, you never kissed Mom like that, and you loved her."

Zane wanted to shake his head like Holt. Eli certainly had some confused ideas. "I loved your mother, yes. A part of me will always care for her, because she's the mother of my children. But the rest of me, the person I am now, wants Abra."

"For sex. Holt said you were crazy about her."

"I am crazy about her, Eli. She's intelligent, kind, caring, and sex is only a part of what I want to share with her."

Eli sat down and stared at his father. "So what are you saying? Are you gonna marry her?"

"What if I wanted to?" Zane asked. "What if I wanted to marry anyone, Eli? How would you feel about it?"

"Not good. I like it with just us guys."

Holt stood up. "You selfish little pig. Don't you want Dad to be happy?"

Eli looked at his father. "You're happy, aren't you?"

Holt snorted. "He'd be happier if he had someone, stupid. Mom has someone and you get along all right with him. What's the difference?"

"I *live* here."

Zane smiled and tousled his younger son's hair. "Find something else to worry about, would you?"

Eli wasn't satisfied. "Did you ever think you might like her so much because she's the first woman who wasn't turned off by the way you talk?"

"I've thought about it," Zane admitted. "But enough has happened between us that my speech is now a non-issue. I didn't think we were ever going to be together, and I'm still not sure where we're headed, so just relax and let me enjoy the time I have with her, all right?"

Eli's nod was grudging. "All right."

"What do you guys want for dinner?"

"Hamburgers," said Eli.

"How about salad and sandwiches?"

Eli made a face. "We never get hamburgers. Mom lets us have hamburgers."

Zane ignored him and opened the refrigerator door. He prepared a hasty salad and took out the sandwich fixings to let the boys help themselves. Then he went to take a quick shower and put on some fresh clothes.

When Holt saw him he said, "You headed out?"

"I'm going to spend some time with Abra. I'll be right next door if you need anything. The number is in the address book by the phone. You guys don't go anywhere."

"We'll be fine," Holt assured him. "Stay as long as you want. I'll make sure Eli doesn't leave."

Zane smiled at his older son. "Thanks, Holt. I'll see you later."

"Have fun," Eli said with a leer, and Holt punched him.

Zane went out and walked across the lawn to the Conlan house. The front door was slightly ajar, so he knocked lightly and opened it to go inside. There was no sign of anyone in the foyer or the hall. He closed the door behind him and started a search of the rooms, walking quietly so as not to disturb the sleeping Thomas.

When he heard voices inside Thomas's room, he knew the man was already awake. Zane cursed softly to himself and waited in the hall.

It seemed forever until Abra came out of the room and jumped at seeing him there. She put a finger to her mouth and Zane followed her quietly down the hall and into the kitchen, where she looked ruefully at him.

Zane took a guess. "He's not going to sleep again anytime soon, is he?"

"Doesn't look like it." Abra moved closer to him and inhaled deeply. "You smell good."

Zane put his arms around her and gave her a squeeze. "Eli saw us in the shed earlier."

"And?"

"And he was full of questions about us."

Abra frowned. "Is he upset?"

"No." Zane looked into her eyes before kissing her on the mouth. "Will I see you later?"

She smiled at him. "You don't give up easily, do you?"

"Not when it comes to you," he said, and he kissed her again, leaving her breathless this time.

"How will I let you know?" she asked when she could speak. "I don't want to call and wake up the boys."

"Turn on the light by your bedroom window. If I see it, I'll know he's asleep."

"You won't mind leaving the boys?"

"I'll be right next door."

"So is Craig Peterwell, so to speak." Abra leaned away from him. "My mother called and said he's a patient of hers. Today he had a brain scan and the neurologist who examined him claims he's dangerously unstable."

Zane was taken by surprise. "A brain scan? I guess that explains it. People with brain tumors often change their behavior patterns, don't they?"

"It happens," said Abra. "I thought I'd warn you, in case of any more confrontations. He attacked the doctor who tested him, so who knows what he's capable of."

"I'll watch him," Zane murmured. He looked longingly at her lips again and was leaning to kiss her when the beeper in her pocket sounded.

Abra bussed him on the lips. Then she pulled away to fix the glass of fruit juice she had come for. Zane was left to show himself to the door. He cursed his luck again and stepped onto the porch. His eyes went immediately to Craig Peterwell's house. A single light was on in the living room.

Zane briefly considered going over to talk with him. God knew Craig would want someone to talk to. But Zane decided he was the wrong someone, and if Abra's mother was right, then Craig Peterwell was a man to stay away from. Zane went home and let himself in the front door.

Eli sat up from the couch where he was watching television with Holt.

"Wow. That was quick."

"Watch it," Zane warned him. "Thomas was awake and needed attention. I might go over later."

Eli started to say something else, but a dark look from his older brother silenced him.

Zane took a magazine from the rack in the living room and went to his bedroom to lie down and wait for Abra.

Mark Vaughn was in his garage with a flashlight, pushing the spiders around in their boxes. He was still jumpy around them, but he had to keep the damned things alive, so he spent a good part of that afternoon trapping flies and other insects outside in the backyard. Valerie had watched him for a while and asked what he was doing. Mark told her he was passing time, was all. His wife shook her head and went back to watching a talk show on television.

She was in bed now with the baby, both of them already asleep at just after eight o'clock. His two tired little sweethearts.

Mark closed the box he held and turned off his flashlight. As he walked into the house, the phone rang, and he ran to pick it up before it could wake Valerie.

"Hello?"

"Vaughn, this is Zane Campbell. I wanted—"

"No, I haven't changed my mind about talking to you," said Mark. "I'm going back to work tomorrow and my life's going back to normal."

"That's good. I called to tell you Craig Peterwell was diagnosed with a brain tumor today, and people who know say he should be considered dangerous. That's nothing we didn't know, but I'm telling you so you can steer clear of him if you see him."

"You're kidding me," said Mark. "A fucking brain tumor?"

"He doesn't know we know, so keep it to yourself and do your best to avoid him."

"Yeah. I will. Thanks for calling and telling me. This puts things in a whole new light, doesn't it?"

"I guess. It explains a lot, anyway. Goodbye, Vaughn."

"Bye." Mark hung up the receiver and immediately picked it up again. He dialed Peterwell's number and listened to the phone ring and ring.

"Pick it up, you bastard."

On the twelfth ring, the phone was picked up. As always, Peterwell said nothing.

"Brain tumor, eh?" Mark said into the receiver. "Oh, my, isn't that just too bad? Poor old Peterfell went and got himself a bad old brain tumor. I bet you're blaming all kinds of shit on that tumor, aren't you? Yeah, I bet you're calling up heaven and saying, 'None of this was my fault, right? I had a brain tumor.' Well, that shit may wash with some, but we know the truth, don't we? You liked doing what you did to me and Louise. You enjoyed—"

The dial tone sounded in Mark's ear and he slowly eased the receiver back into the cradle.

"One for us, Louise," he said, and he made a mark in the air.

For the next few hours he waited, tensed, ready for anything to happen. By midnight he decided to go to bed. Peterwell wasn't going to retaliate that night.

Mark wondered if maybe he should stay home tomorrow instead of going to work. It would be just like Peterwell to come over while Mark was gone and do something to Val and the baby.

"Just one more thing I could say I brought on myself," Mark muttered aloud.

Then it hit him. He could ask Valerie to go to her mother's house while he was at work. He would use Peterwell's brain tumor as an excuse. Valerie knew Peterwell had attacked him in the yard. Mark could say he was concerned for the safety of his wife and daughter, so it was best if they weren't around when he wasn't there to protect them. There was no telling what a man with a brain tumor was going to do.

When he went in the bedroom, he found Valerie awake and looking at him. He went to pat her on the shoulder and she turned away from him. She said, "I heard you make a call a couple of hours ago. I heard you whispering to someone."

Mark sat down on the side of the bed. "I didn't want to wake you up, honey. It was Alan, at work. I—"

"You're lying," she said in a dull voice. "Again. What else have you lied to me about, Mark? Were you actually chained up in a field out west, or was it in a trailer with an old girlfriend or something? Why don't I believe anything you say to me anymore? Why do I feel like everything you say and do is a lie?"

"Valerie, I'm not—"

"Start with the first lie, Mark. The one that keeps getting you into trouble. Who really raped that little girl? Was it you or your partner? And if you say it was him, then be prepared to tell me why you heard that child screaming and did nothing about it. Why you stayed in the other room and heard everything but did nothing. Tell me, Mark."

Mark's hands were shaking. Even his knees were trembling. "I didn't do it, Valerie. I was in the next room snorting China White and hearing nothing. I was an *addict*, goddammit, not a rapist. Why do you think I started breaking into people's houses? My father wasn't going to give me money for heroin. He cut me off completely when he found out I was doing heroin. The only way I got clean was in jail. I could have gotten it in there, too, if I'd wanted to offer myself up and be someone's punk. But I didn't. I got clean and stayed clean.

"As for lying to you about the other stuff, you're right. I wasn't in western Kansas, I was in Craig Peterwell's basement. I went to his house to break in and trash his birds and found his wife on the basement floor with her arms and legs broken. Peterwell came home and hit me over the head with a pipe wrench. When I woke up I was chained up next to Louise and couldn't move."

Mark paused to look at his wife's expression. Her look was incredulous, but not damning. She was listening. He went on and told her the rest, about Peterwell trying to cut off Louise's leg, and about Chance coming in and finding him. When he told her the part about finding Louise dead, she started crying. Finally she dried her eyes and said, "That's why Chance came to the door that night, isn't it? He wanted to talk about Louise. Mark, why didn't you call the police the minute you found her dead? What were you thinking of?"

He turned away from her. "Revenge. I wanted to make him crazy. I wanted him to suffer the way he made me and Louise suffer. But he burned up the house with her in it and made everything look like an accident. He took care of everything but me."

"That's who you called tonight," Valerie said slowly. "You called Peterwell."

Mark nodded. "Zane Campbell phoned earlier and told me Peterwell has a brain tumor. He was diagnosed with it today. I called Peterwell and told him the tumor excuses nothing. He's still going to pay."

Valerie closed her eyes and fell back on the bed. "This is a nightmare. Oh, God, Mark, what a nightmare."

"I need you to go to your mom's house tomorrow," he told her. "Peterwell might come after you and Melissa while I'm gone, so I want you safely away. Will you do that?"

It was a long time before she nodded. "I'll be staying with Mom longer than just a day. I have to think, Mark. I really need to think about all this. About us."

Mark started shaking again. "You don't believe me. I've told you the truth and you don't believe me."

"I believe you," she said. "It's too bizarre to be anything but the truth. The fact that you lied to me in the first place is what disturbs me. And putting us in jeopardy is inexcusable. I have to get Melissa away from the craziness."

"You're not going to leave me," Mark said, and he tried to make his voice firm.

"For a little while I am. Go to bed, Mark."

He opened his mouth to say something further, but her eyes were shut and her face was closed to him. Nothing he said tonight would alter the situation. Mark got up and took off his clothes to go to bed.

# CHAPTER
## 24

AFTER ELI AWAKENED HE jumped out of bed and ran down the hall to his father's room to see if he was in bed. His dad was asleep in his clothes on top of the comforter. Eli smirked to himself and went back down the hall to his room to get dressed. He guessed last night hadn't worked out after all. Too bad so sad for old dad.

Eli liked Abra. It wasn't that he didn't like her. It was just that seeing his dad kissing her had made him feel funny, like his dad was doing something he shouldn't. Eli didn't know why he felt that way. He guessed it was okay if his dad wanted to kiss Abra. He wasn't married to Eli's mom anymore, and Eli's mom was married to someone she kissed all the time. But not like that. Not the way his dad had kissed Abra. Watching them had made Eli feel strangely hot and disgusted at the same time.

He left the house before either Holt or his father was awake and took off on his bicycle. He would probably get in trouble for going off by himself without telling anyone, but he didn't care. He wanted some time to himself. He rode to the walking bridge and parked his bike before crossing over to the brushy bank on the other side. Eli picked up a big stick and began walking through the trees and brush, beating his way with the stick. Soon he crawled inside the green denseness and sat down to think.

He thought about all the good stuff that would happen if his dad married Abra. His dad would probably be nicer, and continue to talk better. Eli would have something female to look at, and someone's underwear drawers to go through. They might have hamburgers once in a while, if she liked burgers. Christmas might be nicer, too, he conceded. Less quiet and lonely.

Then he thought about the bad stuff that would happen if his dad married Abra. He'd have another grownup to answer to, and a female to share the television with. His dad would probably want to do fun stuff with her instead of with Holt and Eli, and he wouldn't be able to turn the living room into an obstacle course anymore. He would probably have to take his showers at night, since grownups liked to shower in the morning. And he would have to meet and be nice to all her relatives. Eli hated that part.

He picked up his stick and held it like a sword to slash at the limbs and leaves around him.

What would his dad say, he wondered, if he asked to go and live with his mom?

Did he really want to do that? he asked himself.

Nah. Not just because of Abra. She was pretty nice, after all. And smart. Hey, she could probably help him with his homework once school started.

Eli drove the stick into the ground and watched it stand straight up.

Wow. He didn't realize the ground was so soft. He pulled it out again and drove it into the ground on the other side of him. The stick went into the dirt again, but it struck something this time and angled off. Eli stood up and dusted off his pants. He grabbed the stick and pulled it up with both hands. He heard a ripping sound, like the tearing of fabric. Eli got down on his hands and knees and pawed at the dirt. Six inches down he began to uncover what looked like a piece of clothing. He pulled at the fabric and felt no give. He dug some more and began to get a sick feeling in his gut.

He uncovered a pink backpack that had *Claudia's After School Club* written on the side in black marker. Then he uncovered an arm.

Eli screamed and leaped up. He tore out of the brush at a run and didn't stop until he reached his bicycle. He pedaled like mad for home and threw his bike down in the front yard to race to the front door. The door opened as he reached it and Eli came face to face with his white-faced father. "Where the hell have you been?"

Eli opened his mouth, but nothing came out. He threw himself at his dad and began to sob. Zane held him and tried to look into his face.

"Eli?"

"I-I f-f-found h-h-her."

"You found her? You found who?"

"Cyndi."

His father's eyes rounded. "You found Cyndi Melo? Where, Eli?"

It was several moments before Eli could speak. Zane held him and soothed him and patted him on the back. "You won't have to see her again, son. Just tell me where she is. Can you do that?"

"No. I'll have to show you. I can't explain the spot where I was."

"Will you take me now?"

Eli nodded bravely. "Aren't you going to call the police?"

"Not until I can tell them where to go. I need you to show me what you found first. All right?"

"Okay. Let's go. Where's Holt?"

"Right here," said a sleepy-eyed Holt from behind his father. "What's going on?"

"I found Cyndi Melo," Eli told his brother. "She's dead. She's buried on the bank in the trees." Just saying the words made Eli start crying again.

Holt's jaw fell. Zane told him to hurry up and get dressed.

"All right, Eli," he said when Holt was ready. "Let's go see what you found."

"It's her, Dad," Eli said as he got in the car with Holt. "I recognized her backpack. She carried it to school last year."

Zane drove where Eli directed him and parked on the street beside the walking bridge.

Eli went across the bridge with his father and brother walking behind him. He followed the exact same path he had taken and walked directly to the thick copse of trees he had chosen to sit down in. His face crumpled and his throat started hitching when he saw the pink backpack. His dad told him and Holt to stay put and went to view the body closer. He went to a squat and brushed more dirt away, and when he turned to them his expression was grim. "Holt, take the car back home and call the police. Tell them I'll meet them at the bridge. Eli, go with him."

"Are you staying here?" Eli asked.

"Yeah."

"Why?"

"Go, Eli."

The roughness of his voice sent the boys on their way. When he was upset he didn't talk so good anymore, Eli noted. His words got all scrambled and nothing was clear.

Eli started crying again when Holt told the cop on the phone who he was, who his dad was, and that he thought the body found by his little brother was Cyndi Melo. Eli couldn't help it. He kept thinking about kissing Cyndi last year on that stupid bridge. He kept thinking how pretty she was and how awful she must look now.

He wiped the snot from his nose on his hand and tucked his face into his arm as Holt glanced at him. When Holt hung up the phone he came to Eli and put an arm around him. "It's okay."

Eli wanted to be a tough guy, but all he could do was lean against his older brother and cry like a little baby.

Zane stared at the pink backpack with the scrawled *Claudia's After School Club* on the side and thought about the tattered book he had seen on the floor of Clyde Conlan's car. He thought about Clyde's open dislike of him, and his innate distrust and suspicion of not just Zane but all his neighbors.

John Ptacek, his former partner during the years he spent in homicide, appeared at the crime scene on the heels of two different uniformed units. The area was quickly roped off and sealed, and Ptacek thanked Zane for attempting to maintain as much as possible the integrity of the crime scene. The ground would be scoured for trace evidence and the entire scene would be videotaped and photographed from every conceivable angle. While his partner worked at sketching the scene and measuring landmarks, Ptacek went home with Zane to talk to Eli.

Eli answered each question truthfully, wincing a little as he recounted driving the sticks into the soft ground. He said he hadn't noticed any tracks there before him, but he hadn't been paying attention. Eventually, Ptacek thanked him and got up to leave.

"Wait," said Eli. "Are you going to tell Cyndi's parents?"

"Not yet. We're going to need positive identification before we do that."

"It's her," Eli swore. "It's her backpack."

"Sorry, Eli. We need more than that."

Eli swallowed. "You want me to come back and ID her for you?"

Behind Eli, Zane shook his head.

"No thanks, Eli. We'll get someone else to do that. I'm grateful for all your help."

Eli nodded and looked relieved. "Okay."

Zane put a hand on Eli's shoulder and squeezed it before following Ptacek to the door.

"Let me know on this one, John," he said.

"I'll call you after we get an autopsy report," Ptacek promised.

When he was gone, Zane asked himself why he hadn't mentioned seeing the book in Clyde Conlan's car to Ptacek. It was one of those weird, offbeat things that could possibly mean something. Clyde Conlan might have something to hide concerning the book and bag business, which would explain most of his anti-social behavior. Zane usually ignored him and talked only to Thomas, who was much more affable.

That was before Thomas became so ill. Which reminded Zane of Abra, and the fact that her light had never come on last night, or if it had, he was already asleep and never saw it. He thought of calling her to find out, but the troubled look on Eli's face prevented him from picking up the phone.

"You okay?" he asked, taking his son by the shoulder and sitting him down on the sofa.

"I'm okay, yeah. I just . . ." He looked around, as if searching for the words. "I was sitting *on top* of her, Dad, and I didn't even know it."

"You couldn't have."

"What do you think happened to her?"

"I'm not sure."

"How do you think she was killed? Her arm looked okay, I mean there was no blood or anything."

"We won't know that for a while. Not until the autopsy report comes back."

Eli blanched. "Autopsy? They're gonna cut her open?"

"It's standard procedure in homicides, Eli. It's necessary."

"Oh, man," he whispered. His face was stricken. "I don't wanna think about that."

"Don't. Shut it out of your mind. Think of her the last time you saw her and don't think of her any other way."

"The last time I saw her she was *dead*," Eli said on a sob. His lower lip was quivering.

"You know what I mean, son. The last time you saw her alive. In class, or in the neighborhood, or at the pool."

"She was gonna be my girlfriend this year," said Eli. "I kissed her on the bridge the first part of the summer. Then I went to stay with Mom for a while and didn't see her until I got back. The last time I saw her was at the pool. She was making faces at me and calling me a retard for talking to Chance. I splashed her and went after her, but I never caught her. She was too quick for me. That's the last time I saw her alive."

"Hold that picture of her in your head then, and let that be your last memory of her."

Eli wiped his nose on his hand. "Dad, how did you handle it when you worked with dead people all the time? What did you think about?"

"Catching the person who did it to them. I didn't let myself focus on anything else."

"Did it work?"

"Most of the time, yes; sometimes, no."

"What did you do when it didn't work?"

"The wrong thing, usually. I drank myself blind so I wouldn't see their faces."

Eli studied him a moment. "Do you still see them sometimes?"

Zane nodded. "Sometimes."

"It's good to be away from all that, isn't it?"

"Yes."

"Dad, I love you."

"I love you, too, Eli."

"Whatever you decide about Abra, it's okay with me. I didn't mean to sound like such a baby about it. I like her and everything."

Zane smiled at him. "This is all pretty premature, you know. A week from now Abra may not even be here."

"Why not? Is Thomas gonna die that soon?"

"Thomas could die at any time. I'm just saying Abra may not be interested in marrying, living with or even seeing me again after she leaves here. It's too soon to tell where the relationship is headed."

"Besides into bed, you mean."

Zane looked at the ceiling. "Where did this perverted streak in you come from? You didn't learn it from me."

For the first time, Eli cracked a smile. "I didn't learn it from anybody. It just comes naturally to me."

Zane looked at his crooked smile and reached out to give his younger son a warm hug. For the first time in months, Eli hugged him back hard.

# CHAPTER
## 25

CRAIG CALLED IN SICK that morning. He saw no point in telling them anything other than that he wasn't feeling well. He saw no point in going back to work, period, but he wasn't able to make himself utter any notes of finality. He wanted to give himself an option to return, should he find merely existing unbearable.

But it wouldn't be mere existence, he reminded himself. He had some presents to deliver. Some Christmas-in-summer surprises for a few people.

Like Dr. Ahrens.

The way Craig figured it, she had told her daughter about his brain tumor. The daughter told Campbell, and Campbell told Vaughn. Craig thought about it all night and all morning and he knew it had happened that way.

The part he couldn't figure out was why Dr. Ahrens had told her daughter.

Because she thought he might do something *drastic*? Like maybe try to commit suicide?

Or was it because she was worried about him becoming violent and *hurting* someone?

Craig chuckled to himself suddenly as he sat on the sofa and stared at the droning television. She had good reason to worry. She—

A noise outside the house made him bolt up suddenly and

creep to the window to look outside. In the next second he jerked open the door and lunged at the cringing Chance, who was on his knees under the windows.

"What do you think you're doing?" Craig snarled as he stood over the guilty Chance.

"I wasn't d-doing nothing."

Craig trembled in anger. "What are you doing sitting under my windows?"

Chance only stared at him, speechless.

"Answer me. Answer me right now."

"I-I was listening for b-birds."

Craig blinked and stared at him. "What? Why?"

"I don't know."

"You don't know. What kind of—" Craig didn't finish. His nostrils flared and his eyes narrowed. "What kind of birds were you listening for?"

"Any kind. The kind you had in here before. Or the other kind."

"What other kind?"

"The—" Chance saw his mistake and stopped too late.

"It was you, wasn't it?" said Craig. "You let my crows out. Who else did you let out, you sneaking retard? Mark Vaughn, maybe?"

Chance was shaking his head furiously. "Don't call me names, Mr. Peterwell."

"I'll call you whatever I please, you crazy, bug-eyed moron. Who told you to come in my house and let my birds go?"

Chance's lips were quivering. "They did."

"They? Who's they?"

"The birds."

Craig's eyes rounded as he stared at the idiot. "The birds told you to break into my house and let them go?"

Chance nodded.

Craig put a hand to his head. The headache he had awakened with that morning was suddenly much worse. He looked around the neighborhood to see if anyone was watching, then he leaned down close to Chance and said, "I cut off my wife's leg with an axe before I burned her up in the house. I still have the axe, Chance, and some night when you least expect it, I'm going to break into your house the way you broke into mine and cut off both your legs so you can't come sneaking around my windows anymore."

Chance's face grew slack. He stared in openmouthed horror. "I'm g-gonna tell m-my m-mother."

Craig winked at him. "Do that, pea brain. Tell her how you broke the law, twice, and came into my house to let my birds go. And be sure to ask how much jail time you'll get, if I don't get to you first. I'll be coming for you with my rusty old axe, so don't even think about going to sleep tonight, or the next night, or the next . . ."

The terrified Chance scampered away from him on all fours and dug divots in the grass as he leapt to his feet and tore away from Craig.

Satisfied with Chance's reaction, Craig went back in his house and, after looking at all his empty bird cages, thought he might possibly turn threat into fact. Who but a warp-brained retard would think the birds were asking to be let out of their cages? "And they say I'm the one with the brain tumor," Craig muttered to himself.

He sat on the sofa once more and soon returned to a trance while staring at the television. He went back to thinking about Dr. Ahrens, and what he was going to do about her betrayal. Her treachery. She had never truly cared about him or his problems; she was just doing her job, smiling and nodding and pretending to listen to him. Asking stupid, leading questions and making him think there was something wrong with the way his father had raised him. His father had had no choice. He had to work and earn a living. What was he supposed to do with his son? Turn him over to the state? Make him live in a foster home?

Craig's eyes burned and his lips began to contort as he fought against a sudden, unbearable urge to bawl. At that moment he would take even his former neighbor, the man who beat his daughters, if only he could have someone there.

When the ache passed, Craig turned off the television and went to the main window to gaze at the empty lawns and quiet houses. While he was looking at the Conlan house his mind began to work. Soon the weepiness and sorrow left him completely. He even forgot about his headache and the tumor that was causing it.


Chance was sobbing incoherently in his room when his mother found him. She hastened in and sat down on the bed beside him to take him in her arms. Chance resisted and turned away to bury his face in his pillow.

"What is it, honey?" his mother soothed. "Tell me."

"I can't, Momma. I can't tell you."

"Whyever not? You always tell Momma everything. There's nothing you can't tell me now."

He shook his head and went on crying in noisy sobs that shook his broad shoulders.

"Let me help you, son. Please."

"You can't help me, Momma. No one can help."

"I can sure try, can't I? Will you at least give me the opportunity to try? Haven't I always told you that you were my one chance to do something worthwhile on this old earth? Let me make it better for you, son."

"You can't help," Chance repeated.

His mother sighed and leaned back on the bed. She looked at the window and frowned in surprise. "What is that on your window, Chance?"

"It's a scary face, from our Halloween stuff."

"But honey, Halloween's not for a couple months yet. You know that."

"I know. But I wanted something scary up there, to scare bad things away."

"What bad things?"

"Just bad things, is all."

"Chance, has something frightened you?"

He said nothing.

"Did you watch a scary movie when I wasn't paying attention?"

"No, Momma. I don't like scary movies."

"Did you have a bad dream last night and think something was coming in to get you?"

He shook his head; then he changed his mind. "Yeah, I did," he said. "I think that's what happened. I think it was a dream that scared me."

"And you just now remembered it?"

"Uh-huh."

"What was the dream about?"

"It was about Mr. Peterwell coming in my room with an axe and trying to chop off my legs. He said he chopped off his wife's leg, and that he was going to chop off mine if I didn't stay away from his house."

His mother was looking at him with an expression of dismay on her face. "Oh, my goodness, Chance. What a terrible, terrible dream. Where did you ever come up with such a gruesome nightmare?"

"From Mr. Peterwell. He called me all kinds of bad names."

"Bad names?"

"Really bad names. He called me a—"

"I don't need to hear them, Chance, and don't you go repeating things you heard in your sleep."

"But I . . ." Chance stopped and looked at his wet pillow. "I think it's more than a dream, Momma. I think he's coming to get me for real."

"Why would he do that, Chance?"

"Because I . . ." Again, Chance stopped. "I just think he is. Can we put my dresser against the window?"

Mrs. Morley stood up. "What? Chance, don't be silly. There's no need to put your dresser against the window."

"There is," Chance insisted. "He's going to come in and chop off my legs."

"Oh, for heaven's sake." Mrs. Morley was going to say more, but the ring of the telephone interrupted her. She went to answer and left Chance in his room, staring at his window. They had some tape in the kitchen. Maybe if he put tape all over the window it wouldn't break and Mr. Peterwell couldn't get in.

Or red pepper. Maybe if he put red pepper on top of the windowsill, then Mr. Peterwell would start sneezing just like in the cartoons and not be able to stop.

Chance sneaked into the kitchen to get the tape and the red pepper. His mother was on the phone and didn't see him. He stopped when he saw her face. She had that bad news look in her eyes, like someone was telling her something she didn't want to know.

He took the tape and the pepper into his room and had put on three strips of tape when he heard his mother call his name. Chance told her he'd be there in a minute and went on taping. Soon his mother called to him again and Chance figured he'd better go in there before she came in and saw what he was doing.

When he entered the living room he saw the look on her face hadn't changed. Her skin was even grayer than before.

"What is it, Momma?" he asked worriedly. "Did Mr. Peterwell chop up someone else?"

"No, Chance. Mr. Peterwell didn't do anything to anyone. It's the little Melo girl. The girl whose bike you found? This morning Eli Campbell found her buried in the trees on the bank across from the bridge."

"Buried?" Chance repeated.

"Someone put her under the ground, Chance."

"Like in a funeral?"

"Without the casket. They buried her under the ground to cover up a crime. They might come looking at you again, son. They might come back and ask more questions."

This was almost as frightening to Chance as the idea of Peterwell cutting off his legs.

"What will we tell them?" he asked fearfully.

"The truth, honey. We always tell the truth when it comes to the law."

The truth. Chance swallowed. Did that mean he would have to tell them about letting Mr. Peterwell's birds go? If he did, he would go to prison. But he didn't know any other truth. He didn't know anything about the Melo girl, besides the fact that he hadn't liked her very much. She laughed at him and made fun of Eli Campbell when Chance was with him. That wasn't very nice.

But neither was being buried beneath the ground to cover up grime.

Chance told his mother he was going back to his room. Once there he picked up his tape and started taping again. When the dispenser was empty, he discarded it and reached for the red pepper. The whole lid came off while he was trying to pry up the corner, and the contents of the tiny container spilled in a pile on the carpet. Chance said a naughty word, a word Eli Campbell taught him, and reached down with his fingers to pick up the pepper and put it on the sill. When he was finished, he realized he hadn't sneezed once.

He guessed it only worked on bad guys. He hoped it did.

# CHAPTER
# 26

MARK WATCHED VALERIE PACK more than a week's worth of clothing in a suitcase while he sat on the end of the bed and said nothing. He could think of absolutely nothing to say. She was right. He had behaved like a fool. The minute he found Louise Peterwell dead he should have gotten out of there and called the cops. When they asked why he went there in the first place, he . . .

. . . couldn't have told them anything, unless he wanted to end up in jail again. He couldn't say he had heard her screaming, because that wouldn't explain the car he had parked on Laurel Street. He was screwed all the way around, and he had done it to himself. He had no one to thank for the mess he was in but solo mio Mark. Valerie didn't understand what he was dealing with. People like her never could. She came from a world on a different level, where people were generally polite, mostly civil, and usually did what they said they were going to do. People rarely got fucked-over in Valerie's world, and if they did, it was with the utmost subtlety and consideration, so it was rarely acknowledged, but happened just the same.

Mark's view was different. His father had started as a used-car dealer, and his mother worked as bartender in a club known for its under-the-table gambling. As a child Mark had gone into the clubs with his mother to clean and set up for the next shift. He had tasted liquor while still a toddler and called a dozen different barflies "uncle." His mother was arrested twice for gambling, playing blackjack at the bar and shooting craps in the back room. Mark's father had managed to avoid arrest on both occasions, although he too was present. As his father's business grew and he became more respectable, Mark's dad decided to divorce the embarrassment that was his wife and move into a different circle of people. He took Mark with him.

The liars, cheats and adulterers in this group were no different, they simply wore better clothing, had bigger bank accounts and drove newer cars.

The higher the caliber of people his father introduced him to, the lower Mark's estimation of his dad became. So he did what any other red-blooded American male would do and declared a rebellion against his father's values. The form of rebellion he chose was inhaling illegal substances into his body. Next came breaking into people's houses for money to buy heroin and listening to a little girl get raped in the next room but not caring because getting the heroin into his body was more important at the time.

Now he guessed his rent was due. Time to pay for all the abuses and stupid mistakes of past and present and watch his wife and baby walk out the door.

Mark wanted to cry.

But he didn't.

He helped Valerie load her things. He helped her put the bassinet, the playpen, the baby's tub, damn near everything but the crib into the car. Then he told his little girl goodbye and touched his lips to her forehead.

"I'll call you," said Valerie. Her eyes were red. She refused to meet his gaze.

"Please," was all Mark said.

She nodded and slid behind the wheel. Mark stood in the driveway and watched them back down the drive and out to the street. He waved as they sped away. When he could no longer see the car, he turned to go inside the house. He stopped when he saw Peterwell's van in his driveway. Why hadn't he gone to work that day? Then he remembered Peterwell's brain tumor and guessed he wouldn't go to work, either. Mark smiled a little as he opened the door. He walked across the room and out to the patio. He had over a dozen spiders now, big fat brown ones with hairy bodies and long, long legs. He was becoming an expert at catching them—and insects, particularly flies. All he had to do was leave a melon rind in an open container for a few hours and then go out and pop a lid on it, trapping all the flies and other insects inside. He cut a small hole in the lid and placed a cardboard tube inside, the other end of which was clamped to a size to prevent the spiders escaping but was big enough to let the flies through into the box with all the hungry spiders.

In the yard his flooding plan still worked to good effect, and he did it again that afternoon while keeping a surreptitious eye on Peterwell's house. It wouldn't do for Peterwell to see him catching spiders. He might suspect something.

Again, Mark had to shake his head. Valerie would never understand this. This need to win over the man who had held him captive and made him a prisoner. This wasn't something that could be politely discussed in an afternoon. It wasn't something a therapist or the courts could deal with, and it wasn't something that would go away with the passage of time. There had to be a showdown of sorts, a final battle between them that would declare the winner once and for all. As far as Mark was concerned, the brain tumor was only incidental. He and Peterwell had hated each other forever.

He caught two more medium-sized spiders that day and added them to his shoebox collection. He was almost ready. All that would be required was a simple tool and a moment when no one was looking.

Mark winced when he saw the five o'clock news that day. He had seen the news van at the Campbells' house earlier, but had no idea what Eli Campbell found that morning. Mark looked at the picture aired of the little girl and thought of his own daughter.

He fixed a ham sandwich for dinner and peered out his curtains while he chewed. The block was eerily silent, as if the news of the Melo girl had forced everyone indoors.

At nine o'clock, Mark said what the hell. There was no reason not to give his plan a try that night. He went to bed and set his alarm for a quarter to two. He didn't get to sleep until nearly twelve, so he wasn't exactly rested and refreshed when the alarm went off. The sight of his spiders in the garage woke him up. He put on a pair of plastic gloves and emptied the contents of all the boxes into a single box without fingerprints and cut out a square piece of flat, slick-surfaced cardboard to rest on top of the box. Holding his package carefully, he turned off the light and slipped outside. He walked slowly so as not to trip and fall, and his head swiveled around in a search for anything out of the ordinary, or any being who might be watching.

When he felt confident, he moved soundlessly over to Peterwell's van in his drive and carefully set down his box of spiders while he took a tool from his pocket. The locked door of the van was open in seconds and Mark eased himself quietly onto the floorboard. He reached for the box of spiders and carefully lifted it up and brought it into the van with him. He placed the box beneath the driver's seat and carefully centered the flat, square piece of cardboard over the top. After a few turns the cardboard top would slide off, releasing the spiders inside. A few seconds more and old Craigy would be doing the stomp dance of his life behind the wheel of a moving van.

Nothing to spray with, and nowhere to go but out.

It might not be fatal, but if Mark was lucky, it would seriously screw him up, *a la* his late wife, Louise.

The curtain behind the driver's side of the van would prevent the spiders from going into the back of the van. They would have nowhere to go but forward, onto the floorboard, and hopefully up Craig Peterwell's legs.

A maniacal urge to laugh gripped Mark and it was all he could do to keep from cackling madly as he eased shut the door to the van.

Bursting with mirth, he slipped over to his own house again and made a crazed dash for the garage before he finally let himself howl.

Abra was awakened by what sounded like hysterical laughter. She rose from her bed and looked out her open window. The August night was unusually cool and her skin began to goosepimple. She listened, but heard nothing further. Frowning, she went into the hall and on to Thomas's bedroom. He was awake and watching his television. His brows lifted when he saw her, and he lifted a feeble hand to point to his television, as if to ask if it were keeping her awake. Abra crossed her arms and said, "I heard someone laughing outside."

Thomas's brows lifted again, but he made no comment. In the last day or so he had gradually stopped talking, and now used grunts, eye contact, and pointing with his fingers to make his wishes known. It wouldn't be long now, Abra thought sadly as she looked at him.

"I'll make some tea and bring you some," she told him, and she left him to go to the kitchen. He wouldn't be able to drink the tea, perhaps only a lukewarm sip or two from a straw. The sores on his body were now inside his mouth, on his cheeks and even on his tongue. It was the strangest thing Abra had ever seen. After she made tea she sat with him and finally went to sleep, only to awaken in time to see the noon news and the story of Eli finding the missing girl's body. She called Zane and had a brief conversation, during which he asked if Abra had noticed anything strange about Clyde Conlan.

"Other than his personality, temperment and behavior, no," she replied frankly. "What makes you ask?"

"I'm not sure. The night I carried Thomas into the house I

noticed a book in Clyde's car. The cover was half torn away, but I could see it was a juvenile book. A book about *Claudia's After School Club.*"

"I asked him about the book myself," Abra said. "He explained that it was a gift for the daughter of the man he and Thomas were to visit, only Thomas said there was no visit. He said they went to a lab, instead."

"A lab? Did you ask Thomas about it?"

"I tried, but he looked strangely at me and changed the subject. Why do you want to know?"

"I'm curious. Cyndi Melo had a backpack with the same words written on it in black marker."

He heard Abra's intake of breath and said, "I probably shouldn't have told you, because it might not mean a thing, but if you stumble across anything, let me know, would you?"

"I will," she promised.

There was no mention of trying to meet again, or to contact each other in any way. Abra hung up feeling at a loss, though she had no idea why.

She went to Thomas's room and sat down with him to watch a movie. When a commercial interrupted, she said, "Thomas, I have to ask you about the lab you visited with Clyde. What exactly did the two of you do there?"

His eyes shifted and he gazed mutely at her. There was no other movement.

Abra tried again. "The gifts Clyde talked about before he took you away. I found a *Claudia's After School Club* book under Clyde's door before you left the other day."

A frown appeared at the bridge of Thomas's nose.

"It's a book for teenage girls. He said he was taking it to give to your friend's children."

Thomas shook his head. His hand lifted and hovered helplessly in the air before falling to the mattress again.

"If you didn't go to visit a friend, Thomas, if you went instead to some lab, then why did Clyde have the book?"

The balding head moved back and forth.

"It was right there on the floorboard of the car," Abra said, echoing what Zane had told her.

Thomas turned his head to stare at her. His lips parted and a hiss of air emerged. Abra watched and leaned down close to him to hear what he was trying to say to her.

"*Stop it,*" he said in a weak whisper.

Abra leaned immediately away from him and gazed into his face. The anger in his expression caused her to leave the bed entirely. His anger was directed at her, for asking questions. After a moment she excused herself and left him to his movie while she went into her bedroom to think.

She didn't think long. Brothers would always protect each other, no matter what. With a spurt of righteous anger of her own, she slipped surreptitiously down the hall and stepped into Clyde Conlan's office.

A quick, thorough search turned up nothing of interest. She went to Clyde's bedroom and repeated the search, and she was still in his bedroom when the phone rang and made her jump nearly out of her skin. She snatched for it and said a breathless hello, half expecting to hear Zane greet her.

"Is this the nurse?" a quavering voice asked.

"Who is this?" she responded.

"Craig Peterwell, across the street. I've gone and done something stupid and I need your help."

"What? What did you do?"

"I took a knife and cut myself. Bleeding pretty bad. I don't know what made me do it. I found out I have a brain tumor and I guess I thought I would just—"

"I'll be right over, Mr. Peterwell. Stay where you are and put pressure on the wound if possible."

She hung up the phone and ran to Thomas's room to tell him where she was going. Thomas was sound asleep, his chest rising and falling evenly. Abra was loath to wake him after their previous peevish encounter. She decided against it and hurried to her bedroom to slip on a robe and shoes and to grab her bag. She closed the front door behind her and crossed the street at a run. Peterwell's door was open and she burst inside the house. She looked all around the room for Peterwell and stepped forward to call his name.

"Right here," he said from behind her, and as she turned he slammed the door shut and locked it.

"Oh, no," Abra breathed as she saw that his wrists and arms were just fine.

"Did you tell your patient where you were going?" Peterwell asked. "Not that he can tell anyone. I was looking in the window at the two of you earlier. He can't say much of anything anymore, can he?"

"I told Zane Campbell I was coming," Abra blurted.

He smiled. "You're lying. Just like your psychiatrist mother." Before Abra could scream, he lifted his arm and brought down a sawed-off two-by-four on her head.

The pain was brutal and immediate. Abra lost consciousness and her body slumped to the floor.


Clyde Conlan came driving down the street ten seconds after Peterwell slammed his door shut. He yawned as he parked his car and thought how much he hated clandestine meetings and the time it took to change the labels on all Thomas's medications. But that was finished now. Clyde had decided to hurry things along. His brother was taking too long to die, and the risk of infecting others increased daily, since Abra turned out to be the complete opposite of the woman he had imagined her to be.

He frowned to find several lights still on inside the house. He put his briefcase in his office and went to see about Thomas. His brother was resting fitfully, his television still on. He left his brother's room and stopped at Abra's door. When there was no answer to his knock, he opened the door and peered inside. Her bed was empty. A quick search of the rest of the house found her nowhere on the premises. Clyde was angry. She was probably next door with Zane Campbell. Thomas had been right about there being a romance brewing between the two. If she thought she could hop into his bed at night and skip next door in the morning, she was mistaken. Clyde had hired a full-time nurse, and that's exactly what he was paying for.

He went to his office and proceeded to write a list of the points he wished to make to her when he saw her again. The list was to help him remember everything he wanted to say. He used lists frequently in his work and in his personal life and felt incomplete without them. Not that Miss Abra Ahrens would care. Clyde found her nosiness irritating, and when he opened his desk drawer and found his paperclips scattered, he knew someone had been in his desk.

"Damn the woman," he snarled to himself as he slammed shut the drawer. "What does she think she's going to find?"

He would hate to think he needed locks in his own house. But that's exactly what he would do if he found any other evidence of her snooping. Clyde liked his things to be just so, and he knew immediately when they were disturbed. When he entered his bedroom he knew instinctively that she had been there as well. The shirts in his drawers rested at an angle rather than perpendicular as he always had them. His sock drawer, too, had a distinctly ruffled look.

The temerity of the woman amazed him. Exactly what did she think she would find in his sock drawer? Pornographic magazines?

Clyde's affront went deep. His home had been invaded, his stronghold pierced by the nails of a feminine hand. He would never be able to sleep in his room tonight, knowing she had been there.

He thought he would be much more effective in the living room, where he would awaken at whatever hour she chose to creep in after her tryst.

Thinking of her dishonesty made Clyde's lip curl. Because she was Lee Ahrens's daughter apparently made no difference. He had mistakenly thought it would. He thought she would be serious-minded like her mother, and less frivolous than most single young nurses he knew. Obviously she took after her father, the man whose license to practice medicine was stripped away when his dishonest nature was revealed. What kind of woman would leave a dying man alone in the house while she ran off to be with her lover? What kind of callous, uncaring, indifferent female would take such a risk, knowing anything could happen at any moment?

Maybe the two of them deserved to get smallpox. But apparently it wasn't going to happen.With each day Clyde gained hope that the virus had been contained, since Abra was still fit and free of ailment. Ever since Thomas's brief exposure at the hospital, of which Thomas was unaware, Clyde had lived in fear of an epidemic and the public relations disaster it would surely cause for the hospital. He vowed never again to work on government projects, no matter how vital to so-called national security interests.

Clyde took a pillow from his bed and went out to the sofa in the living room. He removed his jacket and shoes and settled down on the sofa, facing the living room door. From a pocket in his jacket he removed the book he had been reading. After holding the book in his hand for several minutes he got up and turned on the light beside the sofa. The cover was torn and creased from Thomas attempting to grind the book beneath his feet on the floorboard of the car. Clyde was so upset he had hit his brother squarely on the chin. Thomas had of course passed out, and Clyde had endured unbearable guilt because of it. Thomas could be so hateful sometimes.

He settled down on the sofa again and opened the book. After reading half a chapter he reached down to touch himself. Just reading about the thoughts and dreams of young girls had the power to arouse him like nothing else could. Young girls were unspoiled. Untainted by experience. And the young girls in fiction had such purity, unlike young girls in real life, who had trashy mouths and sullen, sulky ways.

Clyde sighed to himself as he masturbated and lovingly read each perfect little page. When release came, it lifted him slightly above the sofa cushions. He earmarked the page he had been reading, it was a good one, and placed the book back in his jacket. He got up to turn off the light and settled down one last time.

His thoughts returned to Abra and his need to control her movements. He must have been out of his mind to bring her to his house. He didn't know what he was thinking of in opening his home to a deceitful stranger. He should have left his brother to die by himself and fired her on the spot. The hospital was in need of a staff reduction. Maybe there was still time to do it.

# CHAPTER
## 27

ZANE HEARD FROM John Ptacek early the next morning. The autopsy showed Cyndi Melo had been strangled and beaten.

"Which killed her?" Zane asked.

"The beating," said Ptacek. "Keep your eyes open for me, partner."

"I'll do it." Zane hung up the receiver and sat staring into space. The image of the little girl in the grave haunted him. He squeezed his eyes shut after a minute and made himself think about something else. He had a patient coming that morning, a teenager who had lost an eye in a car accident. The boy was only a month or so older than Holt.

He guessed he didn't want to think about that, either, particularly since Holt and Eli had taken the car to the mall that morning to find some new clothes for school. Eli had needed to get away. The news of the day before had made him something of an unwilling celebrity; he had broken down and cried again once the cameras were turned off. Kelly Cameron had brought him a T-shirt from her station, and Eli bluntly told her it was the wrong size and a stupid color. He would never wear it. Normally, Zane would have chastised him immediately for such rudeness, but in this case he did not.

The phone rang again and Zane picked it up and said hello.

Mrs. Morley wished him good morning and asked if he could come over for a minute or two.

"What's wrong?" Zane asked.

"I don't want to talk about it on the phone, in case Chance hears me. Could you please come? I won't keep you long, Zane."

He said he would, though he warned her he had to be back at his house by nine. She said she understood.

Zane looked at the Conlan house as he passed, but he saw no signs of movement inside. Everyone was still sleeping, he guessed. He had been disappointed the day before at the distance in Abra's voice. She sounded like someone with regrets.

Mrs. Morley met him at the door and opened it for him to come inside. "I've got a problem with Chance," she whispered. "Yesterday he told me he had a bad dream about Mr. Peterwell, and last night he sat up all night, watching his window. He said he was afraid Mr. Peterwell would come in and chop off his legs with an axe. I thought maybe you could talk to him, tell him Mr. Peterwell would do no such thing. He needs somebody other than me to make him believe it."

Zane cleared his throat and told Mrs. Morley about Peterwell's brain tumor. The woman stepped back and put a hand to her chest. "Oh, my lord, is there no end to that man's misery?" She shook her aged head. "Is there anything we can do for him, Zane? Anything at all?"

"I wouldn't know. Is Chance still in his room?"

"Yes, he's back there cooking up new schemes to keep himself safe. You should've seen the mess he made with my tape and red pepper."

The corner of Zane's mouth curved and he went down the hall to find Chance. He heard him mumbling to himself in the last room on the left, and when Zane poked his head in the room, Chance screamed in fright and jumped three feet in the air.

It was a struggle for Zane to keep from laughing at the expression on his face. The moment was ridiculously funny, made even more so because of Chance's appearance. On his upper lip was a penciled-in moustache and on his ear lobes were two of his mother's clip-on earrings. He had a large red bandanna tied around his head over his ears, and beneath the bandanna was a brown wig.

"Excuse me," said Zane. "I was looking for Chance Morley. I didn't mean to frighten you."

"That's me," said Chance. "I'm him."

Zane squinted. "Chance?"

"Yeah. It's me."

"What are you doing, Chance?"

"Disguising myself."

"Why?"

Chance looked at the floor and said nothing.

"Your mom said you had a bad dream about Mr. Peterwell. She said you dreamed he tried to chop off your legs."

"No, he said he was *going* to," Chance corrected. "Just like he chopped off . . ."

Zane felt the caution in his pause. "What? Tell me."

"I don't want to."

"Why not?"

"Because you're Eli's dad, and you're an ex-policeman. I might get into trouble."

"For telling me about a dream?"

"Yeah."

Zane eyed him and came to a quick decision. It was worth a try, anyway.

He said, "Chance, I already know you were in Mr. Peterwell's house the day it burned."

Chance's eyes rounded as he stared. "You do?"

Zane nodded. "You and Mark Vaughn."

"Who told you?"

"Vaughn did."

"He did? But he told me not to tell anyone. He said we shouldn't say anything."

"He decided to tell me. You can tell me, too, but only if you want to. I won't make you tell me anything."

"You won't?"

"No."

"I can say anything, and nothing will happen to me?"

"If you want to, Chance. Why don't you start with why you went into Mr. Peterwell's house?"

Chance hesitated. Then he said, "To get the birds out."

"And you found Vaughn inside?"

"Yeah, he was on the floor, and he had chains on him so he couldn't move very good."

"You helped him get out?"

"Yeah. Then we went to check on Mrs. Peterwell, and then we opened all the cages and let the birds go."

Zane's breathing quickened. "Back up just a second, Chance. What was Mrs. Peterwell doing while you were in the house?"

"She was sleeping on a bed in the back bedroom."

"You saw her?"

"Uh-huh. She didn't look too good. She looked all puffy and purple. Mr. Vaughn looked funny when he saw her, and he touched her arm. I thought he was going to cry."

"Was she alive, Chance?"

He shrugged. "She was sleeping."

"Why did you let the birds go?"

"Because they were screaming at me. Please don't tell my mother, Mr. Campbell. I'll be in big trouble if she knows I broke Mr. Peterwell's window and went in his house again."

"Again?" Zane echoed. "What do you mean? Were you in there before?"

"No, I . . ."

"You mean you went back again."

Chance swallowed and Zane could see him kicking himself. He

said, "He had some more birds. Big, black ones. I let them go, too."

"You broke into his house a second time and let more birds go?"

Chance's nod was guilty.

"When was this?"

"I don't remember."

"All right. And then what happened? Why are you so afraid of Mr. Peterwell? Did he catch you?"

A sudden, fat tear rolled down Chance's cheek as he nodded again.

"He caught you the day you broke in again?"

"Yesterday. It was just yesterday, I remember now. He said he was going to chop off my legs, same as he chopped off his wife's leg before he burned her up in the house. He said I should watch for him and not sleep, because he was going to bring his rusty old axe to my house and break in the same as I broke into his house."

Zane was staring at the disguised Chance. "He knows you broke into his house?"

"Yeah."

"Does he know why?"

"I told him."

"He said he cut off his wife's leg before he burned her up?"

Chance rubbed his nose with the back of his hand.

"Yeah."

Zane went on staring at him. "He was trying to scare you, Chance. You know that, don't you?"

"He *did*."

"What I mean is, he probably didn't do the things he said he did. He was probably just saying that so you would be scared of him and stay out of his house."

Chance blinked. "You think so?"

"It worked, didn't it? You don't ever want to go back there again, do you?"

"No," Chance swore. "Not in a jillion years."

"That's why he said those things and made those threats to you, to keep you off his property. Promise me you'll stay away from him."

"I will."

"And promise me you won't tell anyone else the things you've told me today, not unless I tell you it's okay."

"Okay."

"All right. Stop worrying and get some sleep."

Chance exhaled in gratitude. "I can take off my disguise?"

"Save it for Halloween." Zane left the room and ran into Mrs. Morley in the hall. Her eyes were bright with fear as she followed him back to the living room.

"You heard everything?" Zane asked.

She nodded. "What's going to happen to him?"

"I'll be honest, Mrs. Morley, and say I don't know. I don't think your son was in any way responsible for Mrs. Peterwell's death, but his connection with Mark Vaughn is bound to turn up in any investigation."

"What went on in that man's house?" she asked, referring to Mr. Peterwell.

Zane could only lift a shoulder. He told Mrs. Morley to try not to worry and then he left her. What he wanted to do was go straight to Mark Vaughn's house and confront him with everything Chance said, but his watch showed ten minutes to nine and a strange car was sitting in his driveway, so he knew his patient had arrived. He hastened across the lawn and waved to the woman and boy in the car while he stepped onto the porch and opened his front door.

Three hours later he took a break for lunch and decided to call Abra. Clyde Conlan answered the phone on the first ring, and Zane said, "Hello, Clyde, this is Zane Campbell calling to speak to Abra. Is she available?"

"No, she's not," Clyde said, and he hung up.

Zane called him a jerk and replaced the receiver. Abra must

have gone somewhere now that Clyde was home. He would try again later.

The boys returned while he was finishing lunch and showed him their purchases. Zane's eyebrow lifted more than once, but he smiled and nodded and attempted to appear enthused over each item. Soon he returned to his patient and finished out the day by sending a happy, normal looking sixteen-year-old into the world again. The minute the car left the drive Zane tried once more to call Abra.

"She is not here, Mr. Campbell," said Clyde's terse voice in his ear.

"Could you please tell me when she'll be back?"

"I have no idea."

"In that case, would you tell her I called?"

"If I see her, certainly."

"Thank you."

Zane hung up and called him another choice name. He made spaghetti for dinner and was eating with the boys when he got up to see if Mark Vaughn was home from work yet. He was.

"I'll be back in a little while," he told the boys. "I'm going over to talk to Mark Vaughn."

"You want the rest of your spaghetti?" Holt asked, and Zane told him he could have it.

As he stepped outside and walked across the street, he saw Craig Peterwell looking out his front window. Zane nodded to him, but Peterwell ignored him. He watched Zane walk over to Vaughn's house before leaving the window.

Zane frowned and knocked on the door. It opened immediately, and a white-faced, queasy looking Mark looked suspiciously at him. "Yeah?"

Zane decided not to waste any time. He said, "Chance told me everything. I know you were chained up in Peterwell's house. I want you to tell me the rest."

Mark went still. "The sonofabitch was in my house today."

Zane eyed him. "What makes you say so?"

"Because he shit all over the floor. He smeared it everywhere."

Mark opened the door and Zane poked his head inside to have a look. The smell that assaulted him was intense and he reared back again. Something else made him look inside again, an odor beneath the gagging smell of excrement. Five seconds more and he recognized it.

"Gas," he said, and he looked at Mark. "Get out of the house. You're already poisoned."

"What?"

"Out," Zane repeated and he grabbed him by the arm and dragged him into the yard. "He's turned on the gas, Mark. Didn't you smell it?"

Mark's eyes rounded and he stared at his house. "I couldn't smell anything but shit. Oh, man, what do I do?"

"Stay here and breathe deep. I'll go turn it off and open some windows. Are you all right?"

"Yeah." Mark sank down to the grass and put his head between his knees.

Zane held his breath and went in the house to turn off the gas. He opened a window and filled his lungs with air, then he moved to the next window, and the next. All the while he was thinking of Craig Peterwell. When he went outside, he stood over Mark Vaughn and said, "It's time to tell me what happened to Louise Peterwell."

Mark shook his head. "I'm not that stupid, Campbell. I'm not talking to you."

"Chance said he found you all chained up. He said he let you go and you went to check on Mrs. Peterwell. She was purple and puffy, he said. Was she already dead? Did he kill her while you were his prisoner?"

Mark's skin was still a pasty white. "Doesn't make any difference now, does it?"

"So why does he keep messing with you? Why did he shit all over your living room and turn on your gas?"

Mark shrugged. "Neighbors hate each other. Happens all the time."

"Right," said Zane. "You wouldn't be exercising any form of torment, would you? Trying to make him pay for keeping you chained up as a prisoner after you broke into his house?"

"What?" Mark didn't get any of that.

Zane slowed down and repeated himself.

"Do I look stupid to you?" Mark asked. "Do you think I'm going to send myself back to the joint? I keep asking you, man, what possible difference could it make now? Peterwell's going to die, and I've got one last chance to make my life work. I've done some stupid things, and I've screwed up most of my life, but I'm through breaking into people's houses. I'm through with everything but being a husband and a dad."

"You're not going to retaliate against Peterwell?" asked Zane.

"I've already done everything I'm going to do," said Mark.

The statement appeared to be an honest one, but doubts lingered. Zane said, "Call the police and tell them what happened. They'll probably send someone from the gas company out, to make sure everything's all right."

Mark nodded. "Yeah, I will."

Zane paused. "Are you going to implicate Peterwell?"

"Nope. No way to prove it, unless there's some kind of test for shit." Mark grinned crookedly and Zane stared at him. He was certain there was something else going on.

"Come over to the house and use the phone," Zane suggested.

"Thanks," Mark said, and Zane extended a hand to help him to his feet. His legs seemed to wobble a little, and he reached for Zane's arm again.

"You okay?"

"Still a little shaky. Didn't realize what was happening to me in there. Thought I was getting sick because of all the crap. Think I could call someone to come and clean it up? Is there anyone who does that?"

"Not that I know of," Zane told him. "I'm afraid you're on your own on that one."

"Great. Val's going to be supremely pissed if I don't get those walls clean."

"Where is she?" asked Zane.

"At her mother's house. She and the baby are visiting this week."

"Where does her mother live?"

"Across town."

Zane frowned at his neighbor. Mark shrugged and said, "Just one of those things. Don't ask."

As the two of them crossed the street, Zane swiveled his head and saw not only Craig Peterwell watching them, but Clyde Conlan as well. The antipathy on Peterwell's face Zane understood, but the blatant animosity twisting Conlan's features defied explanation. Unless something had happened and Abra had somehow let on that they were suspicious of him. Was that why she had gone? Zane wondered. Had Clyde come home and caught her looking for something? Surely she would have called Zane by now, if that were the case.

If she could call him.

Zane inhaled and forced himself to stop thinking about her. He was eager to believe any explanation other than the probable one, that she had decided against getting involved and was avoiding seeing him again.

He helped Mark into the house and showed him to the phone. He listened to the call and marveled at how innocent Mark Vaughn could sound. The more he heard, the more he was convinced that some form of retaliation against Peterwell would indeed occur. The question was when.

# CHAPTER

## 28

ABRA LAY CURLED UP in the dark cupboard beneath Peterwell's kitchen sink and wondered if her spine would ever stretch normally again. She had been breathing on her knees for what seemed like forever and could not move or flex even one of her larger muscles. The cramped condition of her body in the tiny enclosure gave rein to a trilling claustrophobia that warbled insanely inside her. Every second she expected to hear a snapping sound and feel her mind go running out her ears in the form of warm, viscous liquid. She had no idea of the hour or even the day, since she had been unconscious when he put her under the sink. Not once while she had been conscious had he come to check on her. Her throat was parched and her eyes burned when she closed her lids. The gag in her mouth reeked of motor oil.

She believed she was going to die, and in between the frantic, silent screams of her trapped and suffering psyche, she experienced the deepest sadness imaginable. She regretted having spent so much of her life with death, for she was in no way ready to welcome it for herself. For the first time she understood the tortured ramblings of dying patients in the first days of decline. She understood what they meant when they claimed there was much too much left undone. She hadn't lived yet. She had only just won the first battle in giving herself over to sensation. She would give anything to see again the man who was responsible. Anything to hear him or touch him.

Abra wanted to tell him how desperately she was in love with him, how just looking into his eyes *moved* her, and how the touch of his hands stirred the most incredible passions within her. One hour of fervent need and naked emotion was not enough. She wanted more time with him.

She thought of his face and closed her eyes, wanting to hold the image firmly. Zane was a branch to hold onto in the dark, swirling pool that was her mind.

In time she slept again, and when she awakened it was to see Craig Peterwell peering inside at her.

"You gonna be good?" he said with a grunt.

Abra nodded and felt her eyes fill with moisture. He was going to let her out.

Peterwell saw the tears and became angry as he dragged her roughly from the cabinet. "Stop that," he said. "Stop that right now. I don't want any crying."

Abra blinked and tried to stop, but tears she couldn't halt fell out of each eye and coursed down her cheeks.

Peterwell made a grunting noise and slapped her hard, twice. Abra squeezed her eyes shut against the stinging pain and balanced on her knees in front of him. She looked at her wrists and ankles and saw that they were bound with thin, black electrical cord. She kept her face averted.

"We're going into the other room to make a phone call now," he informed her. "I want to call your mother. I have a few things to say to her."

Abra's eyes rounded slightly and she took a quick glance at him before he grabbed her by the arm and dragged her into the living room. He sat down on the couch and pulled the phone to the edge of the occasional table while he punched in the number. Abra recognized the number as her mother's.

"Dr. Ahrens, please. This is Craig Peterwell calling."

There was a pause while Peterwell listened to the receptionist. Then he said, "Tell her she had better talk to me. I've got a very good reason for her to talk to me right now, I don't care if she is with a patient."

The receptionist said something else and then hung up. The look on Peterwell's face was first incredulous and then enraged. Abra felt a stab of fear as he slammed down the phone and turned to her.

He started to say something; then he stopped. "Don't look at me like that, little girl. Don't you ever look at me like that. I'll whip the tar out of you."

Abra shifted her eyes away, but not before she saw him reaching for the belt around his waist. She cringed when she saw the silver studs on the brown leather, and when he saw her cringe he lost control. He lifted his arm high and brought the belt down viciously hard across her back.

"Don't look at me like that, girl! What the hell is wrong with you?"

Abra screamed around the gag as the metal studs bit into her flesh. The noise was strangled and puny and seemed to urge him on.

"Sassy little smart mouth. I'll teach you to backtalk me. I'll teach you to give me ugly looks and stick out your tongue when you think I'm not paying attention. I'll bust your butt for you."

As he beat her, Abra had the fantastic notion it wasn't her he was talking to. But it certainly was her he was beating, and the thin gown covering the tender skin of her back was in bloody shreds when he finally stopped. Abra struggled to breathe through the gag as she bit back sobs of agony. Her back felt as if it were on fire.

"Look what you made me do. You think I like doin' that? You think I like beatin' little girls? You make me crazy, damn you."

Abra kept her head down and didn't look at him. She heard the noise of his breathing and smelled the stench of his perspiration and finally she heard him pick up the phone again. When he spoke to the receptionist this time he was much calmer. He said, "Tell Dr. Ahrens I will rape her daughter if she doesn't call me back immediately." Then he hung up.

The phone rang again in less than thirty seconds. Peterwell chuckled as he picked it up.

"Hello, Lee. Is that you?"

There was a pause, then, "It wasn't a threat. I don't make threats. You don't believe me? No? Then I suggest you try to reach your daughter."

Peterwell hung up again. He poked Abra in the back once while they were waiting, causing her to wince.

"Look at me," he said.

She looked at him, her face expressionless.

"I hate your mother," he said.

Abra went on looking, her eyes giving away nothing.

"My doctor said she was the best, that's why I went to her. But she couldn't help. All she did was make things worse. She sent me to that idiot who gave me a brain tumor, and you know how those things start growing once you know they're there. She might as well have taken a gun and shot me."

The phone rang again and Peterwell casually picked it up. "Hello?"

Abra swore she heard her mother's voice, firm and controlled.

"That's all he said?" Peterwell said into the phone. "You mean he didn't sound like anything was wrong?" He listened, then said, "I know it's not like me to play games, but the rules have changed."

There was a lengthy pause. Then his voice took on a wheedling quality. "I don't know what you mean. I don't know what I mean, either, can't you see that? I'm acting on impulse, Doctor, and not thinking anything through. Yes, that's right, I am lying to you about Abra. I saw her drive away from the Conlan house a few minutes ago and knew I could make you believe I had taken her. All I want is for you to come and see me. I'm five minutes away and I need to be with someone because I keep thinking about dying before this tumor can kill me. Will you help me stop thinking this way, Dr. Ahrens?''

*No*, Abra silently told her mother.

"You will?'' said Peterwell. "Is that a promise?''

It evidently was, because he smiled widely and thanked her profusely before replacing the receiver.

He lifted his arms and smiled at Abra. "Your mom's coming in a few minutes. Isn't that nice?''

Abra leaned away and he reached out to pinch her cheek.

"You girls just have a way of ticking me off, yes you do. Little ones, big ones. Live ones, dead ones.'' He paused and looked out the window. His eyes went far away.

"I heard they found her yesterday. Didn't remember anything about it until they found her. Still can't remember a whole lot, but I can feel my hands around her neck if I think about it. Had to whip her hard. Smart-mouthed little girl. I nearly ran over that stupid bike with my van. She had it parked right in the middle of the street, and she came up to me sassy as you please and started telling me she could park her bike anywhere she wanted to, and, well, I picked up her skinny little butt and threw her in the van.''

He rose from the couch then. "That's where you're going, too. I got a box just big enough for you. Louise's exercise bike came in it. I'll act like I'm hauling it out to the van. Thinking of selling it, you know. A man with a brain tumor doesn't need an exercise bike, he needs money for chemotherapy.''

His unemotional confession of the killing of Cyndi Melo chilled Abra like nothing else could. She wanted to laugh hysterically at the idea that she and Zane had suspected the stiff, utterly proper Clyde Conlan of harming the little girl. Clyde wouldn't walk on dirt, much less dig in it. He was much too concerned with order to deal with the mess of murdering someone.

Craig Peterwell was different. But his putting Abra in the van gave her hope. She could maybe move in the van. She could kick her feet against the sides and cause some noise and hopefully attract someone's attention.

Peterwell must have anticipated her intentions, for after shoving the box with her inside into the back of the van he taped the lid firmly in place, moved the box into the corner and placed a tire in front of it. There would be no spilling over and jarring the sides of the van. Abra was once again in complete darkness, and this time she had pain to keep her company.

Lee Ahrens drove as quickly as she could to the home of Craig Peterwell. This wouldn't be the first time she had rushed to the aid of a despondent patient, and God knew she had handled crazier people than Craig Peterwell.

It surprised her when she saw him. He appeared calm and polite as he escorted her out of the car and led her to his door. She stopped on the porch. "I'm not going inside with you. Let's stay out here and talk."

He blinked. "Are you afraid of me?"

"I'm afraid *for* you. Why did you threaten me with my daughter?"

Peterwell smiled. "You wouldn't have come otherwise."

He sat down on the porch at her feet, forcing her to look down at him. She stepped off the porch and he simply sat and grinned at her, as if he were a naughty child with a big secret.

"Craig," said Dr. Ahrens calmly. "Let's talk."

"Right. Okay. I want us to talk. We haven't had a good talk in a long time."

Dr. Ahrens was suddenly wary. Something wasn't right. He was acting entirely too strangely. She straightened her spine and clasped her hands together. "All right, Craig, I realize that the idea of an abnormal scan has sent you into a downward spiral and you feel as if you're out of control and completely and utterly powerless. But you're not totally at its mercy. Give yourself a chance and show up for the additional tests. I've told you before that, whatever the results, we'll sort through them together and try to understand more about it. Give yourself a reason to hope and a chance for renewal of spirit. I'm begging you, Craig. For the sake of your soul, turn this around and stop—"

"Before I hurt someone?" he finished for her. His eyes were red and brimming. "You liar," he whispered. "I could listen to you forever. I could sit here and look at you and feel myself be touched by you, by your sweet words, until the sun burns out. But it wouldn't change a thing. I'd still have a sick brain. Louise would still be dead. That little girl they found yesterday would still be dead, and I'd still be the one responsible. My soul is worthless, Dr. Ahrens."

The doctor was staring at him. "Are you talking about the Melo girl?"

"Memory's a funny thing," Peterwell responded. "Comes and goes. I was sitting here trying to remember if you told me you were married or not."

For the first time, Dr. Ahrens felt a frisson of fear. She forced her hands to remain clasped in front of her while her mind raced. He was telling the truth. The man had killed his wife by trying to chop off her leg. He had burned her corpse. And now he was telling her he had killed a twelve-year-old girl and buried her body in the ground. God knew what else he was capable of.

Instinct told her to turn and make a dash for the car.

Common sense told her she would never make it.

She looked around and said, "I'm a widow, Craig. My husband died a long time ago."

"Have any boyfriends?"

"I've dated some, but there's been no one special."

This seemed to please him—for about a second. He snorted and said, "You're too busy making everyone else feel special, aren't you? That's your job, isn't it? To tell people like me that I'm supposed to feel happy about just being alive and having the time that I have?"

He put a sudden fist to his forehead and Dr. Ahrens stepped forward. "Headache?"

He nodded, and once again he reminded her of a little boy, sick and sullen. "I already took eight aspirin today. It doesn't go away anymore."

"You can obtain a prescription for something much more powerful than aspirin, you know," she said.

"I know that!" he said with sudden anger. "I work in a hospital, remember? I don't want to turn into a slobbering fool, and that's what most of that stuff does to you."

Lee Ahrens watched him and came up with an idea. In her most soothing voice, she said, "Would you like me to go and buy some birds for you, Craig? Would that help you feel better?"

He looked at her in surprise. "Birds?"

"Yes. Didn't you tell me that the birds always helped you when you were hurting? I can go and buy some birds for you."

"What kind?" he asked, no longer a sullen little boy now but a hopeful one.

"Any kind you like."

"They cost a lot of money."

"I have money, Craig. Let me help you. Let me go and buy you some birds."

He thought about it for a long time, so long that Dr. Ahrens's palms began to sweat in anticipation.

Craig stood up suddenly. "Okay, let's go."

Dr. Ahrens blinked. "You want to come with me?"

"Yeah. I know where the best places to buy birds are. Come on. We'll take your car."

With a sinking feeling, Dr. Ahrens rose from her seat and followed him down the drive.

He turned and smiled at her. "You really do want to help me, don't you? You remembered about the birds."

"Of course I want to help you, Craig. You're my patient."

Once they were seated in her car, Dr. Ahrens turned to him. "Craig, why did you kill the little girl?"

"What?"

"Cyndi Melo. Why did you kill her?"

He shrugged. "I dunno."

"You don't know?"

"I got mad."

"You got mad."

He looked at her. "I'm about to get mad again."

Dr. Ahrens closed her mouth and started the car's engine.

# CHAPTER

# 29

MARK VAUGHN WAS LOOKING admiringly at Zane's sample eyes when Zane gestured for him to look out the window.

"Who's that with Peterwell?" Mark asked.

"Your guess," said Zane.

"Huh?"

"I've seen her in the neighborhood before. Maybe a realtor."

"Sorry, man. Sometimes it's hard to understand you. Damn, these eyes are great. Wish I'd known about these sooner. I'd have scared four kinds of shit out of him with these things. Not that he didn't shit enough."

Zane looked questioningly at him, but Mark ignored him and went on about how great the eyes were. Zane turned back to the window. Neither the gas company nor the police had arrived. With the cops it was understandable; no one was going to rush right over to check out a house smeared with excrement.

"Let's go over and look inside the box he put in his van," Mark suggested.

"Why?"

"To see what's in it."

"What do you think is in it?"

Mark lifted a shoulder. "Far as I know, there was no exercise bike in the living room, so it must have been in one of the bedrooms. And if it was in one of the bedrooms, it got burned up.

Might be another little girl in that box, Campbell. You never know."

Zane stared at him. "What the hell are you talking about?"

Mark snorted through his nose. "Come on, cop, put it together. That's when everything started, when Cyndi Melo turned up missing."

"Doesn't mean a thing." Zane was thinking of Clyde Conlan.

"Maybe, maybe not, but Peterwell drives a van, and how else would you snatch a girl off the street in broad daylight unless you had a van? It's not like a car, where someone could see her even if she was lying down in the backseat. Nope. Had to be someone with a vehicle that covered up what he was doing."

"You've spent a lot of time on this, obviously," Zane commented.

"Huh? Thought about it? Yeah, I have. Who around here hasn't? It used to be a nice neighborhood, man. Throw in one asshole with a brain tumor and the whole place goes to shit."

Zane heard muffled laughter behind him and he turned to see Eli come into the room.

"Who has a brain tumor?"

"No one," said Zane.

Mark looked over his shoulder. "Hey, kid, you want to earn some money? My house needs—"

"Forget it," Zane interrupted. "Find someone else."

"Who?"

"I don't know. Try the Yellow Pages."

"What do I look under? Pooper scoopers?"

Eli gave a raucous laugh.

"This isn't funny, man," Mark said soberly. "If you could see and smell my house, you'd know this isn't funny."

"What happened to your house?" Eli asked.

"Don't ask," Zane told him. "Go and find something to do, would you? Where's Holt?"

"Right here," said Holt as he entered the room. "What's going on?"

"Somebody crapped in Mr. Vaughn's house," Eli guessed.

Mark moved away from the window. "Thanks for letting me hang out, Campbell. I'll get out of your hair now."

Zane didn't see any vehicles belonging to the gas company in Vaughn's drive. "Where are you going?"

"Out. See you later."

"If you go near Peterwell's van, I'll have you busted," Zane told him.

Mark stopped and snorted. "Aren't you curious about what's in there?"

"Whatever it is, it's his business and not ours." Zane looked at his watch. "You want something to eat? It's time we had supper."

Mark looked at Holt. "Can you drive?"

Holt nodded.

"You wanna drive that Firebird sitting in my drive?"

Holt's mouth opened slightly. He nodded again and looked at his father.

"Why?" Zane asked Mark.

"Go get us some chow. I'll buy."

"I can fix something here," Zane said.

"*Dad,*" said Holt.

"You do that every day?" Mark asked in surprise. "I mean, do you cook?"

Zane ignored him and looked at Holt. "If I say yes, I want you back here in half an hour, no more. No driving by to show off the car to your friends, no leaving tread on the asphalt at stoplights, and no hot-rodding."

"I'm going, too," said Eli.

"No, you're not," said Holt.

"Yes, I am."

Mark took the keys from his pocket and tossed them to Holt. He removed his wallet and fished out a twenty. "Get me the biggest cheeseburger you can find, big fries and a big iced tea."

Eli beamed and snatched the twenty.

Zane's mouth twisted. He declined to order anything and put his hands on his hips as he watched his sons race out the door and across the street to the Firebird in Vaughn's drive.

Mark was watching him. "You must be a pretty strict dad."

Zane said nothing, only looked at him.

"That's okay," said Mark. "I respect you, and your kids obviously respect you too. You got a good thing going."

The moment the Firebird left the drive, the gas company arrived, and Mark went out to meet them. Zane watched him walk across the street.

A second later he stepped out the door and went across the yard to the Conlan house. He rang the bell twice before an irritable Clyde Conlan opened the door. "What is it?" he snapped.

Before the man could react, Zane pulled the door open and pushed past him to step inside.

"What do you think you're doing?" Clyde blustered, his face turning an angry pink.

"I'm going to ask you nicely," Zane began, "so I expect you to answer nicely. Where is Abra?"

"Mr Campbell, I'm going to call the police. You have just forced your way into my—"

"Don't threaten an ex-cop with the police, Clyde. It's irritating beyond belief. Now kindly answer my question."

"I might answer if I could understand you."

Zane's skin prickled with anger. "Where . . . is . . . Abra?"

"I . . . don't . . . know," said Clyde.

When he saw the smirk on Conlan's face, Zane couldn't control himself. He grabbed the smaller man by the collar and brought his face close.

"My son found a little girl's body yesterday. She had a backpack with her, and the backpack had *Claudia's After School Club* written on it. You had a *Claudia's After School Club* book in your car the night I carried your brother in the house for you. I know the police will find that interesting."

For the first time, Clyde looked uncomfortable. "What are you saying? Are you saying you're going to implicate me in the murder of that girl?''

"I . . . don't . . . know," mimicked Zane.

Clyde swallowed. "I came home last night and found Abra gone. She wasn't in the house, so I assumed she was with you. Thomas said he thought the two of you had something going. I slept on the couch and waited for her to come home, but she never arrived. This morning I checked her room and found everything still here. All her clothes and belongings are right where she left them.''

Zane released the man. "May I have a look?''

"If you must.''

He found the room by remembering which window he always saw her at. Everything was as Clyde had said. There were no signs of disturbance.

"Did she say anything to Thomas?'' he asked.

"Nothing.'' Clyde cleared his throat then. "He said she asked him about the book you referred to earlier. I told her a fib about it, and my reason for having it. Thomas wanted to protect me.''

Zane frowned at him and Clyde led the way into his office, where he opened a hidden panel in the wall behind his desk. Inside were dozens of books, each of them bearing *Claudia's After School Club* on the spine. Zane stared at Clyde.

"You read these?''

Clyde's nod was stiff. "Fiction for young adults has been a passion of mine for many years. I'm a collector.''

Zane eyed a book on top of the row on the shelf. On the cover was a picture of a girl in a nurse's uniform with a play stethoscope around her neck. The pages of the book were well worn.

"Her bag,'' Zane said suddenly, and he wheeled away from Clyde to return to Abra's room. After scouring the contents thoroughly, he went down the hall to Thomas's room. Thomas looked at him with round eyes as he searched.

"Abra?'' the man in bed rasped.

"Not here,'' said Zane. "But her medical bag is gone and the car is here, so she must have gone somewhere on foot.'' Without waiting for a reply, Zane left Thomas and strode past Clyde to exit the house. All he could think about was Abra warning him to watch out for her mother's patient, and the big box in the back of Craig Peterwell's van.

Mark couldn't believe his eyes when he saw Zane Campbell trying to get into Peterwell's van.

"Sonofabitch," he whispered, and the man from the gas company looked at him.

"Excuse me?"

"Nothing," said Mark. "Is everything okay now?"

"As far as the gas is concerned, yes. I assume you'll talk with the police about the rest of it?"

"Yeah." Mark was impatient. He wished the guy would hurry up and leave so he could go over and see what the hell Campbell thought he was doing.

"You certainly have a mess on your hands."

"Yep, I sure do. Gotta get started on it, too, so thanks for coming out."

"I wouldn't start cleaning it up until the police have had a chance to look it over."

"Okay, yeah, I guess you have a point there. I'll just go back to my neighbor's house and wait for them. Thanks again for coming out."

Mark started away before the man could say anything further to detain him. He slipped over to Peterwell's house and was approaching the drive when Peterwell and the woman in the Jaguar pulled up beside the van.

Peterwell's eyes narrowed and his nostrils flared when he saw Mark. Mark put out a hand and thumped the side of the van hard.

"Campbell, we've got company," he said loudly.

Zane came around the van and stopped when he saw Peterwell

getting out of the car. In Peterwell's hands were two bird cages, with two birds apiece inside. Peterwell held the cages away from his body and advanced on his two neighbors. "What do you people think you're doing?"

"We want to look in the van," Zane told him. "Open it now."

Craig looked incredulously at the woman with him. "See what I have to deal with around here? Who do you think you are?"

"The wrong people to mess around with," Mark supplied. "We want to know what you have in the box."

"I don't know what you're talking about," said Peterwell, and he gestured to the woman behind him. "Come on, Dr. Ahrens, let's go inside and call the police."

Zane's head swiveled. "Dr. Ahrens? You're Abra's mother?"

Her face was pale as she stared at him in confusion.

Mark tried to interpret. "Are you Abner's mother?"

"Abra's missing," said Zane, gritting his teeth.

Dr. Ahrens went on staring. "What?"

"I think he said Abner's missing." Mark looked at Zane. "Who's Abner?"

Dr. Ahrens turned her stare on Craig Peterwell. She began to shake. "You did something to her, didn't you? You weren't bluffing after all. You really took her."

Zane gave Mark a shove. "Go get your tools and open that van." Then he moved on Peterwell and grabbed him by the throat. He squeezed until Peterwell's eyes began to bulge and veins stood up under his oily flesh. "If you touched her, I'll take out that tumor myself."

Peterwell tore himself away and swung hard with one of the bird cages, catching Zane in the face and opening a long gash in his forehead. Zane staggered and Peterwell shoved him to the ground and ran to his van. He inserted his key, threw open the driver's door and jumped behind the wheel. He shot down the drive in reverse and squealed up the street as Zane sprang unsteadily to his feet and attempted to wipe the blood from his eyes.

"Here!" Dr. Ahrens shouted as she slid behind the wheel of her car. Zane opened the passenger door and climbed in beside her. Mark Vaughn came running out of the house in time to see them race down the street after the van.

"Hey!" Mark shouted. "Wait for me!" He ran after them several yards, until he realized it was crazy and stopped and turned back. He looked for his car and kicked himself when he realized it was gone. He saw Campbell's car in the drive and ran across the street to do a quick hot-wire job. He could still catch up before they were out of the twisty, curvy streets of the addition.

In seconds he had the locked door open and had slid behind the wheel. When he went to yank the wires under the dash he stopped and jumped back, startled at what he found.

From the looks of things, someone had been there before him. Someone who knew about wiring cars. Someone who knew how to wire a car to catch fire and go boom when the ignition was turned.

"Peterwell, you sneaky bastard," Mark whispered. "Had something planned for all of us, didn't you? My house, Zane's car." He wondered what was planned for Abner.

At that moment the police cruiser he had asked for an hour ago rolled down the block toward his house. Mark left the car and crossed the street, wondering how he was going to explain everything.

*I was set to hot-wire this car, officer, when I noticed that someone else had already done an extremely deadly and efficient job of wiring it.*

He inhaled deeply as he thought of the van, and for the first time since his incarceration in Peterwell's basement, he said a quick prayer. "Please, God, don't let me screw up again."

Holt and Eli returned as he stepped onto the curb, and Mark gestured for them to park the car in his drive. They got out carrying sacks from the burger joint and stared at the police cruiser. Mark approached them and said, "Your dad's gone after Peterwell. We think he had Abner in his van."

"Abra?" said Eli.

"Oh. Okay. Whatever. Listen now, I don't want you guys to worry too much. Your dad can take care of himself. And listen, don't either one of you get behind the wheel of your car. Peterwell's wired it to blow."

Each boy dropped his jaw and stared. "He wired our car?"

"Who wired whose car?" asked an approaching officer.

Mark looked at him and exhaled slightly. "I think we're going to need the bomb squad."

The officer frowned. "Wasn't this the house with the shit problem?"

Eli and Holt looked at each other.

"He didn't stop there," Mark said, and while he had everyone's attention, he began to tell them about Craig Peterwell and his brain tumor.


Craig Peterwell was racing west on US 54 while Mark Vaughn was talking to the police. He didn't know where he was going, but where wasn't important. The important think was to keep moving. He knew Dr. Ahrens and Zane Campbell were behind him; he could see Dr. Ahrens jabbering away on her car phone, probably talking to the police. Craig wanted to shout at her to stop, to put that ridiculous phone down and turn the car around. *He* wasn't going to stop. Even if the police showed up to block him off, he wouldn't stop. He was going to take his van right through them.

He was going to drive until he couldn't drive anymore, and then he was going to get out and run, run like he used to run when he was a kid, back when he lived by the field that hid all the crows he caught. He could almost hear the noise they made as he drove. He could hear the clicking and cawing; he could see their blank, round eyes and the black sheen of their feathered bodies.

Craig was hoping they would shoot him. If they shot him, he wouldn't suffer anymore. It would all be over in an instant, and it wouldn't be his fault. None of it would be his fault if the police shot him. He was convinced of that.

He went on driving and dreaming of crows, and when a fat brown spider crawled onto the vinyl between his thighs, Craig's eyes bugged out as he stared at it. A scream like a woman's ripped through his throat when the spider moved, and Craig jumped.

The van swerved violently while he frantically attempted to knock the spider off the seat and away from him. He shuddered as his fingers touched the hairy thing.

Then he felt something on his right leg and gave a startled yelp. He couldn't have knocked the spider onto the floorboard. He had knocked it much farther away, to the other side of the . . .

Two more spiders, both of them bigger than the first, climbed over the seat and into his lap.

Craig froze. He couldn't tear his eyes away from the spiders, and he couldn't seem to move his hands or any other part of his body.

He heard a loud, blaring horn and jerked his eyes up to see the van moving directly for the railing at the side of the road. He grabbed the wheel and missed the rail by inches. The movement startled the spiders and sent one of them scurrying across his thigh and onto his arm. When his horrified gaze dropped again he saw more spiders climbing up his leg and onto the seat with him. Craig screamed and began to brush frantically at himself. Another horn blared, and another, but this time he couldn't tear his eyes away from the spiders. They were everywhere, crawling all over him.

When he felt something on his head, Craig lost control and threw up both arms to bat wildly at his hair. The van careened toward the overpass and crashed through the railing to go over the side. The van turned on its side and then flipped end over end down to the bottom of the hill. When it came to rest on its side, Craig was dazed and covered with blood. But he was still aware of the spiders. They were on his face and arms and running down his neck. He shrieked in terror and lifted an arm to knock the spiders away. He saw shreds of flesh hanging down from his arm, like wings made of skin, and he began to scream all over again.

Zane slid down the overpass on his backside and reached the van seconds after it came to a stop. He heard Peterwell screaming, and when he peered in at him, he saw what had to be a dozen spiders running around the inside of the van. Zane made a face and crawled on top of the side of the van to jerk open the door. Peterwell clawed at him, his face the picture of desperation, but Zane avoided him and reached back to unlock the side door and slide it open. The big box lay on its side in the bottom of the van. There was no movement, and for a moment Zane wondered if he had been wrong, if in fact there was nothing in the box.

He lowered himself into the van and took out his pocketknife to slit the tape that held the lid in place. He lifted off the lid and felt all the breath leave his body as he stared inside the box. Rage filled him and he shouted something unintelligible at the still shrieking Peterwell. Then he groped inside the carton to feel for a pulse. His legs went weak with gratitude when he felt the strong beat of her heart. He reached carefully inside and lifted her out. Anger gripped him once more as he saw the thin black electrical cord binding her arms and feet. He opened his pocketknife again and began to saw through the cord.

Dr. Ahrens reached them and Peterwell began to scream for her to help him kill the spiders. He grabbed hold of her arm as she tried to climb past him, but his hands were slick with blood and he couldn't hold on when she jerked away from him. Strands of hair fell in her face as she made her way to her daughter. Her cheeks were glowing with exertion as she performed a quick examination.

"Was she unconscious when you found her?"

"Yes."

"Nothing feels broken, thank God. Let me feel her head while you check on Peterwell."

Zane eased Abra into her mother's arms and moved to see about Peterwell. Peterwell lunged at him, his eyes still round with panic, and Zane held him off with one hand while he looked around at the spiders. Before he fully realized what he was doing, he had brushed most of the spiders out of the van and into the grass outside. He told himself he was doing it to spare everyone further trauma, but he knew better. He had a pretty good guess as to where the spiders had come from, and what their purpose had been.

Peterwell was sobbing. "Thank you, thank you so much."

Zane removed the last spider and tried to push Peterwell away. Peterwell held on tighter, his nails digging into Zane's arm. "I'm not letting you go," he said through his teeth. "I'm not letting go, Daddy. You're not leaving. I won't let you. You can't go."

At that moment, two policemen appeared and looked inside the van. Peterwell saw them and something in his eyes changed. He shoved Zane at them and tried to scramble out past Abra and her mother.

"Shoot me!" he yelled. "Shoot me! I'm going to run! I killed her! I killed Louise and I buried the little girl! Shoot me!"

Peterwell started to run. Within ten yards, one of the officers tackled him and pinned him to the ground. Peterwell screamed in agony and began to squawk and shriek like an angry parrot. The officer who held him lifted his head and looked at his partner in disbelief.

Zane saw Abra's eyes open and he moved to look at her. When she saw Zane she opened her mouth in a soundless cry and immediately opened her arms to him. He gathered her to him and held her as tightly as he dared, pressing his lips to the side of her neck and swallowing hard at the sight of her striped and bloody back. She leaned away to look at him and her eyes fastened on the deep gash in his forehead. "You're hurt," she croaked.

"No worse than you."

"She needs to go to the hospital," her mother said firmly.

Zane was reluctant to let her go, but he could hear an ambulance coming, and he could see people milling above by the bent and twisted railing.

"I have to talk to the police," he told Abra, and he eased her gently out of his arms.

"I'll talk to them," said her mother. "You ride with Abra to the hospital and have someone look at your head."

The paramedic who examined Abra agreed, so Dr. Ahrens was left to explain Craig Peterwell and the flattened van to the officers on the scene.

"Mother," said Abra, before her mother could get away. "This is Zane."

Her mother smiled and hugged her daughter hard.

"I know."

# CHAPTER
## 30

ABRA SAT WITH THOMAS in his bedroom and held his hand while Clyde sat on the other side of the room and watched. In the short time that she was gone Thomas had slipped into a coma. His marked face was sunken and already waxy in appearance. His half-lidded gaze stared at nothing. Her sole function now was as a sentinel, and Abra watched each breath with the knowledge that it might be the last. She didn't want to be there. She didn't want to be in the same room with Clyde Conlan, who watched her with slitted eyes and gave off waves of animosity. His clipped speech grew imperious when he informed her she would have to forfeit pay for the time she had been away, hostage or not. And she could consider her career as a nurse at Riverpark finished.

Stunned, Abra had called her mother and told her the news, only to learn that the chief of staff had let go at least ten people in the last few days. The odd thing was that most of the people let go were the staff who had attended Abra and Zane in the emergency room the day Peterwell crashed his van. Formal complaints had been lodged with the board and the union, but standard layoff procedure had been followed and there was little anyone could do. Abra had the ridiculous notion that it was because of her that all those people had been fired from Riverpark. She had the insane idea that Clyde Conlan thought she and Zane had talked to those people, or passed on some kind of information that made him look bad. She had no idea what to think. Her mother told her not to worry. She had other things to think about. Zane, for one. He was thinking about her, too; thinking about her and making room for her things, though she had not yet agreed to live with him. He had asked her while she was in the hospital, and she told him she would consider it.

Craig Peterwell was still in the hospital, under constant guard. The doctor in charge of his case was baffled by his behavior. He had stopped eating and made no sound but to caw like a crow.

The police closed the case on Cyndi Melo. Louise Peterwell was thought to have been murdered by her husband as well, after Zane and Mrs. Morley talked Chance into telling the police what Peterwell had told him. The neighborhood had been infested with newspaper and television reporters for two days afterward, and today was the first day no one had asked to interview anyone.

Abra enjoyed the quiet, more than she enjoyed staring across Thomas's bed at the stiff features of Clyde Conlan.

Zane had told her about the books. About Clyde's professed passion for young adult fiction.

Abra thought over everything Thomas had told her, all the family stories and anecdotes about his older sibling, and decided Thomas himself wasn't sure of his brother. He had wanted Abra to know of his doubts, even while he protected Clyde. His fears were justified, Abra believed. Like their father's uncontrollable passion for his sweet young sister, Abra saw something uncontrollable simmering in the imperturbable Clyde.

With a start Abra realized she was staring at Clyde, and that he was staring at her. She shifted her gaze and made her posture more erect, to still the ache in her bandaged back. The side of Clyde's mouth curled, as if he knew of her discomfort and was secretly pleased. Abra blew breath out her nose and decided to give him what he deserved. "Now that your secret's out, Clyde, why not trade books with some of the little girls in the neighborhood? I know they'd love to see your *Claudia's After School Club* collection. You can't imagine the joy I brought to everyone at Riverpark when I told them about it. Really.''

Clyde stared again, rendered temporarily speechless. Abra smiled.


Zane looked longingly out the window until the doorbell rang and drew him to answer the door. Mark Vaughn stood outside. He smiled when he saw Zane.

"How's it goin'?"

"Good," said Zane. Instead of inviting Mark inside, he stepped out to join him. The evening was cool and the air felt good in his lungs. "What's up?"

"Not much."

"Your wife back yet?"

"No. She said she's thinking about coming back next week."

"That's good."

"Yeah. I've, uh, been wanting to ask you something, Campbell. About when Peterwell's van crashed—"

"Must've taken you a while to catch them," Zane interrupted.

Mark looked at him. A slow, guilty grin spread across his face. "I was wondering. I never saw anything about it in the papers or on TV. Who, I mean, what happened to them?"

"I cleared them out of the van before the police arrived."

"You got them out?"

"Yeah."

"You knew where they came from?"

"I had a pretty good idea." Zane eyed him then. "You think quick, Vaughn, I'll give that to you. Holt and Eli admired your story for the police, about how you had loaned the boys your car because something was wrong with mine, and how you were being a nice guy and checking it out when you found the nasty wiring job."

The guilty grin spread even farther. "I do have a certain talent for lying, I must admit. What can I say? I'm a salesman."

"But you'll stick to selling cars," said Zane.

"You got it." Mark grew serious then. "If I want to keep my family, that's the way I have to play it." He stuck out his hand then. "Thanks, Campbell. Thanks for everything."

Zane shook his hand and gave a brief nod. "You want a beer?"

"Nah, I better not. You'll get me drunk and make me start talking about things you think you ought to know."

Zane smiled. "I hate loose ends."

"There aren't any. Trust me."

"Maybe in my next life."

Mark looked at him. "Huh?"

"Never mind. See you later, Mark."

His neighbor waved and started off across the street. Zane stared at the empty, blackened Peterwell house and wondered what would happen to it once Peterwell was sent away. It was hard to imagine the block without the noisy birds or the rumbling black van.

But he thought he could live with the silence.

His own house was quiet without the boys, gone to visit their mother again for the weekend. The excitement of the last days would carry them for weeks and make them popular beyond measure during the first days of school. Zane had to smile when he thought about it.

Then he thought of Cyndi Melo's parents and grew sober again.

A part of him thought he should have been able to see the madness growing in Peterwell. He should have recognized the signs and done something to prevent what had happened. But he wasn't a cop anymore. His senses weren't as sharp as they used to be, and he didn't have the eye for strangeness that he had in those days. He was just an ocularist with a speech problem.

He took a beer from the refrigerator and went out to walk through his garden. Things were starting to turn brown. The zucchini was still growing and the tomatoes were still plentiful, but other crops were shriveling and dying away. Zane retrieved his bucket and picked a few tomatoes before going back to the kitchen for another beer. He sat on the porch and drank it while listening to the cicadas and the crickets.

A half-hour after dark the mosquitoes chased him inside. He went in and turned on the television for a while, then he turned it off and went to his bedroom. He left the light off and looked at the Conlan house. There was no light in Abra's room. Zane watched for a while, then went to bed, wondering how many more days he would have to wait before she came to him.

Around three o'clock his doorbell roused him and he went in his underwear to answer it, half-expecting to see Craig Peterwell escaped from the hospital and come back for revenge. It was Abra. Her arms were bulging with bags and suitcases, and there was a small, sad smile on her face.

"He's gone," she said.

"Thomas?" asked Zane. "It happened tonight?"

"Yes. They just took him away. I've been officially released from my position. May I come in?"

Zane held open the door and reached for some of the items she was struggling with. "When?"

She was looking at his briefs. "An hour ago. He just stopped breathing."

Zane wasn't sure what to do. "Do you want to talk? I can fix you something to eat, or drink."

She shook her head. "I'm not hungry, thanks."

They stood looking at each other, neither sure of the next move, until Zane glanced down at himself.

"I can put something on if you're uncomfortable."

"I'm not. I'm tired and sleepy and really happy to see you again."

Zane put down her things and smiled. He approached her to pull her into his arms. Abra pressed her face against his flesh and heard him ask, "Are you going to stay with me?"

She kissed his chest. "If you say, we can move to another house. I can't bear the prospect of living next door to Clyde, the book collector."

Zane smiled. "He's hardly ever home."

"That's true."

"In spite of all that's happened, this is a nice, normal neighborhood."

"Did you say normal?"

"I tried. What I meant to say is that the people here are just like people anywhere."

Abra rested her head against him and closed her eyes while she exhaled.

"That's the part that scares me."